ASTEROID

MADE OF

DRAGONS

G. DEREK ADAMS

Published by Inkshares, Inc., San Francisco, California, as part of the Sword & Laser Collection
www.inkshares.com

Edited and designed by Girl Friday Productions
www.girlfridayproductions.com

Cover design by David Drummond

Cover images © NagyDodo/Shutterstock, © Oceloti/Shutterstock

ISBN: 9781941758731
e-ISBN: 9781941758748
Library of Congress Control Number: 2015951149

First edition

Printed in the United States of America

To the Lodestar—and all that have stood before the mast

Sing in me, O Muse
of the moment when
of the moment then
her gray fingers
wrapped
and coiled
around my heart,
a circle.
Help me sing of the circle
the circle that cannot break
the center that should not hold
but does.
For now.

PROLOGUE

The players' cart was in need of repair. The wheels were missing spokes, and the clapboard panels creaked and moaned as the cart traveled and did little to halt the rain and wind. A small collection of moss had sprouted on the back wall of the wagon near the prop bins and had flowered into a surprising eruption of lavender flowers. Sand was more concerned about the state of their repertoire. Their adventures had grown stale, their comedies overripe, and the romances rotten. So, as all wise troupe leaders know, when the choice must be made between spending the company hoard on repairs, costumes, and comfortable lodging or a new play to perform—the choice is clear.

So Sand found an out-of-the-way corner of the city to park their nearly immobile wagon and called his players together. Vincent was a tall, lean man with a sallow complexion, all angles and bone. Toby was an escapee from a maiden's love poem, all blond hair and white teeth. Vincent was the company Villain, and Toby the Hero—chasing each other through endless scripts and scenes and usually into each other's beds after the curtain fell.

Sand was the Fifth Business—playing whatever else the script required: servants, fathers, wizards, apothecaries, guards, mothers, maids. His own clean features and balding pate allowed him this license with the aid of the right wig or cape or turnip. The troupe had lost its Damsel not long ago, and they had not had the heart to replace her.

Toby munched on an apple, his handsome face bored. Vincent laid a fond hand on his lover's shoulder and nodded to Sand with expectation. They both knew a new play was about to begin, and even through hunger and hardship and the bumps in the road, no actor can truly resist such a thing. It had been a lean time for the players, and this new show was a gamble; if it failed they would all be back to factory work for months and months until they saved up enough to start out again.

"Now we are gathered." Sand smiled. "And we can begin our rehearsal. This new play—"

"Better be good," Toby groused, his mouth full of apple.

"Is different than our normal fare," the lead actor continued without a bend in his voice. "I have commissioned it, rare and unique for our troupe alone. It is written for three players; no Damsel required. The parts are thus: a Demon, a Paladin, and a Sage."

"Doesn't sound that different. I'm to be the Paladin, of course." The blond hero stretched and tossed his apple core at a passing stray cat with unfortunate accuracy.

"Toby." Vincent sighed.

"No, no. Not this time." Sand bowed and pulled the folios from his pouch with a flourish. He tossed one each to his players and continued. "You are to be the Demon, for in this tale the Demon must be beautiful and valorous. And you, Vincent, you are to be the Paladin—for this paladin must be cruel and swift."

"We're playing against type," the tall Villain whispered reverently.

"Oy! I don't want to play the cruddy Demon." Toby shook his scroll with disgust.

The bald player hid his smile with professional care. This was not unexpected. "I think you should give it a try, Toby. This Demon is a most tragic figure. He knows what he is, you see. And he has learned of a sacred fountain that can wash him clean— transfigure him from a monster to a man. If the Demon can only reach it . . ."

"But the Paladin would prevent it!" Vincent cried, already scanning through his script.

"Yes! The Demon is too great a danger in his eyes, has already spilled too much blood to ever allow surcease or mercy." Sand nodded. "Before the end they will face darkness and grand but glorious death—not something you can resist, if you're the actors I know you to be."

"Wait, wait, wait." Toby started flopping through his folio as well. "Where does the Sage come in? What does he have to do with it? And I know you always save the best roles for yourself, Sand!"

"Ah." The player's eyes twinkled and he stepped forward until his back faced the wagon and his heart pointed out toward the world, toward the audience invisible. "The Sage makes a discovery—learns of a power most fell—and we meet them in the first scene. Why don't we give it a read through and see if this is something that we can make sing?"

Vincent immediately trotted away to the wagon to find a hero's sword, practically giddy that he would not wear black this time. Toby watched him go, frustrated fondness warring with his natural recalcitrance. Then the handsome man shrugged and sat down with his script to watch Sand begin the prologue.

Sand filled his lungs with air and held his hands out in the Penitent Statue Position—palms flat, arms at shoulder height. Prologues were always best when the audience understood that they were not watching a real character yet, just a piece of the play to set the wheels in motion. The arcane position reminded that this voice was Other, outside the tale to be told in the Twilight Kingdom.

His voice filled the empty square as he began:

"Far away in the sands, a lone searcher does find
hidden and horrible a secret that binds
their hands and heart and blood to the road
of Calamity, Darkness, and Sorrow untold.

How lonely the travels, how heavy the bones,
of gray pilgrim walkers carrying stones.
The stones of Tomorrow, the stones of Unless—
you cannot forgive what you cannot confess.

Songs of Forever, Songs of the Lost—
the innocent sapling withers with frost.
Take my hands, gentles, and help me forget
the darkest memory that I have told yet."

Sand bowed and moved quickly to take his place for the next scene. It was time for the Sage's first entrance.

CHAPTER ONE

XENON

Quiet pen scratch by lamplight was the goblin's comfort. She sat on the edge of a stone obelisk etched with post-exodus Sarmadi cuneiform, her bare feet dangling against the stone words, feeling their ancient meaning rubbing against her skin. Her campsite was nearby. The fire was nearly embers around a pair of potatoes—a forgotten, quickly carbonized meal. She had only stepped away for a moment to enter the day's findings in her journal, only a moment with her paper and quill. Xenon's green nose wrinkled at the dense odor of burning starch. It was not entirely unpleasant; perhaps she could still eat when her hungry journal was satisfied.

The second chamber is a marvel! I am eager to press on farther into the site, especially after my frustration with the Pass Wall [R1]. The early worshippers of Nasirah seemed to be even more zealous than their current-day descendants, and their determination to make that damnable puzzle nigh unsolvable was obvious in every part of its construction: the concave face of each activation stone, the obscuring of each glyph with sand pitch, the Sarmadi koh blades that erupt upon each incorrect sequence. Tsk! It's as if they didn't want me to enter. As I'm sure the nearby tribes of the Sarmad would agree, it is fortunate that I chose the lull in this region's seasonal migration.

But the week was well spent, even when I ran short of healing salve for the knife cuts on my fingers. All the tedium and irritation swept away as soon as that damnable block of stone—clicked—and swung slowly into a recess, scattering hundreds of years' worth of silicon and mica in its wake. I collected samples as per standard procedure, but so far it is of little note. Average AR score for this location and period, no sign of anything really shiny. But when I stepped into the second ch—

Xenon looked up, not quite sure why. The potatoes were not getting more burned, that was certain. Had she heard a noise? She peered up and down the two rows of obelisks, next to the fallen one she sat upon. She gave a long look at the oval-shaped opening to the site. When all that came back to her ears was the vague hiss of night wind on sand, she went back to her quill.

—amber, I was astonished to discover an overwhelming source of AR. The chamber is divided into six alcoves of equal size, circular, four-foot radius. They radiate like spokes around a low depression in the center, the largest part of the chamber. The central depression is a prayer wheel, consistent with Sarmadi priests of the period. The cuneiform text is a very early form of their "Way of Fire" canto, matching some similar rubbings I read in Pice. [Dated 108 VA]

But back to the AR readings! I didn't even need my dowse-stones; the tertiary signs were impossible to miss.

Two of the six alcoves were glowing, easily discernable by the naked eye. One with a long bier, the other had a series of sealed urns. The other four were cold and dark, preliminary conclusion: natural arcane erosion. The—

Her head jerked up again. She hadn't heard a sound, more like the space where a sound should be. Like the swing of a pendulum on a tall grandfather, the empty breath before the certain tock. Keeping one avocado-green finger on the page, Xenon closed the journal and tucked the quill behind her ear. She craned her neck looking systematically across the obelisks and her crude campsite. Nothing moved; still, the same whisper of the wind across the sand. The site was in a low depression between larger dunes, so it was shielded from the worst of the wind. Her free hand moved slowly to the hilt of the dagger strapped to her calf. The Sarmadi sands were a place of peril: the law tribes, fire serpents, skull wolves, the Shuddering Behemoth Balustrade. Even cautious travelers could find an unremarkable death.

Xenon was a very cautious traveler. The dagger slid free from its oiled sheath without a whisper. She tucked her journal into the wide pocket stitched inside her square-cape. Long ears and eyes still straining, gauging every shadow, she reached to shutter the light on her lantern.

The lantern gave a loud crash as she knocked it spinning to the sand. Xenon hissed in frustration and did her best to roll off the back of the obelisk to take cover, but her feet lost purchase as she swiveled around, resulting in an ungainly flop into the sand. She pushed her dark hair out of her face with exasperation and pulled herself up to peer over the stone.

"Yes, I am just that graceful!" she yelled in challenge. "Vicious with a blade! And I . . . I . . . spilled ink all over myself."

The inkpot had gotten tangled in her cape in her hasty movement, and now the ink was quickly staining the front of her white tunic. Xenon sighed. No desert beast or mustachioed fiend had leaped out of the dark to accost her, so while her disarray was provoked by only her own apprehension, at least it had gone unobserved. The desert wind blew again, then slacked, and Xenon heard the empty sound again.

It was coming from the entrance to the site. The stone oval waited like a black eye, open and fixed.

The goblin picked up her lantern. It still burned, though it had earned a new dent near the top. *It sounds almost like something moving, like a massive door swinging. All I'm hearing is the air moving.* She set the inkpot back on top of the obelisk; she would collect it later. Xenon hurried to her tent and swung her tool case over her shoulder. She noticed absently that the potatoes were nothing but cinders as she hurried toward the entrance to the site. *Something moving! A hidden chamber? Something activated?* Some goblins' eyes glow when excited or angry; Xenon was not of that ilk, but her eyes did turn from their customary black to a mute periwinkle.

This was why Xenon had traveled so far for this expedition, for a chance to learn about the early Sarmadi, while they still burned in the crucible of their exodus, letting the "impurities" of the Empty Island burn away. The site was built by Sarmadi zealots not long after the schism from their homeland of Al-Hazaar. The cuneiform, the way they had beveled the edges of each stone, the facing of the entrance due south: all markers of their shared heritage with their fiend-loving brethren. In later centuries they would break from many of these lingering cultural vestiges as new practices were developed. It was a moment of change, of crisis, the turning of the stone when stories change. She had always been fascinated by these, the before and after and the tiny, tiny decisions that spun the world off into strange new directions. The Sarmadi had left their island far to the south and come to this unforgiving desert to begin anew. And not soon after, they had built this place. To her, it was made not of stone and desert glass but of stories and answers.

Xenon stepped through the dark portal, dented lantern held high. A new story was already whispering in the darkness: the strange sound of something swinging through the air. The first chamber revealed nothing out of the ordinary, but she surveyed it carefully all the same. Only the mute stones of a Sarmadi way site met her eyes, already catalogued earlier in her journal. The sound of movement was growing slightly clearer; her ears pricked and guided her toward the defeated puzzle door and the second chamber.

She had to kneel to enter the second chamber, as the tunnel had become only a few feet high. Her lantern was no longer needed as the chamber was bathed in a brilliant yellow radiation. Xenon wanted to update her journal; this chamber had been completely without sources of illumination earlier, which was how she'd spotted the faint spectral display of the Arcane Resonance the two unspoiled alcoves had given off. But now the light in the room was nearing the sun at midday. The source of the illumination was obvious and astonishing. In the center of the prayer wheel a metal circle had appeared, bright silver and gleaming, as wide as the span of her arms. The stone walls surrounding the chamber were unmarked, as were the floors. It was as if the circle had appeared out of thin air. It was hovering a foot off the floor and slowly rotating. The gentle press of air against the tunnel opening had created the slow rush of air that had brought her this far.

Xenon pulled free her journal, eyes wide, fingers jittery as they retrieved the quill from behind her ear. She had left the inkwell behind, so without taking her eyes off the spinning circle she dabbed the quill into the still-wet ink on her chest. Flipping open to a clean page in her journal, she began to sketch. The goblin had no idea where this object had appeared from, but she was determined to record as much information as possible in case it decided to disappear. *Are those Dwarven runes on the sides? Or early Gilean? Dammit, is it spinning faster? Hold still!*

She shook her head and settled her eyes. She had unconsciously started wobbling her neck to follow the circle's rotation. *It's clearly the source of this light, but I can't make out an origin point. Magical illumination?* A fair wind was picking up as the circle began to spin faster and faster. In a few moments the circle was spinning so fast that it appeared a sphere to Xenon's eyes. Her quill flew, but she nearly dropped it when the first word appeared on the sphere's exterior.

It wasn't really a word. It was a letter. Or rather, a numeral. It was the number zero. Xenon's quill stuttered as she copied it into her journal.

0

The sphere (or rapidly spinning circle) seemed to be making small gaps in its surface, allowing the brighter light within to shine through. *It looks like a zero, tall oval with slash, common rendering. Don't assume, could be some other symbol.* She gasped reflexively when the sphere went blank for a moment, and then she blew the air out slowly as it began to flash a series of new characters. *Cold brain, girl, get it down exact and accurate. Don't try to read or decipher, just copy!*

FIELDSYNC. 1.
LANGSET. 1.
RCVR.1.
USER.0.
TRANSMIT.1.

Xenon risked a quick glance at her paper. She was unconsciously putting periods when the sphere went blank in between characters. *I'll clean that up later. It will serve for now.*

YOU ARE NOT OF ZERO.
YOU ARE NOT AUTHORIZED.

Is it talking to me?!? She forced her eyes to stay focused and her quill to keep moving, pausing only to dredge up more ink from her tunic.

REPORT REQUIRED. NO APPROVED USER IS PRESENT.
  LIMITED REPORT WILL BE MADE.
  TRAJECTORY ADJUSTMENT SUCCESSFUL. MISSION
    COMPLETED OUTSIDE DURATION PARAMETER.
  SHAME RETURNS. 10.10.7171

The yellow light in the room and the center of the sphere began to darken to orange, then red. The temperature in the room and the speed of the rotation did not change, but Xenon took an unconscious step back all the same.

YOU ARE NOT OF ZERO.
YOU ARE NOT AUTHORIZED.
YOU WILL BURN.
ZERO WILL AWAKEN.
ZERO WILL RISE AS SHAME FALLS.
NOTHING MORE REAL THAN THE CHAINS YOU FORGE.
NODE DESTRUCT.1 . . .

Xenon blinked and realized that the sphere was no longer pausing; the strange message was complete. Also the spin of the strange device was growing more and more erratic, the sphere seeming to wobble and bob as if trying to escape. The goblin looked down at the last line she had written.

"Oh. Oh! That can't be . . ."

With a sudden wrenching kinetic force, the steel circle tore itself apart. Xenon threw herself flat on the floor, bits of twisted metal whipping through the space she had just occupied. She covered her head and kept her journal safe beneath her body.

The yellow light quickly faded from the room. Only a dim, mottled green illumination coming from the bits of broken metal provided any visibility—that and her beleaguered lantern, sitting calmly at her feet, completely untouched by the arcane event. Xenon took a long look. The exploding sphere had wreaked havoc with her site. One of the AR-laden alcoves was completely demolished; the other had a single spear of bent metal buried into the long bier. From the shattered pots she had planned to transport and open with great time and care, brittle bones spilled out across the floor. What little resonance they still had, completely despoiled and overwritten by the massive discharge of the circle. Her entire excavation was ruined. Months of research and no little expense completely exploded in a matter of moments. Xenon grinned feverishly and laughed with excitement as she pushed herself up. She had no idea what she had just witnessed. She had no idea what it meant. The magical prowess required to create such a device was on the level of master enchanters in Valeria or the sublime technology of the Precursors.

"What the hell was that?" the goblin asked out loud, almost chortling with nervous energy. "What the *hell* was that?"

She didn't know. It was an amazing feeling. The light that burned in her mind's lantern, that spilled across the pages of her soul's journal, was always the feeling of not knowing. She loved that feeling, along with the belief that she could find out, the answers waiting just over the horizon. Xenon picked up her actual lantern and held it close so she could read the sphere's message. *Or "Node," I suppose. That's what it called itself.*

The first part was gibberish as far as she could discern. *The text is in the Common style, which is curious. That dates the device after the Vardeman Accords.* The Node seemed to have completed some sort of task and was attempting to report back. The task itself didn't sound like anything she had ever researched in the history of Tel, or Eridia, or any of the other continents. *Ominous, though. Definitely ominous. What is "Shame"? Where did it go? Where is it falling from?*

Xenon reached over to a piece of the bent metal, it's light beginning to dim. It was lighter than she expected: a foot-and-a-half section of it weighed less than her lantern. Her nostrils flared in scholarly delight as she recognized the Precursor sigil for "Jump," two parallel lines with a dot between. *This was made by the Lost!* Scholars such as she generally referred to the vanished civilization as the Arkanic race, the general public called them Precursors, but the strange culture of singers and technological geniuses only ever called themselves the Lost. She tucked the ravaged metal under her arm and made a few more notes in her journal.

The site is ruined, but I'm on to something much bigger and stranger. Plenty of physical specimens, but very little to start my investigation. The Arkanic sigil for "Jump"! Why would the Precursors make such a thing? Best start there. Other than that, I have only a name. Or a number?

She drew the number large, with the careful slash from shoulder to hip.

Ø

"What the heck is Zero?" Xenon asked the gathering dark.

CHAPTER TWO

JONAS & RIME

The roof of Waters & Moore Fiduciary Exchange was a small wonder of unnoticed architecture. Each tile was made of thinly cut marble in a most flattering shade of faded green. The builder, a famed goblin crafter whose name was remarkably silly even by local standards, had used an enchanted chaos saw to transform massive blocks of the stone into finger-thick slices. Most importantly, each tile was slightly curved with a simple notch on the bottom. The roof was assembled with no mortar at all, only a proprietary binding spell and hundreds of creature-hours to construct the roof piece by piece. It allowed excellent airflow in the summer but kept the heat inside better than thatch or slate in the winter. Rainwater passed over and off the roof with the gentlest of kisses and a faint apology. It was a marvel of roofs. A competitor Roofmaster Jeprodain's slide into alcoholism and financial ruin the winter after the installation was attributed quite correctly to his all-consuming jealousy at the accomplishment. "Damn you, your silly name, and your beautiful, beautiful roof," he howled outside the goblin crafter's home two or three times a week before sobbing his way into the shadows.

Knowing none of this, Rime exploded through the roof, sending a geyser of marble tiles spinning off through the air. The heat from her blue nimbus melted and seared each piece of marble, rendering them absolutely useless for any future repair.

Across town, Roofmaster Jeprodain woke with a start from his drunken doze in a pig cart—but soon fell back to sleep, not knowing of his vindication until some days later.

The blue fire bit into the tiles with ravenous heat. Rime was held aloft by a blooming flower of her magic, already swiveling to look down at the gaping hole in the bank's roof. She had a large sack in her hands, and her face was covered with chocolate and a rainbow of tiny candy dots. Her eyes blazed a pure white, searing the confection around the orbs a crisp black. From between clenched teeth, a furious stream of end-to-end curses hissed a litany of hate.

"Not the plan. Not the plan. Not the *fucking* plan," the wild mage spat.

As if to punctuate her wrath, two massive hands made of lacquered oak appeared at the hole behind her and clamped on to the melting tiles. The first few feet ripped away feebly in the golem's claws, but at last it found enough structure to bear its considerable weight. Rime soared to the western edge of the roof, blue fire keeping her feet inches above the tiles. She flew backward, keeping her eyes on the golem's bulk.

It was of a simple bipedal design. Green crystal eyes deep set into its wooden face, the symbol of a crashing wave on its forehead in brass, the letters "STC" just above. Rime had only passing knowledge of these constructs' manufacture and design, but she was quickly learning how devastating a theft deterrent they could be. As the golem finally stood on the bank's roof and clenched its fists in mechanical pride, she gave a faint mental salute to whomever had built this savage block of wood.

The gigantic cannon in its chest was just excessive, however.

Rime ignored the growing exhaustion in her limbs and the vibration in her vision and took stock. She had the gold in hand. It was her gold, deposited some weeks ago. The irony of stealing her own money was irrelevant to her current predicament, so she flicked it aside. Far more germane was the iron cannonball that the golem pulled from a slot in its hip and began to insert into the barrel protruding from its chest. She made her mind go faster. Her magic was burning hungry and fast—maybe thirty seconds before she lost consciousness. The bank sat in the middle of a wide plaza. Her vision filled with lines, angles, numbers: the clarion vision of mathematics and order, calculating radii and distances and the surface areas of each piece of skittering tile as it fell from the roof. The comfort and mastery that some find in song or color or the secret knowledge of good grain from bad, Rime had always found in numbers. They were her ablest allies and most assured sentinels. The closest golem-less roof was 162 feet away— she could fly there before blacking out, but there was no way to guarantee the bank's defender couldn't follow—or hit her with a well-placed cannon shot. She would need to see a volley or two before she could calculate the exact range of the golem's cannon, but no time or folly to allow such experiment. The wooden construct had bounded across the vault's polished metal floor with startling speed: too risky to leave it operable. She would need to destroy it before making her escape. Absently, she jammed the sack of gold into the waistband of her pants.

A distant shout came from the streets below. Rime rolled her blazing white eyes. That meant she would need to trust in her guardian. This was never a welcome part of any strategy.

". . . ime? Rime! What's going onnnnn?" The voice came from the plaza beneath her.

Four ticks of the clock. The golem was bracing itself to fire, small pitons on its feet digging into the tile roof. The construct had surprised her, and she had pulled far too much magic in alarm, hurling herself through the roof. *Stupid. Wasteful. Dangerous. I don't have time to dance with this thing.* She pointed a finger toward the open plaza below and drew a circle on the ground in heatless flame. As a quick afterthought, she put a block letter "J" with a blinking arrow right above it. *Even he should figure that out, right?* It was easily forty feet to the blackstone streets; a fall would kill her. She would just have to trust her guardian to figure it out.

The golem's cannon fired.

Rime clenched both hands until her power burned white. The ball of iron and flame seemed to slow. She was the master of the Magic Wild and all she could see was a toy that needed breaking. Her laughter came quick as she flew to meet her foe. The lines of force were easy to follow, sketched in the air for her in sapphire blue, each vertex carefully annotated with the proper numeric notation for angle, speed, and force.

The golem was fuzzy, indistinct, already loading another shot; Rime's focus was on the cannonball. It would be easy enough to avoid it entirely. The mage didn't bother. She punched the ball with all the might her magic could generate. The lump of hot metal reversed course, fast as a flicked peapod. Rime burned her magic to go even faster, a frenetic arc to arrive before the first cannonball—just as the second cannonball spewed forth from the golem's chest. She didn't know if the golem had been designed to show surprise, but the glint in its crystalline green eyes was in the neighborhood of aghast.

Rime laughed and placed herself parallel to the imminent collision of the two cannonballs. A spike of pain circumnavigated her head, but she ignored it. She spread her small hands wide, wrapped in bright power, and smacked the two colliding lumps of iron together. Her magic reached into the kinetic frenzy of colliding metal and bent and twisted it to the image in her mind's eye. Before the golem's (perhaps) startled gaze, she formed the metal and fire and magic into a grotesque sledgehammer. The weapon seemed to grimace, dark iron burning red in the fires of its birth.

Rime grunted, wrapping her small hands around her creation's haft. It was a waste of time; the edges of her vision were already getting dim. She should have just dodged the cannonballs and eviscerated the golem with surgical fire. But there was style to be considered. And the way the Magic Wild sang in her veins: werewolf-golden howl of power. *Why can't it be this all the time? Why can't it be always this?*

The hammer came down, crushing the golem's head. A similar echo of nausea pealed inside her head. Rime ripped the dark sledge free and brought it down again and again, shards of wood and enchanted brass flying. *Not much time left. Need to finish.* In three heartbeats the hammer fell a dozen times. Rime took a ragged breath, a trickle of blood making its way from her left nostril down across her lips. The mage blazed away toward the edge of the roof, allowing herself one heartbeat to turn back and watch the golem topple and fall. As a parting gesture she squeezed the sledgehammer until it disintegrated into hundreds of burning iron pellets. They fell on the roof like rain, pitting and warping every moss-green tile they touched. The white flame of her magic began to dim, turning light blue and growing ever darker as it faded. She bobbed in place, her magic guttering like a torch in the wind. Wasting no more time, she stepped off the edge of the roof and sailed toward the glowing target she had drawn for her companion.

He was twenty feet from the target. *Of course he is.* Rime sighed.

Her companion was a square-faced young man, only a couple of years older than she. He was wearing a moth-eaten cloak of mud brown and a sword strapped to his back. Currently, he was shuffling back and forth in the plaza between the edge of the building and the illuminated target she had drawn for him.

Indecision was clear on his face, gone at once when he spotted her sailing toward the target. Jonas immediately backpedaled, his eyes locked on the falling girl.

Rime summoned forth one more erg of magic to keep herself aloft as the vision in her left eye went completely dark. It changed her smooth arc of a descent into a sudden updraft, raising her fifteen feet above the target. She held consciousness between her teeth and allowed the last bit of power to dribble away and vanish. Her body folded and dropped, deadweight, and she braced for impact with the stone plaza floor.

She landed square in Jonas's sweaty arms. Her guardian grunted with exertion, dropping to one knee. Rime could still see from her right eye and her fleeing vision was filled with the squire's mop of brown hair, flushed face, and broad grin.

"A glowing target. Your initial. An arrow," she complained.

"I couldn't tell what was happening up there. I wasn't sure if I should try to climb up the drain spout," Jonas apologized.

"Just . . ." Rime's voice faded as her awareness ebbed. "Just get us out of here."

The girl let go and sank into her private darkness.

Jonas pushed himself up to his feet. Rime's body was thin and small, light enough to be no trouble. *I really need to rig up some sort of sling. This is becoming a habit.* He balanced the mage in the crook of his left arm and pushed the hair out of her face with his right. Rime's hair was brown, but a swath of it had gone bone white over the past few months. It had begun as a small collection of locks, but now nearly a third of her hair was drained of color. *Why is her face covered with chocolate and candy sprinkles?*

Okay. Simple job. Get us out of here. Right. Jonas trotted away from the ruined bank, doing his best to look innocuous and not at all like a bank robber.

The city of Carroway was quiet just a few moments after dawn. Rime had picked this day and time with care. The day prior had been some sort of financial festival and one of the busiest days of the month for the establishment; the next day should be lightly staffed. She had concluded that entering the bank bare seconds after it opened would mean easy access to the hallway near the vault and a minimum of onlookers to cry alarm if a small girl suddenly made the intricate locks and gates fly open with a bolt of lightning. After her recent experience solving and disassembling a most intricate lock, she had been eager to try her hand at whatever the bank had to offer. Jonas had wanted to accompany her, but she had only instructed him to sit on a marble bench outside and wait for her. "You'll knock over something and track mud on the floor. Just wait here."

He had a pleasant time on the bench. A couple of sparrows flew by and ate some peanut shells in a nearby gutter. A stitch had started to give way in the hem of his cloak, so he had pulled out a needle and thread and set to mending it. Jonas had just started to whistle an old marching tune when the first muted rumble had come from inside the bank. He had sighed, tucked away his sewing kit, and stood up. The next explosion that blew glass out of every window in the bank found him ready with one hand already on the hilt of his good steel. The squire had made it as far as the tall archway that led to the entrance when he heard the explosion coming from above. The rain of melting roof tile had made it easy for him to guess where his companion was.

Now he ran through the streets of Carroway with his armful of unconscious mage. This was the trade district of the town; no residents to be disturbed by the predawn rooftop battle, but more than a few clerks, guild bonds, and one fat dwarf pushing a bagel cart were coming into the plaza with wide eyes and fearful questions. An attractive goblin with blue hair and a sharp business cloak eyed his flapping brown one with disdain. Jonas put his head down and ran.

He ran out of the plaza and down mimic streets of blackstone, repeating again and again. They all looked the same, so he turned wherever felt right. The squire did his best to keep moving east toward the port. Rime breathed shallow and thin in his arms. He briefly considered throwing her over his shoulder for convenience, but he decided that it would be better to avoid the wrath of an upside-down wild mage. The girl's blackouts were never of certain length: sometimes a few minutes, a few hours, and once or twice over a day. Jonas was on his own until she woke up.

To his great shock, the squire made it to the docks without incident. The dawn light gleamed on the streets of Carroway, just picking up the barest sparkle of the minerals pulverized within. He had nearly wrenched his neck out of socket, craning at every open alleyway or opening door expecting a horrendous wooden golem to come smoking forth or armed bank rangers to loose a volley of golden arrows. *This is one of those times that Master would talk about. Where you were supposed to run into trouble, but Trouble spilled morning coffee on his tunic and got a late start.* Jonas could see his master's lean face spreading into a low chuckle. *But don't worry, young man. Trouble always keeps his appointments, late or no. Enjoy the days you missed him because he'll be double furious next time around.*

The docks were busy, even this early in the morning. Four dwarves were tossing sacks of meal from a battered crate up onto the deck of a ship while singing lustily. A fat wood-elf bellowed over the side of his ship either demanding more cats or less cats, Jonas wasn't sure. Two Minotaurs were standing chest deep in the bay applying pitch and resin to a new patch in the side of a low sloop. The squire puffed up the stairs to the warehouse attic he

and Rime had rented yesterday. The sun's gold made a black outline of his form on the cracked stone sea break running alongside
the warehouse. Jonas had to bang his shoulder twice against the
splitting wood before the salt-crusted doorjamb gave way.

The attic was a drafty loft facing the ocean with one wide window, snaggle-toothed with broken glass. Rime had pressed her
last three copper coins into the hawk's talon yesterday in return
for two nights' lodging. The fat bird had squawked a warning
about gem crabs in the loft and defecated all over its perch as
way of punctuation. "It's a roof; that's all we need. We'll be gone
tomorrow," his companion had said, plopping her bedroll down
in the center of the attic.

Gone tomorrow. Jonas shook the words off. They fell down in
the folds of his cloak and set to smoldering. He knew where they
were going, though Rime had never named their destination. A
witch of his acquaintance had left little doubt in his mind where
the wild mage was taking them both. *Home.*

He placed Rime's sleeping body carefully on her bedroll and
propped her head up with his satchel. The squire splashed the
edge of his cloak with water from his canteen and did his best to
wipe the scorched confection off the mage's face. He noticed the
jingling sack of gold in the girl's pants making an uncomfortable
bulge in the thin fabric. Jonas was already reaching to remove it
when he abruptly realized what he was doing and hastily pulled
his hands back, cheeks growing warm. *It's safer there anyway.*

A few steps to the broken window and Jonas looked out over
the bustling dock. He gave the crowd a slow scan: no followers
or hard-eyes, no one paying the attic the least bit of attention.
Certainly the morning's bank robbery turned bank demolition
would be attracting heavily armed notice from the Third Regiment
of Carroway, but for the moment they appeared to be safe. He
squinted at the sun. *One—no, two—hours. I'll let her sleep for two*

hours. If she isn't up by then, I guess I'll move us somewhere else. Maybe hire a ship?

A ship was a decision. Jonas had made that sort of decision before, when he begged his way onto a ship heading north, away from Gilead. Now he was about to get on a ship going south, back to Gilead. *"Gilly-son, gilly-son, come 'round the bend."* The old doggerel came to his mind unbidden. *"Stones in the river and your own grave to tend."* It was a march; most of the songs he knew were marches of one sort or other. In the Academy that was what they sang, excepting a rare ballad or two on feast days and hymns at the turn of night.

I have to tell her. I have to tell it all. Jonas looked down at Rime. *If she's going to Gilead, I'm going too. But I don't know how far she'll get with me at her side.* He pulled the red cord of his sword-strap, wrapping both hands around it.

"I'm a murderer," Jonas said to the sleeping girl. "The last person I was supposed to protect, I cut his throat. I killed my master."

Rime began to snore muzzily into the leather satchel.

"Hey. That went pretty well." The squire sat down and pulled his sewing kit back out. His cloak was not going to mend itself.

RIME'S DREAM #1

Bricks bricks bricks
Fingertips on bricks
Counting the bricks
Counting the bricks
There are many bricks
Climbing the bricks or crawling the bricks?
Another brick another brick
Brick brick cold brick colder brick

Ice on the bricks
Ice brick ice brick ice brick brick brick

Rime woke up. A small puddle of drool had formed on the leather satchel under her face, but the smelly bag had gotten revenge by imprinting the thick outline of the buckle on her left cheek. She growled and pushed herself up, rubbing the indention in irritation. Jonas was across the room with needle and thread and the hem of his brown cloak supported on his knees. They were in the stinking loft next to the docks.

She opened her mouth to berate her guardian but checked herself. Jonas was sitting in the perfect position to look out the broken bay window and keep an eye on the street below. A quick glance at the position of the sun told her only 113 minutes had elapsed since her blackout. A skilled, swift, savvy citizen of Carroway could run from the bank plaza to the docks in thirty-five minutes at a dead run. Jonas was none of the above, so probably between forty-five minutes and a flat hour for him to find his way back here. That meant that they had been resting here for a reasonable amount of time. This was their only base of operations in the city, and it showed sound judgment on the squire's part to retreat here when left without other instructions. The squire had performed his duties well. Rime snorted and concentrated harder. There must be something she could find fault with. She shifted on her bedroll and felt the bank pouch dig into her hip.

"Why is there money still in my pants?" Rime groaned and pulled the sack free with a sigh.

"It didn't seem, uh, proper?" Jonas said primly, tucking his needle and thread away into its tiny leather clutch.

"Proper." She let it drop and pulled the bank sack open. It was an unfamiliar fabric, a durable and tough purple weave laced with gold thread. *A question for another time. I'll make a note of it . . . later.* Rime made a quick count of the steel coins within, letting them trickle through her fingers. Like all currency minted in Valeria, the coins emitted a dim blue radiance to prove their authenticity. In a city populated by dozens of wizard colleges, the opportunity for illusory or ensorcelled coinage was a legitimate concern, but the proper coins were embedded with a cunning enchantment. Local vendors were taught a simple cantrip that could identify them. And here in the wide world they were considered of almost inarguable value, one of the most stable currencies in Aufero. Perfect for traveling.

Traveling. Rime looked at Jonas's waiting face as she considered. The coins here were a pittance compared to her family's total wealth but a small fortune for her needs on the road. With the first half of this she had paid a group of caravan guards to escort her, bought rations for two weeks, paid for lodging at a few fine inns. What would she do with the other half of it? *I will do what I must.* The sun's clock moved forward, and not even her power could confound time. She needed to book passage on a ship; she needed to be gone. The hounds of this city would be at their door before noon at her estimation. She needed to go now.

Which meant that the Conversation could no longer be avoided. She had been formulating it for days. The shaggy-haired guardian and his sword had become a comfort and a surprising place for her trust. From the first days of their quest searching for the Gray Witch, through the terrible night in Bellwether Manor, he had lumbered into a special space in her esteem. Together they had defeated the nefarious Hunt, leaving its commander Linus dead and forgotten on the lonely shore. Thoughts of journeying on across the sea without him were brittle and thorn edged. Rime shivered. *Am I buying one ticket or two?*

"Time is short, so I'll speak swiftly. You've known that I have a goal. I appreciate your courtesy in not demanding to know our final destination all these long days and miles," she began.

Jonas blinked.

Rime gritted her teeth and plowed ahead. "Much to my surprise you have been an *admirable* companion"—she had finally arrived on that epithet after much deliberation as it meant that Jonas was capable of being admired without explicitly saying that she did in fact admire him—"and have proven worthy of my trust."

"Rime, you don't, uh . . ." Her companion raised a faltering hand.

"I have to go to Gilead. I didn't tell you before because I know you ran away from there. So I will understand if you will not or cannot return." This was where her construction of the Conversation got rocky. She was surprised at how much she wanted the stupid squire at her side and completely lost as to how to convince him to remain there. Rime wanted desperately to withdraw within her own mind—into her place of safety and lore—a library of sorts where she could think and plan, revise the Conversation a few dozen more times, but she hadn't been in there in days and had no wish to risk the long shadows of her mind now.

"I'll go." Jonas grimaced. "Though you may not want me to."

Rime felt a burst of relief followed hard by disgust with herself. She pushed it aside and latched onto the thread spinning off the squire's words that led into the past. "Trouble in Gilead. You ran away from it. How bad?"

"Bad."

"How long to explain?" The mage felt the sun's time press against her.

"Uhh . . . well . . ." Jonas's eyes searched the ceiling for inspiration.

"Too long. You want to go. I want you to go. You can tell me on the boat." Rime reached down to roll up her bedding, then tossed their battered satchel to the squire. She wished she had thrown it harder when she saw his creased smile beaming across the salt-air loft.

"It's really bad, Rime." Jonas's face sobered. "You may not want me along when you know. Even less with the whole story."

"Tell me on the boat." Rime slung the bedroll over her shoulder and pulled her wide-brimmed hat from the rust-green nail where it waited. She was still wearing borrowed finery, a blue dress surmounted with a white half cape and hood. It was more than a little spattered with travel and chocolate but could still help her pass as a noble's daughter. She thought about what she had done in those halls—thought about the bard's blood she could still feel wet on her left hand. *Whatever Jonas has done can't be worse than what I've done. Or what I will do when the magic escapes my grasp.* She knew what was inside her head. *Madness. Death. A ticking clock. My tiny library surrounded by oceans of dark. Got to get moving.*

Jonas swung the satchel over his head and tucked it in beside his sword's scabbard. He followed the mage back down the clapboard steps. As they reached the ground, he very gently pinched the fabric at her elbow. Rime rolled her eyes, stopped, and turned around. Her guardian's face was uncertain, as if struggling to find the right words to say. Impatient, she poked his sternum with two fingers.

"Okay, okay." Jonas rubbed his chest in chagrin. "I just wanted to say that a ship is a decision. I'm glad we're taking this one together."

Rime spun to hide her smile and advanced toward the waiting docks. *Me too.*

CHAPTER THREE

THE HUNT

His armor was heavy. The slow weight of the pauldrons pressing into his shoulders, the bite of the breastplate if he turned too quickly, the cold pinch of the gauntlets on his pale skin: this was how he knew who he was. The weight was memory, the weight was duty, and the weight was home. The weight was dragging him down. He was an old man by any measure: limbs thin, his bones pressing against every line of his frame. What little hair he had on his head was silver. Gray iron, silver hair, and a white sword. The sword was heaviest of all, heavier than forged metal, heavier than Time.

He was Linus the Blue. He had been pulled back from death. Again and again and again, and each time he wept and found his memory in the weight of his armor, in the quiet menace of the white sword at his side. He had a duty, a charge that none but he could fulfill.

But it was heavy.

"The trail leads to this dock, boss." His assassin crouched, perching on the flat circle of a nearby dock brace like a horned gargoyle. "She knocked off the bank, ran back to that attic hidey-hole, then traipsed right down here and got on the boat. I bent a few arms of the sailors around here to make sure everyone's memory was clear. But unless the boat was an invisible boat, it's gone."

The orange-skinned assassin pointed at the empty water at the end of the dock. Linus's companion, Sideways, was extremely skilled and had proved his reputation and reliability time and time again. He still made Linus's head throb, however.

"What was the name of the ship?" Linus asked patiently.

"Boat's called the *Cormorant*." Sideways shrugged as if to suggest he had no strong opinion of the quality of the craft's moniker.

Linus turned and looked out across the waves. Carroway was on the western edge of the landmass, just a few days' travel south from where he had recently been reborn. The port was not as massive as some he had seen in his travels: Quorum, Parajuelego, Pice. But what it lacked in scale, it made up for in variety. Carroway was a hungry city, and ships from many nations found their way to these algae-coated docks. Several of the ships bore the mark of the Seafoam Trading Company. The bulk of their trade was plied across the skies of Aufero, but they still kept a healthy interest in sea travel. *They would not have booked passage on one of those— too much paperwork and the chance of being discovered. A private trader, perhaps, or one from a less circumspect company.*

"Did you learn anything of the ship's captain?"

"Tarwell Blackberry is his name, small trader. Mainly foodstuffs out of Pice. Keeps his crew small, just a few hands and his daughter." Sideways's eyes were focused on the waves as well, following the lightning-quick movement of some fish below. His squashed-coral horns angled down toward the water hungrily.

"Perfect. She chose well. A ship capable of a fair distance but small and flying no banner. A family-owned ship is always eager for extra gold; they are the most defenseless against the vagaries of the sea. Honest enough to carry them to their destination but crooked enough to not ask too many questions. Mouths to feed, bills to pay." The ironclad knight chuckled. "She tore the bank apart at dawn and was already on the water before noon. Splendid, *Doma*."

"What now? That was yesterday. She's more than a day ahead of us. No way to know what direction she headed. I got ten different directions from the salt dogs I questioned." The devilkin leered and cocked his pointed orange chin at Linus. "And we can't trust to luck this time, I think."

Linus nodded. The assassin was right. They had been making their way south from that lonely bit of shore where they had faced the wild mage a few weeks before when they had come across a caravan of silversmiths. They had shared news of the road, but the smiths spoke only of the explosive robbery that had taken place that morning as they were leaving Carroway. Where Rime Korvanus went, explosions were sure to follow. The knight and his cohort pushed on until well past midnight to arrive at the scene of the crime. The bank's magister had recognized his badge of office and was all too eager to enlist the hunter's aid.

His lips bent again into a smile. Seeing the devastation she had caused gave him a feeling almost nearing pride. It was the feeling a hunter got when he found a particularly savage gryphon or a tiger with blood still on its jaws. It made the weight worthwhile. It made it all mean something, something grander.

Linus pulled his left hand free from his gauntlet so he could rub his throbbing forehead with his fingertips. It had been many years since a sleepless night could be had without cost. *I'm still weak from the sword's . . . call.* He had never understood by what strange power the sword could pull him back from the cool waters of death, nor why it would wait three days before doing so. Nor how the blade could rend and erase the very fabric of any magical energy. *I will need to sleep soon. Sleep soon and deeply.* The white sword, all but featureless and blank, was the perfect weapon for his charge, for his Hunt. *I will sleep deeply indeed when she is dead—when the sword cuts the life out of* Doma *Rime Korvanus. Maybe then it will let me go at last.*

He pulled his iron gauntlet back on. He was too old to believe such things.

Sideways hopped down from his perch and crossed his arms, waiting for Linus's word.

"Come. We gather nothing here but sea air." Linus turned back toward the city. "We have resources that we must collect, and you have an errand to run."

The gray-leather boots fell in behind the iron plate. "An errand?"

"When the Hunt was needed more often, we kept supply caches in most major cities throughout the land. We never knew where a new abomination would appear. There is one close at hand, and I believe it has something that will aid us. You must go to the market and obtain some food."

"Oh, of course! You haven't had your breakfast. I'll be happy to run and pick up whatever you need. Bagels, cheese? Maybe a little wine? Your color is looking rough, boss."

Linus gave the devilkin his breakfast order and directions to the Hunt supply depot. Sideways departed with an uncomfortable wrinkle on his brow, his horns angled toward the earth.

He walked with a retinue of ghosts. It was common. It was drab as the steel he wore, familiar and sure, gray phantoms of memory at his elbows nodding and sighing like so many gulls.

Late morning sun arched over his head, illuminating the foul gray bricks of the warehouse. Linus wished he could stop and lean against them for a moment, but he kept his back straight. *I'm the last. The last of the great Hunt. After me there will be no others.*

His stomach rumbled. He was alone in the gray alley, but all the same he was not. The ghosts stood at his elbows, all those who had fallen to the vicious power of his quarry. Friends and followers and strangers on the train, a bread seller's wife with her head split open by emerald fire, one blue eye boiling as she screamed— forever caught in his memory. *That was the tall one with the beard—the Breaker, wasn't it? Or was it the Empty Academy?* He sometimes jumbled his past quarry but could never forget their victims.

Linus and his fellow hunters had given each wild mage an honorific, partly for quick reference, but also for the distance it allowed. It was much easier to feel righteous slitting the Breaker's throat as he slept—not so grand if one thought of his birth name, Pelton Vail. He had been a spindly lumberjack from the Hollow who found one day that he could command the trees to kneel, to snap their branches into neat cords and stacks—all at his will. Wild mages often started that way: a simple miracle, a grand moment, and an impossible talent. But they all ended the same. *Madness and blood.* Sooner rather than late, now instead of then, their miracles would turn to mire. *I should give* Doma Korvanus *a name,* Linus mused as he turned the corner of the drab warehouse.

The alley before him was filled with broken crates and upended canisters that had once held some sort of fuel. He sighed and pushed his way through, feeling the sick twinge of his joints. Linus chuckled, thinking of the great power he could bring to bear both martial and magical, the armies of many nations if it came to that—but it did him little good in getting past a rotting pile of trash. Wild mages had once been all too common—a grand threat requiring the assembled might of many nations. Now there was only one young woman to chase and one old hunter contending with splintered boards and stinking refuse in the pursuit. The alley terminated in a brick wall plastered over with a faded poster worn down to yellow shadows by rain and sun. The hunter placed a gentle hand on the wall.

"Hello, old friend." He blinked and saw the poster brand-new—an advertisement for a traveling show, a hoary wooden galleon slipping through the clouds, a steely-eyed sky pirate hanging from the side with a beautiful blonde nobly trying to pull both the man and her décolletage into some sort of order. On the deck shadowy figures gathered, led by a hooded figure in red. Linus blinked again and the colors drained away—the only part still clear the pirate's hook that was drawn as if made of lightning. Linus had never seen the show—too busy. It was some fantastical fluff spun from the barest threads of history. The hunter's hand moved across the yellow parchment and pressed the hidden switch just below the red hood.

To his right there was a door. The door was simple oak, unpainted, with a brass knob. There had not been a door before he pushed the crumbling brick, but there was a door now. Linus had spent a few idle days throughout his service trying to determine the method of this cache's hidden door but had never proved successful. He had been tempted many times to simply march into the archives and look up the original work order but had determined to respect the craft of this portal with the continued unsolved riddle in his head like a canker sore. Other caches in other cities had much more mundane entrances: trapdoors, toma-gates, a moat filled with rage-spelled pixies. He gave the damnable oak a salute as he passed through it, turning sharply to the left and heading down the metal stairs into the cache below. His iron-shod boots rang on the steps like vicious bells.

The interior was crammed with sleeping shadows; Linus had to rap sharply on a few glow-globes to get them to spring into feeble illumination. He glanced around, watching the lumbering shadows retreat to the corners to continue their interrupted naps. The chamber was mostly round. It had once been used for some function in the city's sewage system—a central pool had long ago been drained and filled with thick leather chairs and racks for weapons, books, and scrolls. A massive map of the globe still hung taut on the far wall; ivory pins with brightly colored heads winked at him in the untrustworthy light. Old Hunts, old lives. The ghosts at his heels filed their way in and took their places in the dust-covered chairs. Linus took a long breath and braced himself as the smell took him back. Back to when his armor had felt light as copper, his purpose bright as the sun. Back before he died the first time.

"Ahem." A very nonspectral voice interrupted his reverie.

Linus looked up the metal stairs to where his associate, Sideways, stood. The assassin came down the metal stairs without another whisper, a dirty green duffel bag tied off with a cord carried over his shoulder. He placed the bag in one of the mold-eaten chairs, then straightened, his eyes carefully empty.

"Your breakfast," Sideways said.

"Not mine." Linus strode across the dusty tile toward a metal cabinet that ran from floor to ceiling, nearly double the old man's height. Black cables, thick and coiled like snakes, erupted from one side, burying themselves down into the tile, hungry for sustenance. The cabinet was not locked, even during the Hunt's height it had not been. *Some weapons are their own warning.* Only in great desperation would a hunter ask to employ the metal coffin's contents; only when the trail had gone cold, as cold as a winter's dawn. Only with careful thought would permission be granted. Linus had only seen these doors swing wide a handful of times throughout the long years. *Some tools require so much wisdom and skill that only the best can be trusted with them.* He paused only a moment as his gauntlets closed on the simple handles, then flung the cabinet wide. *And when the cost is so high for such a tool, couldn't the best find some other, any other, option?*

It sat on its haunches in the cabinet. The head of brass-etched steel lay quiet on its chest, a strange barrel of glass. The hound's paws were held in a neat row as if ready for inspection. Unlike everything else in this chamber, there was not a speck of dust, the glass dog was immaculately clean, as if Time itself had been afraid to slip past the metal doors of its cabinet. Linus's mouth quirked in what was almost fondness. He slid his hand free off the iron gauntlet and placed his palm on the hound's broad forehead.

Sideways leaned so far over trying to get a better view that one mangled horn could have easily scratched his knee. Linus spared his rogue a wry glance; the green sack nearby gave a slight twitch.

The first taste must be from the master, the knight reminded himself and carefully placed his naked hand between the hound's steel jaws. *But just a taste.*

The metal was cool to the touch but soon began to grow colder. Linus braced himself as a faint blue light blossomed in the glass chest of the hound, and her head began to stir. He sagged with weariness as strength seemed to flow out of him and into the dog. The cerulean light flared brighter. It was soon bright enough to see the ceramic shield on her chest—circular and printed with a crashing wave—the sigil of her manufacturers the Seafoam Trading Company. Linus slipped his hand free. A spike of nausea ran through his gut, causing him to lean on the glass dog's shoulder for support.

The hound raised her head, eyes empty hollows of sky-blue light.

"Hello, Nora." Linus sighed with satisfaction.

The devilkin unfolded himself and gave the automaton a wide berth as it stepped down delicately from the metal cabinet. "So this is 'resources'?" Sideways muttered.

"It is. The mage-hounds were designed with great care, a strange synthesis of Precursor technology and some alchemical processes. I admit I've never grasped the underlying lore, but I am intimately familiar with the effect. With the proper resonance achieved they can track almost any type of magic, set and maintained by the hound's core." Linus ran a fond hand down Nora's glass back. "Elemental, necromantic, a summoner's forge, a druid's roots."

"Ah—what kind of range do they have?" The assassin's professional curiosity peeked out.

"A few hundred miles, though it can grow complicated if there is more than one target within range. The hounds always seek the closest, strongest signal." Linus watched as Nora took a few steps into the center of the chamber, her flat head turning back and forth like a slow metronome. "But that will not be an issue in this case. Nora is very special. She tracks only the Magic Wild, and there is only one who bears it, and that is our quarry."

"Wait—how can you be so sure that Skinny Girl is the only one?" The assassin crossed his arms and then snapped his attention in alarm when the glass hound suddenly stumbled to a halt, the blue fire inside beginning to flicker. "Whoa, what's wrong with your pup?"

"I'm sure," Linus said, crossing the chamber to the green sack full of "breakfast." Without ceremony he ripped the cord free and dumped the sack's contents on the floor.

It smelled terrible. It hadn't shaved in weeks, a mud-spotted tunic the only clothing it wore. It was human, not that it mattered. Nora whined, an almost musical thrum like a bassoon. Linus pointed at the vagrant and said, "Feed."

Nora's flat head bobbed with delight and loped over. Her mouth was large enough that the vagrant's chest nearly disappeared inside. Linus saw the human's eyes flutter open and his mouth work, trying to voice a question or perhaps cry for help. The cold of Nora's jaws soon ended that as the human's life was absorbed, energy to stoke her blue flame. The knight nodded. The assassin had done his job well, even though it had been distasteful to him.

"We will return to the docks and pick up the trail." Linus watched the knowledge of death pool in the vagrant's eyes and a pitiful line of slobber pour down his lips. "Then we will book passage on a ship—a large ship with many passengers."

Sideways nodded, turned, then stopped—shoulders tight in his gray leather armor. "Lots of passengers?"

"Yes." Linus patted the glass dog's head as she dropped her breakfast on the floor.

CHAPTER FOUR

JONAS & RIME

The deck of the *Cormorant* was stained a dark nut-brown. Rime did not particularly recognize the wood grain itself, but she assumed that the signature color came from the staggering amount of coffee that the captain continually sloshed and spilled every which way from a dented metal tankard that he carried as a permanent fixture in his left hand. Captain Tarwell Blackberry seemed to be a constant slow dervish, talking and pointing and tying a line here and refilling his coffee flagon there, issuing sharp controlled screams of indistinguishable orders in the direction of his first mate and two crewmen. All the while the tepid brown liquid sloshed and spattered on the deck as unnoticed as the salt spray. His orders were carried out with a certain degree of blithe humor by the crewmen, two boys of ten and eleven, and with a seething disdain by his first mate, a tall black-haired girl of eighteen and a half years. Rime knew each of the crew's names and ages because they were constantly referenced and repeated by the captain. They were his eldest daughter and two sons.

"Londra! Londra! Dammit, watch that throttle now! You have to keep a steady hand or you'll burn through all of our . . ." Captain Blackberry took a long slurp from his coffee.

"Yes, Father. I know." The tall girl did not take her eyes from the seas ahead, accustomed and unaffected by her captain's exhortations.

"Wick! Tell your brother to stow that line properly now!" The captain spun, and Rime ducked underneath the arm of his bright-red coat. The first day she had nearly been tossed overboard by just such a powerful gesticulation and had learned to never take her eyes off the man when he was less than fifteen feet away from her.

The *Cormorant* was a small ship powered by a simple Arkanic reactor. It could burn any mineral of sufficient complexity for its fuel source. A family-owned ship like this mainly used quartz or spike-granite; larger ships required far more exotic and expensive fuel sources—or different means of propulsion entirely. *Another gift of the Precursors, another tiny machine that we use barely understanding how it works. Another shadow . . .* Rime cut herself short. It was a beautiful day. The sun was bright. The sea air was sharp in her nostrils, and she had only had coffee spilled on her once this morning. She would not think about ancient history today.

She carefully extricated herself from the captain's blast radius and made her way toward the prow of the ship. The youngest Blackberry lumbered by with his arms full of some sort of tarp. She gave him a wide berth as well. Fortunately the pile in his arms kept him from having an unobstructed view of her. The youngest was named Warp, and over the past day and a half of travel he had spent a great deal of time staring at her with his eyes moon-wide. *I've already got one boy stumbling around after me; I certainly don't need another.*

Her guardian sat in the prow with his back against the simple wood, his eyes determinedly focused on his cloak and thread. Rime had been amused to discover that while Jonas did not get "seasick" to the cartoonish degree so often portrayed in plays and novels, sea travel did make him queasy, and he preferred whenever possible to keep his attention off the vast horizon of blue water that surrounded them.

"Hey." Rime leaned against the prow, taking a deep breath of the salt air.

Jonas grunted.

"So. Want to tell me your dark secrets?"

The squire sighed, his eyes still on the needle and thread; the hem of his brown cloak that always seemed to need repair. "Rime. I . . . look, I know I told you that I would tell you the story. But it's hard, okay, it's just, I mean—how do I tell it? How do I tell it right? There are a lot of parts to it. I want to make sure I have it all straight and together in my head so I can tell it right."

Rime rubbed her eyes and tried to keep her patience. "I understand, but we're landing in Shiloh sometime tomorrow. We're stepping off this boat right onto the soil of Gilead. You told me it was bad, the reason you ran away. I kind of need to know exactly how bad, and the more time I have to plan, the better."

Jonas tied off a knot in the thread and bit off the excess. He stowed the thread and needle away and replied without looking up. "Tonight, okay? I'll tell you the whole story tonight."

She looked out across the crisp blue waves and closed her eyes for a moment. Impatience did battle with some other less familiar sentiment and surprisingly gave over the field. "Okay, tonight, then."

"Right here, after dinner." Jonas tapped the deck. "Tales like this need the open sky as judge."

That night a storm hit. Captain Blackberry and his brood carefully sealed each hatch and were more than a little mystified when their two passengers insisted on going back on deck.

"It's pouring rain, Miss! The sea and wind is calm enough, but you'll be soaked through in an instant." The captain offered her a sailcloth jacket many sizes too large. "At least take this."

"No," Rime almost hissed. "It's an important religious ceremony for my guardian. Very important. Absolutely no way that it could be performed in the dry comfort of our quarters."

Jonas flushed but pushed past out into the driving rain with stubborn boot steps.

"Here's your hat," Londra said, passing the wide-brimmed item into Rime's hands. The mage bit her tongue, crammed it on her head, and stomped out into the storm.

She found Jonas doing his level best to lash a piece of tarp across the point of the prow to give them some sort of cover. Rime grabbed the back of his tunic and pulled him back. With a quick glance to make certain that the Blackberry clan had sealed the hatch behind her, her eyes flared and she snapped her fingers. The tarp jumped to attention, flinging rain like a catapult. The lengths of rope wrapped around the steel eyes set into the railing for just such a purpose like snakes; the entire impromptu awning drew taut and Rime bent down to get in out of the rain. Jonas shook his shaggy hair like a wet dog and followed.

This tiny burst of magic only whetted her appetite, so Rime went ahead and pulled all of the water from her soaked clothing into a neat ball that hovered over her palm. Her companion watched with interest, brow furrowing when he realized that he was not going to be similarly dried out. The mage concentrated, forcing the water to become solid, to form into a lantern of ice shaped like a crescent moon. With a final nod the lantern began to glow with a cool green light, making the awning a small peapod of illumination surrounded by rain and dark and sea.

Rime sat the lantern down on the deck in satisfaction. It required a small bit of her will to maintain but nothing that would tax her overmuch. She would let it fade when the squire's story ended. Peering into Jonas's face, she saw his gaze fixed on the brown-stained planks, now turned almost purple in her lantern's light. The dull roar of the rain made her lean in close to catch his first words.

"My father was a baker. We baked bread mostly—loaves for the common folk—though every so often we'd do special things for feast days. Cupcakes, cookies, cakes, all the . . ."

"NO." Rime nearly exploded. "You cannot start the story this way. Are you going to tell me the entire story of your life? Can't you just skip to the part that matters?"

"It all matters, Rime," Jonas said, hurt clear in his eyes. "I told you, I have no skill in telling a tale. But this is my story. Please let me tell it the best I can."

"Fine." The mage settled back against the *Cormorant's* rail with ill grace. "Tell it, then."

"My father was a baker. We baked bread mostly, loaves for the common folk. Sometimes we'd do special things for feast-days: cupcakes, cookies, and the like. I thought for most of my life that flour and yeast were all there was for me. I used to play in the streets with the other kids pretending to be in the Legion, pretending to be Alain the White, pretending to fight monsters—but at the end of the day I knew that I was going to live my life making bread. It didn't bother me; it was just the way things were. I never prayed for anything different on church days. When I swung my wooden sword I always knew it was just a game, just a dream. The Academy was for the families with the right blood or the right coin, and mine had neither. But then, one day . . ."

"I get it. You were poor, but you got in the Academy somehow, right? It's a big deal for you and your family. Is this part of the *bad stuff*?" Rime demanded.

"Well, not really. It happened after I had been in the Academy for two years and was ready for the final part of . . ."

"Okay, then! Can we just skip a little bit?"

Jonas flopped wet hair out of his face and managed a rueful smile. "Yeah, okay."

The mage made an imperious gesture and settled back in her spot.

"At the end of our training, all of the cadets have a choice. They can join the regular Legion as soldiers or if they can find a knight to sponsor them, they become squires. They receive special training from their master and one day become knights themselves. To serve in the Legion is an honor, but to become a Knight of Gilead, the Order of the Wand, the Bow, the Sword, and the Scroll. There is no higher honor, no greater calling. To me . . . to me it was . . . impossible." Jonas smiled again. "I didn't even seek out a single knight. I was happy to go into the Legion as a soldier. But on Measure Day, we all stood in rows according to our units. The knights would walk up and down inspecting us—a tradition, a formality—all of the matches were prearranged, of course. But then he put his hand on my shoulder. He chose *me*. Sir Matthew Pocket with his silver sword, Hecate, at his side. He walked right up like he had known me my entire life and put his hand on my shoulder. 'Let's go'—that's what he said. Rime, you have to understand, it was like a piece of a legend walking up and touching me. All the dreams I'd never been brave enough to have, all of the prayers I'd been too small to pray, that wooden sword in my hands in the alley, all of it! Right there in front of me. Choosing *me*."

Rime, for once, said nothing.

"Not that he really looked all that impressive." Jonas laughed, eyes lost in memory. "He had this long white mustache that was always getting caught in his mouth. And his skin was so crinkly that he looked like an old potato. But he was a hero; he was my master. He taught me so much. Everything, really. Everything that mattered. In the Academy they teach you how to fight with a sword; he taught me when not to. Before, everything about being a soldier, about being a knight, was just words; he taught me what they meant, what it could mean for someone to stand against injustice, to stand against evil. To do good, to be a Hero True."

The squire's body was tight with concentration. Rime saw the tears begin to slide down his face and then was startled to find her companion looking directly into her eyes.

"I know I can't really make you understand, make you feel it. I'm not telling it right. He was the best. The best I've ever met, maybe that there ever was. To stand at his side for even a short time was the greatest honor of my life, more than I'll ever, ever deserve. The thought that I could be a knight . . . I'm . . . I'm not telling it right."

Rime reached across the lantern and, without breaking eye contact, took her guardian's hand. "Tell me the rest. You have to. There's no turning back now."

Jonas took a long breath, and then nodded. "It was his sword, you see. I'm sure even you've heard the tales of the monsters he fought—the darkness he could find where all other hunters would give up. Sir Matthew Pocket and his shining blade, Hecate, the sword blessed by the three moons. I was only with him for a few months, but I saw him face things of great evil. Vampires, bog wraiths, an archlich and his skeletal horde. He kept me safe from all that. I wish you could have seen it. It was like watching a god—a story made flesh—he and the silver sword tore through the dark like . . . like light itself. I was with him for almost a year before he finally trusted me enough to tell me his secret. His curse."

The mage leaned in, eyes wide.

"You see, the sword didn't lead him to evil, it *drew* evil to him. He told me one night over dinner in his tower when the Black

Moon was new. The sword was blessed by the moons with great power but cursed as well. As the Black Moon waxed the effect grew worse; every dark heart for miles around would find itself inexorably drawn to Hecate and her master. And he would deal with them, had been dealing with them for nearly twenty years at that point. And he was tired, so tired. Tired of never being able to stay in one place for long, tired of never having any family, tired of the endless nights of blood and death. So he asked me."

"What did he ask you, Jonas?"

The squire looked down at his navel, his hands twined. He spoke very quietly, just above the rain. "He asked me to kill him. That night. He had traveled far with Hecate and knew that the curse could only be passed to a willing bearer. But if he died still the sword's master, then the curse would fade. That's why he'd picked me, he said. I had no prestige or gold to risk. He could train me as best he could, then present me with the facts and trust to my good steel."

Rime gritted her teeth, anger held close. "He *used* you, Jonas. He made you love him, made you worship him . . ."

"Yes. I did. I did love him," Jonas said. "I also cut his throat. We finished dinner; he drank a good deal of wine. He gave me a huge purse of gold for my escape. I stuffed it into my pack. I walked right up to him. He was fast asleep, wine sleep. I took the knife I used to cut potatoes and I opened his throat."

"But why? I know he told you to, but if he wanted to die, why make you do it? Why couldn't he take poison or hang himself or fall on his precious sword?" Rime stood up on her knees, nearly upsetting the lantern. "And why did you just run off into the night like a thief? You had to know there would be a hue and cry, stories told about the 'murderer' of the great hero. Dammit, Jonas, why?"

She was yelling directly into his face now, fists balled into the sodden brown cloak at his shoulders. Their faces were inches apart, and she could see his eyes like empty wells, and down at the bottom Jonas was drowning.

"Because I'm not supposed to be a knight," he said. "Because I was never going to be. I'm a baker's son. It was my charge to keep him safe, to learn from him, to be worthy of the burden he carried. I couldn't do any of that, not really. He was the greatest man I'll ever know, and if the only purpose he found suitable for me was executioner, then it was . . ."

"Shut up. SHUT UP. SHUT UP." Rime's anger tore through the tiny awning, flinging the tarp off into the wind. The delicate lantern of magic and ice she had crafted burst and began to melt, lost among falling rain. Water poured down around them, and her eyes crackled and shone like the lightning the storm itself could not muster. Jonas blinked, unafraid—his slow litany at least halted by her outburst of emotion and power. "He used you. Used you and you *thank him for it.* I don't care how many songs they sing about him or how many statues of him the birds shit on in Corinth. He isn't worth more than you. His quiet little death stinks to high heaven, and only a fucking moron like you would throw away your good name and your life because some gray hair told you to."

"Rime, I . . ."

"I'm not finished." The mage dragged the much taller boy to his feet and snarled through the pounding rain. "I can't believe it. You've been moping around the world, drinking your way from town to town, and this is the story?"

"I failed, Rime. I failed my charge. Only Once." Jonas managed to get her small hands off him. "I did what he commanded, I did what he asked. But I shouldn't have—I should have found another way. If I was a hero or a knight, I could've figured it out. But I couldn't, so I did what he said and then I ran."

"Yeah, yeah, 'Only Once.' You only get one life, but yours isn't over yet. And you are in luck, because we are going to the throne of the king." Rime crossed her arms. "I need to go there anyway— once we're there, you can plead your case. If Gilead is truly the land of heroism and justice that you say, we can clear your name."

Jonas shook his head, startled. "Wait, wait—what? We're going to see the king? Why are we going to see the king? *How* are we going to see the king?"

The mage grimaced. She hadn't intended to be as explicit with her guardian. "The . . . the Gray Witch told me that was where I had to go."

The squire's eyes bugged out, and he had a small coughing fit. Rime understood; the Gray Witch made her feel much the same. She and Jonas had sought her counsel a few weeks back only to be rewarded with riddles. But as was often the case in such matters, the riddles the witch had dangled bore just enough mashed-up truth and prophecy to be irresistible. She and Jonas had only known each other for a few days when they encountered her, and both still bore the scars of that meeting.

"She told you back in the marsh?" the squire sputtered. "And you're just telling me now?"

"I told you we would be going to Gilead. I was working up to specifically where in Gilead later. I thought she was a wild mage, remember? That she could tell me how to not go crazy? She gave me a clue, and it's all I have to go on, okay?" Rime wiped rainwater out of her face. "And why are we still standing out in the rain arguing? Are we done with your little story? Can we go inside now?"

"Yes, I guess we can!" Jonas bellowed and stomped toward the main hatch across the deck. Abruptly he turned back, causing Rime to skid to a stop on the rain-slick deck. "No! Two things. One: What exactly did she say? Two: Did you really mean what you said?"

Rime pulled her wide-brimmed hat down tighter on her head in frustration. "What was it that I said?"

Jonas smiled. "That I'm worth as much as Sir Matthew Pocket."

The mage rolled her eyes, then punched the smirking squire in the stomach with a quick jab. While he recovered, she repeated what the Gray Witch had told her: "'You will go to Gilead, to the throne of the king. There you will find your answer. We will never meet again. In time you will know my price.'"

"Price?" Jonas asked, a haunted look forming on his face.

"No idea," Rime half lied.

"She's tricky, Rime. She asked me all sorts of weird questions and then she kissed me, and then the tower . . ." Jonas stopped and turned his attention to the hatch. "I mean, we should be really careful."

The mage sighed with annoyance, dancing from foot to foot with impatience. "We will, we will. I've got to figure out how to disguise us so we can pass through Gilead, gain audience with the king, and somehow not draw attention to the fact that I'm traveling with a villain from a bard's tale. Are you having trouble with the latch or do you just like slowly drowning?"

"I guess Gilead is the one place where I'm more wanted by the authorities than you, Rime." The squire chuckled weakly, his attention still on the thick steel clasps on either side of the portal belowdecks.

Rime snarled and elbowed the squire away from the hatch. She would never have the strength of his arms, but her magic could part the slick clasps in half a heartbeat. The mage turned to say something sharp and drizzled with molten peevishness, but the look on Jonas's face made her stop. He was very close to her but stared out over her shoulder into the rainy sea. His eyes were wide and fixed on a single point—as if he was staring at the specter of his past, his guilt, his foolhardy murder. She realized that he needed support; he needed comfort, maybe even a hug. *Vomit. I will vomit forever. Maybe the captain's daughter would lend an ear to his troubles?* Rime considered the tall girl's laconic nature and steel-eyed demeanor and decided it was unlikely—at least not without a small crate of wine. The mage gritted her teeth and prepared herself to make some sort of human gesture to ease her companion's despair.

"Jonas, look, I think . . ."

"Pirates," he said, ripping his sword free from its plain leather scabbard.

"Wha . . ." Rime spun, looking out to the rain-stammered waves, just spying the dark outline of a wooden galleon less than a dozen yards from the side of the *Cormorant*. They had extinguished all lights on their deck, but the fickle moonlight still glinted off the edges of a few ragged cutlasses bristling near the prow of the approaching ship.

"Good. Good!" The mage pushed her wide-brimmed hat back until it hung free on a cord around her neck. Rime cracked her knuckles and grinned with relief that they could stop talking about the squire's feelings. A pirate battle is the best remedy for emotional trauma.

Jonas took his place in front of her, his steel held low; Rime reached down into the Magic Wild and called a trill of lightning to dance between her fingertips. The wooden hull crashed into their tiny ship, pouring salt water, pirates, and more rain into their waiting arms.

CHAPTER FIVE

XENON

Xenon shifted in her chair, feeling the warm friction of cloth against wood. Her nose was inches from the scroll splayed out over an untidy regiment of tomes. The scroll was a reproduction of a Caleronai codex, and whoever had prepared it had used an improper blend of sulfur and lime in the ink, resulting in an unfortunate yellow shade that forced the goblin to squint to read the finer lines. She had a small headache rotating between her eyes like a turkey on a spit, and they vibrated with strain and concentration. Her brain rolled with the headache—a crushed up dynamo of satisfaction—rolling flat the path in front of her, bending and sorting the words into their proper places.

"Can we go?" A peapod-green voice slid through the spokes of her brain and flung Xenon away from the scroll to flop in an ungainly heap on the rocky shores of Now.

"No, Mercury, no! No, going is not what we can be doing. We are nowhere in the vicinity of going. 'Go' is a subset of values that we have not yet encountered," the goblin moaned, rubbing both of her eyes. "I *told* you when we got here that I was *staying* until the library *closed*."

Mercury blew out her green cheeks in disgust. "But I'm really, really stillwater. The children's section closed hours ago."

Xenon swiveled her neck to look out one of the stone windows at the angle of the sun. A quick calculation told her that even with the most generous of head-math, the children's section of the Archivus Eldracon had only closed thirty minutes prior. She snapped her head back to consider her younger sister. Mercury was nine years old, feet swinging and not touching the stone floors of the library. Her dark hair was twisted into a sensible clump, fiercely warded by their mother's red bone-clips. The younger goblin kicked back in her chair, freeing her belt dagger, and set to sharpening it on a small whetstone. The rasp made Xenon wince against her will.

"Look," Xenon pleaded, hands covering her face. "I only brought you along because Mom *made* me bring you along. And because you promised that you would wait patiently for me to finish my work today. I know this room must seem very boring compared to the children's section . . ."

"Children's room's got tunnels. And a tree that sings songs. *And* marmalade cookies and fresh milk." Mercury continued to sharpen her dagger.

Xenon spoke from between her fingers: "Maybe a book or two?"

The younger goblin paused her work to deliver a blistering look of Complete Agate Disdain. Xenon recognized it as being one of her mother's signature attacks. Her sister had been learning from the master.

"What I'm working on, it's important, Mercy." She gestured at the scattered pile of tomes overlaid with the eyestrain scroll. "I found something way up north in the Sands. So important that I dropped everything and spent a ton of money to buy airship fare to fly across an ocean to come home, to come home to Pice and deal with Mom and to deal with *you*. And you know the fight that Mom and I had when I left last time." The younger goblin tapped her cheek with the flat of her dagger and gave a grudging nod of recognition.

Xenon herself shuddered at the memory. Her mother had followed her all the way to the terminal, continuing the argument in a firm, measured, and very loud voice—attracting the attention of everyone that passed. When Xenon stopped offering even token resistance, her mother had simply started carrying both sides of the argument. It was perhaps the most embarrassing part that her mother had argued her daughter's position with far more alacrity and skill than Xenon had herself. *Mom's been quiet and calm since I came back, like the sky before a thunderbolt.* The goblin shelved that concern for later and held up the scroll for her sister to see.

"I found this thing—this big spinning thing—made by the Precursors! As far as I can tell they sent it off to carry out some sort of task, and it came back to report on it. But it's been so long that there are no more Precursors, so it reported to me. To me, Mercy! It was this huge metal circle all covered with light and Arkanic sigils, spinning in the air!"

"Don't call me 'Mercy.' I'm too big for that name. " Her sister began to spin her dagger on the table. "Precursor stuff? Like the light globes at home? Or the jukebox at Grandfather's? Or spire-blast airships?"

Xenon's eyes flared with triumph. Her sister was listening. "This scroll is a reproduction, but it's a copy of some scholarly work done in Caleron, trying to get a sense of the Precursor calendar. Did you know our own calendar is based on it? Ten months—each with thirty days—three hundred days exactly in a year. Even the month names are cribbed from poor translations or 'interpretations' of the shapes of the Arkanic sigils. 'Arrowspan,'

'Handspan,' 'Giantspan'—it's really just from people looking at the Precursor word and saying what it most resembled!'"

Mercury spun her dagger, tapping the table between the blade's revolutions in a fixed pattern. Xenon checked her scholarly excitement and rushed toward a conclusion that would keep her sister's attention.

"But! What's important is that their calendar worked just like ours does. We list years from the Vardeman Accords, that's year zero for us. This scroll has records that give some Precursor dates expressed in common. In other words, if I can figure out what year it was on their calendar for our year zero, then I can figure out what date the Node gave me!"

"Zee."

"Because it gave me a year! I left that part out. I've been working on the text of its communication for weeks, and I finally realized that it had given me a date! 10.10.7171—I mean, it could be just a random sequence of numbers, but it corresponds perfectly with calendar notation. Since a random string of numbers tells me nothing and a calendar date tells me *something*, I decided to focus my research there for the moment."

"Zee, I am so bored."

Xenon shook the scroll with adamant fire in her eyes. "This matters, Mercury! If this scroll is correct, then our year zero was Precursor year 6007! If that's correct, that means that their year 7171 is our year 1164! That's *this year*. It's 8.28.1164 *today*."

Mercury slapped her hand down on the table to stop her dagger from spinning. Almost delicately she slipped it back into the sheath on her bandolier. The young goblin folded her hands together and gazed at her sister. "You were doing so good. Then you had to gabble-blab about calendars. Can't we just talk about airships?" she asked flatly.

"Because!" Xenon began, and then stopped. She couldn't truly explain how the Node's message had filled her with dread. "*YOU*

WILL BURN." The goblin bit down on her tongue, torn between not wanting to frighten her sister and the certainty that she would look ridiculous if she tried. "ZERO WILL AWAKEN. ZERO WILL RISE AS SHAME FALLS." What is "Shame"? What is "Zero"?

The archaeologist took a deep breath, then sat the scroll down and folded her own hands. She locked gazes with Mercury. "I do, Mercury. I can't explain it all yet; I barely understand what I've found. But I know that it is real. And I know that it is dangerous. And I know that I have to figure it out as quickly as I can."

"Okay." Mercury nodded.

"Okay." Xenon smiled.

"Then you should probably ask someone smarter than you." The younger goblin slid off her chair. "You've been grubbing away at this for days. You are super, super slow."

Xenon growled with frustration and caught her sister inches from the door. There was a brief struggle, and then Mercury learned exactly how quick her older sister could dispense a thorough beating. The archaeologist had her younger sister in a firm headlock and was feeling Mercury's razor canines sink into her forearm when she realized that the words rang true: *someone smarter than you.*

"Mom, we're home," Xenon called, hanging her hood on the hook to the right of the door and shooting Mercury one last admonishing glance. They had carefully discussed the fallout from their quarrel and made sure that all open wounds were tended and hidden from view Neither party wished to involve the primary governing force of the household in this small skirmish, and so a simple covenant had been struck, one that had become common over the past couple of years during Xenon's intermittent visits.

"Excellent. Please have your sister go prepare herself for dinner. You join me here in the kitchen." Her mother's words were distinct, heavy as if quarried from granite. Mercury snickered and gave her older sister a quick poke. Covenants with her sister were easy. Mercury understood that Xenon's real opponent was their mother. Xenon squared her shoulders and went into battle.

The kitchen was one of her favorite places in the house. The counters were all done in a riot of pastel colors, cheerful tile, and plain black stone for the floor. Some of her happiest memories were from here: fixing breakfast, reading next to the stove, slipping down before dawn to steal a long, cold drink of milk from the frost box. But that was before.

Her mother was a black silhouette in the center of the rainbow. She sat at the plain wooden table in the center of the kitchen, hands folded around a white mug of tea. Xenon's mother almost always wore black; it seemed to complement her skin tone, a much darker green than her two daughters—past olive, past the green of pine needles in the fall. Xenon knew that her lighter skin tone came from her father, who had been nearly cactus; Xenon's mother's skin was very nearly gray—only with slight avocado hints when she smiled, which was infrequent.

She took a seat across from her mother and braced herself.

Her mother raised the mug to her lips and blew across it to cool the liquid within. She sat the mug back in the same spot as before without taking a sip. "I would like it recognized that you have been here for a week and I have not spoken an ill word."

"Yes, Mom. I . . ."

"And I would like it recognized that your choices in life have been supported. Financially."

Never emotionally or materially, but . . . Xenon winced. "Yes, I recognize that—"

"Now." Xenon's mother pushed the teacup away from her, as if she found the beverage unpalatable. "We spoke at some length when you departed last. The problem then is the problem now—only grown worse by the addition of time and another jaunt across the globe."

"I . . ."

"You are out of money. Your father and I provided quite carefully for your future with a significant amount of gold. It was intended to provide for you through the majority of your adult years, until such time as you would begin providing for yourself, with money that you yourself would earn. At that point it would be a resource that you could rely upon in times of need."

"Well . . ."

"Our intentions, however, are a moot point. The money is gone. You have spent it. There is a pittance that remains, but it is insufficient to keep you fed for more than a fortnight. There is no more money. I will not redistribute any amount of gold from the house budget or your sister's trust to replenish your stores." Xenon's mother steepled her fingers. "I have spoken to you several times on this subject, and you have ignored every warning. There was always some justification for your sojourns: the right historical find, especially of Precursor origin, would be of immense value and you could begin funding your research through this method. But that has not happened. You have run out of options."

Xenon forced herself to keep eye contact, difficult as it was. *I really wish my mother were not a lawyer.*

"Now. What will you do?"

I'm not going to panic. I'm not going to beg. I'm going to be an adult and patiently explain my discovery, its importance, and how the possibility of danger is too great to ignore. Xenon took a slow breath and opened her mouth to speak.

"You are going to take a job here in Pice. You will move back into your room here in the house. I have already arranged a position with the Paphyreal Stack. You start at the beginning of next week." Her mother picked the cup of tea back up.

"The Paphyreal Stack?!?" Xenon shrieked, promising herself that she would not *remember* it as a shriek later on. "Mom, their research is garbage! The first librarian banned them from the Archivus Eldracon for six months last year because they spilled barbecue sauce on a first edition of *Hannibal al'Hazaar*! They're hacks, the worst type of opportunistic scholars. They published a paper claiming that the *Precursors were mummies!* Just reanimated corpses the whole time—wrapped up in bandages roaming around—it doesn't make any sense!"

"Well, I'm sure that you will help correct their lack of acumen." Her mother's dark lips closed on the rim of the cup and she took a slow sip. *A victory sip!* Xenon reached across the table, palms up in supplication.

"Mom. Mom, please listen. Normally this is when I'd dig in my heels and we'd have a four-hour fight, but what I'm working on now is too important. And I think too dangerous."

"Dangerous?" Her mother quirked an eyebrow.

Xenon pulled herself up and reached into her pouch to pull out her journal, the scroll she had showed Mercury, and a few other supplemental texts. She spread them across the kitchen table. *Someone smarter than me. Just like Mercury said.* Her mother only had a passing interest in the study of history and the stories of Before, but Xenon could not think of a sharper intellect. She risked a glance up at her mother and saw the telltale angle of her head, slightly cocked to the left. It betrayed interest and a small portion of concern.

"Just let me tell you about it. Just once, let me lay it all out for you. Tell me what you honestly think. I need a fresh perspective. And if you think I should abandon it, I will." *I won't.* "Okay, I told you that I was up on the northern continent investigating a Sarmadi site . . ."

The tea was cold. Xenon's mother had listened. She had asked a few questions for clarification along the way but had mostly allowed her daughter to present her case. Xenon stuttered to a halt, realizing she had run out of any sort of concrete information she could present for arbitration.

Her mother looked down at the table as if assembling the pieces of a large jigsaw puzzle. "I think your basic conclusions are correct. Something called 'Shame' is coming. It is coming in just under a month and a half. And I do think that it presents a danger."

Xenon nearly gasped with shock but covered the gaffe by shifting some of her books around. "Thank you, Mom—thank you."

"However"—her mother's eyes blazed like fireflies—"I believe your core premise to be incorrect. You think that this 'Node' was sent by the Precursors. The evidence does not support that. I am not the expert that you are, but the language that it uses does not match with what I know about them. You say they call themselves the Lost, the Singers, poetic names such as these. I have never heard the Precursors refer to themselves as 'Zero.' The very manner in which the Node communicated seems to suggest it was made by some other force."

"But the metal fragments of the Node! I checked. The sigils inscribed are Precursor!" Xenon argued. "It's what put me on the trail of the calendar in the first place."

"Circumstantial. You need an expert, someone to consult whose knowledge of the Precursor's reign far outstrips your own." Xenon's mother pushed the books and scrolls back toward her daughter. "You must go see the first librarian tomorrow. You will tell him everything—show him everything—then turn this investigation over to him."

"Wait, what?" Xenon demanded.

"The second premise that is incorrect: that you are the best-suited person to solve this mystery. You do not have the experience, resources, or knowledge to succeed. The danger is real; greater scholars than you must be employed to work on this problem." Xenon's mother stood up from the table. "Now, go get your sister. Dinner will be late as we have conversed overlong."

"Mom!" the archaeologist shrieked *again*.

The dark flow of her mother's dress along the graceful curve of her back gave no answer. Xenon fumed and exited the kitchen, only to find Mercury sitting with hands folded on the stairs. She clearly had been sitting there for some time.

"So." Mercury smirked. "Sneak out after dinner?"

"You're not going," Xenon growled.

"If you don't take me, I'll scream bloody murder when you go." Her younger sister stood up and trotted past her into the kitchen.

Every goblin in this house makes decisions except for me. Xenon stomped up the stairs to steal a few minutes to lie on her old bed and stare up at the old poster that her father had given her. It was for a play they had seen as a family, and she had always loved the sky pirate leaning out across the bow, a flying galleon and a sky full of stars behind. She still remembered feeling so small next to her mother and father, watching the players capering around their cart as they fought the Dragoon War with painted faces and wooden swords.

She asked the empty room and the faded stars above. "Who is Zero? What is Zero?"

CHAPTER SIX

JONAS & RIME

Jonas wiped salt water out of his eyes for the dozenth time and barely moved his sword quickly enough to block the green nimbus blade that sliced directly at his stomach. The pirate's skeletal grin filled his vision, and the squire braced for impact, only to see the phantom cutlass pass right through his sword as insubstantial as a passing mist. Jonas growled a low moan of frustration. The past several minutes since the collision of the pirate ship with the *Cormorant* had been a maddening clatter of rainwater, storm-tossed seas, and the assault of the ship's crew. But all the more infuriating had been the discovery of the true nature of the vicious, leering pirates—sailcloth and leather wrapped around rotting flesh and salt-encrusted bones.

"They're the Half-Ghost Armada!" Captain Blackberry had bellowed, emerging from the portal. "Gods help us all! Londra, bring up the belaying pins! Wick and Warp, you stay below and keep this portal shut until I give the right knock."

"Half-ghosts?" Rime had demanded. "What does that even mean?"

Blackberry and his tall daughter had entered, carrying large black wooden clubs capped with steel. The captain had grimly sealed the portal belowdecks behind him. "The Beyond is all too similar to our own world: a vast pile of paperwork and desks. Sometimes things get filed wrong and you wind up with the unexpected: a whole crew of villainous cutthroats dead at the bottom of the sea—meant to haunt the coast as proper phantasms. But someone didn't check the right box, or fill out the right form, and you wind up with things like this—half-ghosts. Not quite undead, not quite gone—mean and angry and cursed by bureaucratic oversight to occasionally spook and slaver the hearts of mortal men. Poor bastards, they're just as confused as we are—but that don't make 'em any less dangerous!"

The captain's words quickly proved true. The pirate's forms were the husks of corpses, knit together by a firefly-green illumination. But from moment to moment they seemed to be only intermittently substantial. Jonas's sword caught nothing but spectral light, but the very next moment the pirate's bone fingers tore a deep gouge across his right breast. It meant that every attack could be real or not, and he had to try and block them all.

Jonas grabbed the pirate's shoulder and prayed that it would remain material. The vicious revenant scowled and tried to spin from his grasp, but the squire managed to keep enough of a grip and shove the pirate over the side into the heaving seas. Jonas caught his hip hard against the wooden rail of the ship in time to see the half-ghost fall toward the water. The tumbling sack of bone and steel suddenly halted, then floated up through the rain, green nimbus flaring with sudden phantasmal motivation. He groaned again with exhaustion, then pushed himself up. *I'll worry about that one later, when there is a later.* Jonas blinked away more water and looked across the *Cormorant*'s deck to survey the situation.

Captain Blackberry was holding fast near the prow of the ship, his daughter at his side. Londra's black hair whipped around her face like a shroud, writhing around the clear ice of her eyes. The only illumination came from the half-ghost pirates themselves and the sporadic bursts of fire and lightning that Rime spun from her hands. The wild mage hovered a few feet above Jonas's head, acting as both lookout and turret. She had kept the area around them clear for the past several minutes, but Jonas could see the telltale set of her jaw that told him she was running short on time. She was pulling from her power and hanging on by pure determination, and before too long she would fall. Three pirates cackled, clattering sacks of cloth and bone. They barreled their way toward his position, green-light daggers flickering. Would the blades be solid when they landed or not?

He took a deep breath, held it, and felt it burn in his lungs.

The half-ghosts were a danger; the pitch of the deck and the constant fall of rain made for an uncertain battleground. But it was the weight in his heart that made him slow, that made his blade feel like a flat board in his hands. Telling the tale of his sin had been harder than he could have imagined. It wasn't like he had forgotten or forgiven himself, but in the day to day it was easy to not think about the Past, to bury it like a slab of granite in the dark earth of his mind. Speaking it aloud, telling the story to Rime, had uncovered the stone. Now it was hard to breathe.

The first pirate carried a halberd, the haft rotten and splintered. Jonas moved his sword to knock the pole arm away, but all he could really see was the dark blood pumping from his master's neck. The squire gritted his teeth and shook the vision free. He landed a firm kick on the pirate's chest, only to have his boot pass right through. Jonas stumbled forward, carried by momentum, and soon found himself standing directly in the center of the half-ghost. The pirate craned its neck, and somehow the phosphorescent green skull managed to look sheepish. Jonas had only a moment to nod in agreement before the thing's two companions pulled him free and threw him up against two crates lashed down with cord and sailcloth.

The air burst from his lungs with the impact, and Jonas thought of the night he had slipped from the tower, the silver blade Hecate wrapped in a spare cloak. *I've got to pull it together. Head in the clouds, blood in the dirt.* His master's words. The squire pulled his good steel into a simple guarding stance and made ready for the pirates' assault. Through the wind and rain the Past came again, faster and sharper than any pirate cutlass—his master's face, his words, his blood.

I am being buried alive. The thought appeared in Jonas's mind. He could not say whence it came, but he knew it to be true. In the tempest and half-ghost dark the stones of the past were too heavy for him to bear.

But then, lightning. And laughter. Wild laughter, Rime's laughter. She erupted, searing his eyes with light—both hands high, calling down fire from the heavens.

"Of course! I don't know why I never considered it. It takes far less energy to"—a yellow-gold bolt of sky-fire tore through the three green phantasms in front of Jonas—"redirect the lightning than to create it!"

Rime laughed again, pulling lightning out of the sky like yarn from a skein, then throwing it down among the green-glow bones. She hovered higher and higher above the deck, her nimbus burning gold, then pure white. Jonas could do nothing but stare, the weight of the past suddenly forgotten in the face of Rime's lightning now. Bolts danced from her hands, shattering or liquefying each half-ghost, dependent on their current phase shift. One of the pirates pulled free a large tome and began to leaf through its pages frantically as if looking for a specific reference. In sudden triumph it raised a bone fist and shook it at the lightning-flinging wild mage.

"*Granich varr septo!*" the half-ghost moaned indignantly, pointing at a pertinent passage in the leather-bound book.

"*Septar do'vash. Septar do'tun malufrego!*" The wild mage laughed. "Lightning works on *everything.*"

To punctuate, Rime sent a bolt of gold coursing through the pirate's book and yellow-bone chest. The half-ghost seemed to implode, its phantasmal energy eaten by the lightning's audacity. His offended expression was the last to go, hovering in the air.

Jonas picked himself up, his eyes locked on Rime. She continued to spin lightning out of the storm as if it belonged to her, sending bolt after bolt to hammer and shatter the few remaining pirates. It never ceased to amaze him, the things she could do. In her company he had seen tiny wonders and gargantuan marvels—called forth by nothing more than the girl's will. But of late, he had started to see a shift, something changing in his companion. The laughter—the way she seemed to revel in her power, it made the squire worry. There wasn't one thing he could really put his finger on, but it seemed that Rime's magic was perhaps beginning to get out of control.

"I'm going to blow their ship up too!" Rime howled with exultation, weaving her lightning into a large ball above her head.

Head in the clouds . . . back to work. "Rime! Do not blow the ship up!" Jonas yelled, waving to get the floating girl's attention. "Just . . . do not do that!"

The girl looked down from her work, her eyes quizzical and annoyed. "Why not? It would be easy."

"Because . . . uh . . . because . . ." Jonas grappled for the words, then his eyes went wide. He slammed his sword back into the scabbard and placed himself directly under his companion, his arms wide. He made his words as calm as possible, even though he had to shout to be heard above the rain. "Because blood is coming out of your mouth, Rime. A lot of it. You've done too much already. Now just come down and let's get out of this rain."

The mage raised a hand to her face, then pulled it back to see the crimson truth. Jonas could see the doubt in her face, but it was soon wiped away by certainty. Rime clenched her fist and reached up into the vast ball of lightning she had gathered.

"Rime, no!" the squire shouted, moving toward the crates, thinking perhaps he could leap and grab her ankles, distract her and get her to listen. The mage moved too quickly, calling one last bolt into her web of light, then with a great cry flung it down onto the wooden galleon that had borne the pirate crew.

The galleon exploded in a torment of screaming wood and improperly released spectral energy from a few half-ghosts sleeping belowdecks. Each drop of rain was outlined in light, and Jonas had no choice but to cover his eyes. Somehow, amid all the carnage, he still heard the shallow thump of his companion's body hitting the deck. When the lightning cleared, he stumbled forward to Rime's body and pulled her up; her eyes were rolled back in her head and her skin was white as the belly of a fish. For a dozen beats of his own thundering heart he could find no pulse and no breath coming from the girl; only by putting his cheek directly against her nose and mouth could he feel the faint exhale of her lungs. *She's alive, now get her out of the rain.* Not his master's words, but they could have been. Jonas stood up, with the mage's limp body in his arms to discover the fear-stricken eyes of Captain Blackberry approaching, knuckles white on his club. His daughter, Londra, seemed less afraid, but more willing to use her own club.

Jonas sighed. *I'm terrible at explaining things.*

RIME'S DREAM #2

Fire sat down next to her. The doublet that Fire wore was immaculate and black.

Fire leaned down and kissed her on the cheek.

Fire's lips were ash and her cheek was cold. She felt Fire's hands make their way up her spine and run through her hair.

"White," Fire whispered in her ear. "White as sundown, white as tomorrow. White as the rib bone that beggars borrow."

Fire held her close and reached for the front of her tunic.

Jonas sat next to Rime in their tiny cabin on the *Cormorant*. "Cabin" was a generous term, as it was merely a storage space, and the captain had pushed a few barrels of lard back, room enough for them to spread their bedrolls and stow their meager gear. He watched his companion's chest rise and fall, slow but sure, by the light of the glow-globe lashed into the corner.

His feeble words on the deck had been cut short by Captain Blackberry. "I don't know. I don't want to know. You get off the ship in Shiloh, just as we agreed. You stay in your cabin with . . . her until we make landfall tomorrow, understood?" The wide man had stomped away to give the all-clear knock on the portal belowdecks.

His tall daughter had looked at the unconscious Rime with cold curiosity. "She's a wild mage, right?"

Jonas had managed not to nod but offered a noncommittal shrug.

"Do yourself a favor, then. Put a knife in her and toss her overboard." Londra had followed her father without looking back.

Now he sat in the cramped space, his back against a barrel of lard, and looked down at Rime. Asleep, she wasn't much to look at, only the snow-white swath of her hair marked her as anything unusual. She was short for her age, too sharp featured to be pretty. *Or is it sharp tongued?* Jonas grinned.

But awake . . . The squire's smile faded. Awake she was a wild mage, a power that Jonas knew he would never understand. He was guardian to a girl who walked the world as a small god. He looked down at his hands, at the sword he was automatically sharpening, even now. *What am I to protect her? I'm just a boy with a bit of sharp metal. And more and more it looks like I need to protect her from herself.*

Rime opened her eyes. Jonas set his good steel down and moved closer. "Are you feeling okay?" He leaned over her.

The girl did not answer, but she slowly pulled a hand out from under her cover and held it out to him. With a vague feeling of shock, Jonas took Rime's hand.

"Tell me . . ." she started, then coughed.

Jonas felt the weight of the Past gather again, breaking through his concern for her. "I told you before the pirates, Rime. I don't think we need to go over it all again."

She shook her head. "Not that. Tell me about Gilead."

The squire opened his mouth and then shut it. A thousand memories pressed forward all at once, becoming a tangle in his head, a dull ache in his heart. *Gilead is home.* Those were the only words he found, but he could not speak them. What did she mean?

Rime closed her eyes. She did not let go of the squire's hand. "Your story, there's a piece missing. Something about the place, about the land itself—about what it means. Some stupid horse nonsense about glory and heroes. You told me about what you did wrong. Now tell me about what you left behind."

Jonas opened his mouth again. *I don't have the words. I'll never have the words.* Then he remembered a song his master used to sing at the end of the day. The squire could not carry the melody, but he could recite the words well enough.

"Last light of the sun against gravestone sky,
dream of the shadows all come to die.
White sand, gray stone, green field bear the scar,
of heroes' blood and silver star.
They walk in steel, they die in stone,
Children of Gilead sing alone.
Black sea, white sand, the lives they fall,
from broken horns still sound the call.
Where Night and Beast dare wear the crown,
Knights of Gilead will throw them down.
Last light of the sunshine across the waves,
bones of valor down in their graves.
Songs of blood and journey's end,
the price of heroes for shadow's end.
Sundown comes and Gilead stands,
sundown comes and Darkness plans."

Jonas did not stumble over a single word; he could hear every verse sung by Sir Pocket, perfect in his memory.

Rime was asleep, a gentler calm than the black unconsciousness she had come back from. She still held tight to her guardian's hand. Jonas nodded and made himself comfortable, taking great care to keep her hand in his.

CHAPTER SEVEN

THE HUNT

Sideways lay on the deck chair, wearing nothing but a handkerchief's worth of fabric wrapped around his mystery. The assassin liked to think that the periwinkle cotton was a perfect match to the shade of paint he had used on his malformed horns and complemented the unabashed carrot orange of his skin. He also liked to think that the glances and whispers aimed in his direction were in reference to his chiseled physique and not the litany of scars that hummed across his skin. The sea air was brisk, the sun was warm, and the devilkin was fairly certain that no one had noticed the missing passengers yet.

He kept his eyes closed to slits; the afternoon heat made him like a fat disco-lizard on a rock. He dangled a hand to the deck, feeling around for the wooden tankard that perhaps still had a few precious swallows of purple alcohol slurry. His fingertips brushed against the hilt of his magic sword, Chester, tucked strategically under his chair. "Sorry, Chet." The assassin burped, then redirected his finger quest to the rim of his cup.

Not too long ago, the devilkin had carried *two* magic swords—acquisitions that had taken him not a little trouble and expense. He had carried the gray blade Chester and a far gaudier weapon known as Sunhammer. *Then the beach. And those kids. Skinny Girl and the Boy. Can't believe they broke Sunhammer.* Sideways slurped at his tankard, then let his fingers fall back down on the remaining sword.

"But they didn't break you, Chet. They didn't even *see* you." The assassin chuckled, then squinted up at the sun.

Almost feeding time again. Sideways sighed and rolled up from the chair like a solicitous cobra. He snagged Chet and his cup and tossed the complimentary towel he had been given over his shoulder. A pair of women in sun-suits, a goblin and a human, gave his mystery a frank look as he swaggered by, but he only had time for a short smile.

They had booked passage on a luxury liner, the *Vacuous Gargantua*. It had been leaving when they needed it to and boasted a passenger list of a few hundred. Sideways had been hoping they could grab a cabin on an actual airship, but his employer had insisted on an ocean vessel. *Air travel would take us too far into the clouds. Our prey is on the waves, and Nora has a clear scent. We must not risk losing it,* Linus had said, iron gauntlet almost caressing the mage-hound's glass chest.

Sideways shivered and didn't blame himself for doing so. *That fucking thing.* The mage-hound had not paid him the least amount of attention, not a flicker of recognition in its gaslight eyes. But he had been assigned the task of feeding it, keeping its furnace stoked. His employer had spent most of the past two days asleep; Sideways had spent it counting.

Counting hours, counting kids, counting the number of minutes a nanny would leave her charges untended, counting the drinks an old dowager threw down at the crystal bar, counting the scars on a young elf's wrist as he swam by in the lap pool.

Nora was hungry, and she only ate one thing. Life. Life for time, life for the blue flame to burn a little longer, a little brighter. The assassin sat on the deck of the *Gargantua* and kept drinking and counting. As best he could tell, one life bought between six to sixteen hours. There didn't seem to be an easy way to gauge what any one life would buy between the hound's jaws. The fat dwarf he'd nabbed on the first night had only lasted six hours, but that might have had to do with the dagger the old lady had needed between the ribs before she stopped screaming for help. He had picked her because she was cruel to one of the serving men at the banquet table. *Some justification is nice. Rude to the help? Fed to the doggy.* The next morning he'd hit on the idea of trying to snag any of the small pets that the affluent passengers brought along, but they proved better guarded than the children. The one golden beetle he'd managed to spirit away had barely stoked the glass dog's furnace; he'd been forced to engineer a seeming lifeboat accident for a pair of wood-elves on the crew to cover up their immediate disappearance. The two elves had blubbered and begged for their lives. Sideways hated that. Although half-devil by birth and a killer by trade, there was an odd sinew of morality in his heart's core, and he'd been forced to knock both of them unconscious. *At least they won't know they're dying,* he consoled himself.

Nora had burned like a full moon on the fuel of the elves' lives. Sideways dumped the bodies overboard. It was most of the following day before the blue light began to diminish, but he had already found another log by then. A young noble had drunk himself into a stupor and left loud orders that he not be disturbed in his quarters. Sideways slithered through his door and scooped up the soused soul, taking care to lock the cabin room behind him.

It was distasteful work, but that's what he got paid for. Linus's gold was good and showed no sign of slacking. Sideways tapped on his heart, hoping it would quiet the persistent ache of his hangnail conscience. They were a day behind the Skinny Girl and would land tomorrow in Shiloh. He would just have to keep counting until then.

The devilkin turned the corner, taking the stairs two at a time down into the B Deck, the passenger level. He arrived at the bottom and spun delicately into the nearest corner, where a convenient pool of shadow seemed to have a Sideways-appropriate outline. Sideways scratched his nose with the edge of the complimentary towel and grinned with sudden excitement. *Someone is following me!*

He knew that tickle in the pit of his stomach well, the slight twinge at the base of his spine. Most people could train themselves to harness this simple instinct, but for rogues of his profession those slight, unconscious signals were as good as trumpets on his shoulders. Sideways wrapped his orange fingers around Chet and made his breath go shallow the way that an empty corner full of shadows would breathe if it suddenly were burdened with lungs.

Linus came down the stairs.

The old man was wearing a clean robe, closed at the waist with a golden strip of silk. It left enough of his employer's chest bare that Sideways could see the horrible, twisting scar that covered most of the torso. The assassin blinked, surprised despite himself. He had more than his fair share of scars, but the ones that the knight bore were something else. The edges mashed together like idle potter's clay, a strange mottled complexion as if the wounds were not healed so much as forced together. Linus looked around the empty hall and then nodded in appreciation. "I know you are hidden, but I cannot discover you. Let us speak."

The assassin stepped from the shadows, still taken aback. He had only ever seen Linus in his iron armor, his long blue cloak draped with care. Seeing him like this, it was like coming upon a naked parent. *No, more like a hawk with all the feathers ripped off. Or a crocodile with no teeth.*

"Nora's light grows dim. She needs to be fed," the old man said.

"I'm on my way now." Sideways shrugged. "There are a lot of people on this boat, sure. But it's like hunting a herd all penned up together—have to be careful that no one notices the missing bucks." *And you've been asleep for two days; I've been handling it, old man.*

"I understand." Linus began to walk down the hallway toward their quarters where the mage-hound waited. "Your discretion has always been a hallmark, and I know . . . I know that at times your tasks are unpleasant."

The old man stopped in front of a closed cabin door. Sideways's eyebrows rose. They were standing in front of the cabin directly adjacent to their own. *Uhh. This is so embarrassing for the old man.* Linus took a step toward the door, then placed his hand delicately on the clean oak, as if it were a windowpane on a summer's day. The devilkin cleared his throat to prevent his employer from waltzing into the wrong room, but Linus's words and straight back showed no sign of error.

"Do you know what it is to be a villain?" the old man asked softly.

Sideways ran a thumb down the cruel edge of his blade. "Yeah, I've got a pretty good idea."

"Not just a life taker, not just the sharp knife that waits in the shadows, my friend. A villain. In my days with the Hunt, we learned quickly. The wild mages were all heroes, each and every one of them. Before they turned, of course. Saviors, miracle men, the breakers of chains—even as they fell into madness there were those who still sang their songs, who still would die to save the shining star that kept their little patch of earth from ruin. We learned quickly that our prey were heroes, and to bring them down, we would need to be villains. We would burn the hero's town to bring her from hiding. We would steal the hero's lover and hold him for ransom. Every fool that stood between us and our quarry were either obstacles or weapons, and we learned to use both."

Sideways felt his mystery itch but decided to ignore it. The old man kept his gaze on his palm and the wood of their neighbor's cabin.

"Because, we knew. We knew what the heroes were, what they would become. Sparing a life in a hunt meant spending a hundred when the mage turned. I slit many a throat knowing that a century of hearts would beat on because of that decision."

"You know that isn't our room, right?"

"That's what it is to be a villain. You will never stop. There is nothing you won't do. Nothing under the heavens that you fear. You can bear hatred, you can bear pain, and you are the shadow on the wall. I answer to no god, no king, no law written in stone or light. I slake my thirst only with the blood of heroes." Linus rapped on the door with staccato courtesy.

The door opened to reveal a wide-faced man with a bald head and a thick brown beard. The sound of a loud family meal came from within: the clatter of plates, the whine of children's voices. "Yes? Something . . . Are we being too loud?" the man half bowed in apology.

"Not in the least." Linus returned the man's bow, then gestured to Sideways. "Bind and gag them all. We'll begin with the parents and use the children only if we are delayed making port. This will be our larder. I'll go instruct the porter that this family has come down with the flu, and their meals can be left at the door."

"I'm sorry . . . uh, what?" The bearded man's eyes were wide, blinking as he tried to swallow the knight's words.

He still has his teeth, old crocodile, that's for damn sure.
Sideways wrapped his towel around Chet, hoping the sword
would not take too much offense. He offered the gaping passenger a shrug before clubbing him sharply on the temples with his
padded weapon. The assassin dragged the fat man quickly into
the cabin amid the shrieking voices of his family. Sideways kicked
the door shut but not before he caught one last glance of Linus.

The old man's face was completely calm, blue eyes set.

That man scares the shit out of me. Sideways turned and
started binding and silencing the screaming family.

CHAPTER EIGHT

XENON

Xenon slipped down the stairs of her mother's home. She was dressed for travel: square-cloak, instrument pouch, a bundle of scrolls and books crammed into a road-sack, dagger freshly sharpened, her sister slung over one shoulder like a glowering satchel.

"This is really unnecessary," the archaeologist whispered.

"Nope." Mercury held on to her back tighter. "You've got long legs; you can beat me in a race. Don't want you getting headtall and trying to ditch me until we're out of here."

They both went silent as Xenon took the last few steps across the front hall. Their mother's room was on the opposite side of the building, but neither of them thought it impossible for her to coalesce out of the cloakroom or the very stone of the house itself. She laid a hand on the front door's handle but felt an insistent tug on her hair. Xenon paused and allowed Mercury to wriggle around and slather some leftover butter from dinner on the hinges. The older goblin nodded with appreciation, and her sister wriggled back into place. The door swung open without a squeak, and the sisters moved swiftly into the waiting night.

The streets of Pice were busy even at this late hour. A cluster of philosophers weaved between a nearby grove of stone trees, swinging on them like schoolchildren as they loudly shouted their positions on utility and personal responsibility. A pair of gnomes walked by holding hands with an empty suit coat, which hung between them like an invisible child. The buildings leaned close, mostly made of simple brick and mortar, but often warring with a sudden span of marble columns or aged dark-wood beams. By current, and often revised, estimation, Pice had been razed to its foundations seventeen times in its history. The denizens kept returning after each war or fire or unexpected zoning ordinance and rebuilding. This resulted in an almost limitless strata of history compressed beneath the feet of Pice, a circle of broken crockery around the Archivus Eldracon, the library. Xenon used to ride on her father's shoulders and make him tell her again and again: *What's beneath our feet? A catacomb of a forgotten prince,* he would say. *A temple to a dark god with daggers for teeth. A broken cistern filled to the brim with robbers and thieves, dancing to the tune of a blind violin. All true, Daddy? All true and more, Pickle.* Xenon smiled and skirted around the edge of her mother's house and headed toward the cramped side yard and the small shed with the slate roof. *How does anyone from Pice become a baker or soldier or singer or scout?* Her father used to say that if you lay your ear on the ground, you could hear the stories of the past just whispering their way up to the top. She, of course, had spent a great deal of time following his instructions and did not consider the time wasted, not a moment of it. She was following his instructions, putting her feet on a honeycomb of history and letting it whisper to her—just like he did.

"Zee, why aren't we leaving?" Mercury hissed in her ear. "Mother could wake up any wandertime!"

"I'm not coming back, Mercy. Not this time. I can't." Xenon made her voice stay calm, even though her heart slammed ceaselessly against her rib cage. She laid her hands on the black chain that was wrapped around the door handles of the shed. It had no lock. The steel links were welded together. It had been this way since her father had stopped giving instructions and telling stories.

"Zee. Zee! You can't!" Her sister writhed with panic. "Mother will . . . Mother will, I don't even *know* what Mother will!"

Sorry, Mercury. Let's see how bad you really want to go. "No turning back." Xenon got a firm grip of the black chain in both hands and set her feet. She would never be as strong as some goblins, but in a pinch she could bend steel carpenter nails without wincing. With a sharp exhale she grunted and snapped the chains apart, throwing them aside. Both sisters paused and pressed themselves against the shed door in a breathless moment of terror, waiting for the sound of their mother's approach.

When only the distant sound of the philosophers stumbling farther down their street came, Xenon slowly stood and turned her head to look into her sister's wide eyes. "I told you before. What I found, it's important and it's dangerous. And it's my job to figure it out. I'm not dumping it on someone else's plate. I took the little gold I have left, but if I'm going to figure this out, I need, well, transportation."

Mercury said nothing, only stared at the shed door with reverential awe. Xenon took a deep breath and flung open the shed doors, where the light of the three moons could fall upon the contents.

It was all curves. It was midnight blue, like the darkest deeps of the sea. It was beautiful and covered with dust.

Xenon swung into the saddle and ran her thumbs along the throttle, the starter switches, the display panel that still gave off a faint light, even as the machine slumbered. She shook Mercury off her shoulder until her sister's bottom was on the seat. A quick wipe with her cloak removed the worst of the dust from the panel and showed that there was plenty of energy still in the reserve. She closed her eyes, just for a moment, and let herself listen to the stories underneath her feet. Then her thumb flicked the ignition switch.

An Arkanic sky-cycle?!? It had been beyond her teenaged capacity to preserve even a semblance of calm when her father had touched down in the backyard the first time with it. It had hummed instead of roared, as if floating made it happy. Just like it hummed now, even though it had sat alone in a dirty shed for years. It was ready to fly, like it had been waiting for her. True Precursor technology did not fade, did not break, did not diminish or grow dull. The sky-cycle was powered by an actual *aerolith*, and with careful use and maintenance, the machine would fly for years. Her father had taught her how to operate it with calm, thorough care, and now it felt only right to be sitting on the back of this ancient machine on the trail of a mystery that stretched back to when the device had been born. Xenon looked over her shoulder, a final question in her eyes. Mercury had already found goggles from the saddlebags. She blinked once through the smoked glass, then passed another pair to her sister without a word. *Answer enough.* Xenon pulled them onto her forehead snugly and eased the throttle and let *Tobio* out into the night.

The Precursor's machine hummed as quiet as a drifting cloud down the length of the house, but both goblins kept an eye on each window, expecting to see the razor silhouette of their mother's anger. Xenon held her breath and felt Mercury's fingers dig into her sides. She kept *Tobio* at his slowest speed until her mother's house was a diminishing shadow. Then she hammered the throttle and made the midnight-blue wonder leap into the sky.

Mercury whooped with delight, pounding on Xenon's back with her sharp fists. Their part of the city was mostly dark, even with the roaming philosophers—but other parts shone with lantern-glass warmth: the bright yellow of the theater district, the cool blue of the torches that burned around the library, the piercing white light that tore into the night sky like a spear that came from the Glass Towers of Vo. The night wind whipped past and Xenon felt free. Terrified and free, she strongly considered turning the sky-cycle right around and parking it back in the shed.

"Where are we going, Zee?" Mercury demanded.

Xenon folded up her fears and tucked them away in a pocket just over her heart, there to be easily found and consulted at need. "Like you and mother said. Someone smarter than me—or at least someone who knows more about the Precursor civilization." *And not the first librarian—that old stick would bury this in committees, rhetoric, and old men's science. If we were lucky, the mystery would be solved some fifteen minutes before Shame arrives.* "We're going to go talk to an old boyfriend."

"What?!?" Mercury shouted in either glee or pure incomprehension over the wind whipping past.

The two goblins soared across the night sky on a machine older than the city below, leaving a trail of magenta energy behind them like a line of bright ink.

Xenon parked *Tobio* on the balcony of the top floor. It was more than wide enough to accommodate the sky-cycle's width, though she had to deploy her sister to scoot a few chairs and tables out of the way. The building itself was an innocuous affair—a squat four-stories of brick in the middle of the trade district. Only the wave symbol made from pearl, obsidian, and gold above the large front doors suggested that this simple building was an outpost for a much greater force. The Seafoam Trading Company controlled the skies of Aufero with their fleets of ever-improving airships and ruled the market on devices of every type and description concocted from recovered Precursor artifacts. Their founder, a bold man by the name of Moore, had dared to lead an expedition to the Unbroken City of Kythera, the last stronghold of the dying Lost. From the ruins of the Arkanic civilization he had found a bounty of forgotten technology, and with it raised a humble tug-boat company to a globe-spanning corporation.

She had listened to the bards' tales of the Great Expedition with wonder, and every novel written of the fantastic journey had found a way into her younger hands. It was no accident that had led her to the doors of the company, fresh from her tutelage at various lore houses and wander-archives around the city. She had dreamed of working her way up to a position of prominence in the field, to where one day she herself could visit Kythera, to walk the singing streets and glimpse the Hall of Gryphons. Xenon had left the company two years later, not bitter but wiser. The STC loved Kythera as a husband does a faithless and beautiful wife—locked behind as many doors and guards as possible. She knew in her heart that the wonder of the Past, the stories of Ago were out there waiting for her. She could sit outside Seafoam's door for years and never get into Kythera or she could go out and find her own miracles. Xenon had never felt more right than when she had marched out the brass-lined doors forever, never more wrong when she explained her choice to her mother that night.

"You watch *Tobio*," Xenon instructed. Mercury opened her mouth, but Xenon laid a firm finger over her sister's lips. "No. We can't play games. I say. You do. The end. This is too important."

Mercury's mouth opened, sharp teeth considering. Then she locked eyes with her sister and kissed the finger in assent. The younger goblin spun into place on the sky-cycle's back and propped her feet up on the handles. Xenon exhaled as she turned away. *I'm really glad that worked.*

She found the glass door leading in from the balcony locked. Xenon freed her dagger from its sheath and quickly forced the simple bolt open and slipped inside. The interior was dark, but light came from a few closed doors down the hallway. Seafoam had many operations running, and it was not out of the ordinary for agents to work all hours in pursuit of the company's interests. The thick carpet smelled of pressed lilacs.

Xenon slipped to his door, clearly labeled with his name. "Enton Blake. Acquisitions Magical & Mundane." She pushed the door open as quiet as mice dancing but wasn't entirely surprised to find him watching the door swing open.

He was sitting at a desk made of dark wood, with rows of books and ledgers neatly filed behind him. He had a ledger open and an ordinary raven's quill in his hand. Enton's skin was almost the same color as the desk, as were his eyes. His short-cropped hair, mustache, and goatee were flecked with gray.

"I need something," Xenon said, shutting the door behind her.

Enton smiled, made one more note in his ledger, then placed his quill back on its inkstone. "What can the Seafoam Trading Company do for a former employee?"

"I . . ." she began, then closed her mouth as it flooded with words. *I need all of your research on the Arkanic race. I need everything you have on pre-Sarmadi ritual sites. Anything that would give me a clue why an Arkanic device called the Node would just appear there. I need your largest battleship and a squadron of scroll-grips, maybe a few trained Burners if this is as dangerous as I think. I need you to have the answers. I need you to not look so unruffled. Ruffle, damn you. RUFFLE,*

Enton chuckled, watching her bite the inside of her cheek. "Do you want me to keep working while you think it over?"

"No! Okay, this is a favor. A favor for me. I found something in the Sarmadi Sands in a dig site. I was convinced it was Precursor, but now I'm not so sure. It's covered with Arkanic sigils, but some of the translation I've done doesn't fit." Xenon tugged on her left ear in thought. "But what I found is a warning. Something is coming; something called Shame. And it's coming in a matter of weeks, so I was hoping that you could . . ."

She trailed off as she noticed that Enton was out of the chair and his back was to her, searching the long rows of books behind him. He had a way of doing that, of moving so silently and swiftly that he was like a shadow. He plucked out a red-leather-bound tome, more battered than the others, and crossed around to her side of the desk. She moved closer and peeked over his shoulder at the crabbed handwritten letters as his hands danced through the pages. *A journal. Written in Dwarven script. Late Syprian, so a modern researcher.* Enton's hand lingered on an illustration of three Arkanic sigils, and Xenon gasped in academic shock and recognition. *"Knowledge." "Will." "Valor." This is . . . this is . . . !*

"This is Bragg Silverhammer's journal!" the archaeologist shrieked in complete dismay. "I've seen this illustration a thousand times in *Finding the Lost: A Researcher's Guide to the Arkanic Civilization*! He's a legend. A god! I once sat outside a coffee shop for six *hours* trying to work up the nerve to go in and talk to him. *He loves cinnamon rolls and takes two sugars, Enton.* He's a pillar of the field. His discoveries are beyond instrumental to our understanding of the Lost. ARE YOU ABOUT TO DOG-EAR THAT PAGE?!?"

Enton held his place with a calm hand and just blinked at her. She made a halfhearted grab for the journal, but his smoothly raised eyebrows forced her to retreat.

"Silverhammer is a forgetful soul. The dwarf scholar's mind is always a thousand years away; it's a wonder he remembers to wear pants on a regular basis. He left this behind after an expedition we funded into Kythera. We are taking him again later this year, and I intend to return the journal at that point. Acceptable

to you?" Dark eyes laughed at her. "This is one of his older jour-
nals, from very early in his career. Much of what he writes here
has been refuted or debunked by his own research, but there is a
passage that you brought to mind with the word 'Shame.' Would
you care to read it?"

Xenon nodded, her eyes wide. Enton stepped back and waved
her forward with easy grace. *I want to read every word. Every word
of this. Just climb under the desk and read and read.* She forced
herself to focus. The older man at her elbow was taking a risk, a
significant one. The STC did not deal lightly with its secrets nor
treat kindly those that would steal them. She concentrated, trans-
lating the Dwarven in her head.

*I told that miserable drunk, Carbunkle, to stay out of my cookie
drawer. But did he listen? NO! Now all my finest macaroons and
chewy gingersnaps are crumbs. Crumbs and betrayal! Never trust a
gnome with the location of your baked goods. Words to live by, and
perhaps words for that bastard to die by.*

Xenon grinned in delight but made herself scan on.

*Stumbled upon the most beautiful urn today. It caught
my eye because right at the top was the Arkanic sigil for
"Shame." At least that's the -face- descriptor we agreed
on for that word; the stacked meaning is far more varied.
Guilt, sin, a transgression against the peace of the city itself,
also it almost seems to mean Fate in some contexts. As in a
crime that bears its own punishment, a reckoning, a dark
day.*

*This urn was most fascinating because of the actual
pictographs around the bottom! Suggesting it dates from
the time when the Lost cohabitated with the other denizens
of this planet. They never depicted themselves in this way;
it's much more similar to some early elven work, such as the
root-glyphs on the gates of Seroholm or the carved spears*

of the sea-elf dolphin tribe. What an amazing age it must have been! To learn and build with the Lost, to watch their glass towers rise and the dark things of this world driven back by the light of knowledge.

It shows figures of light, which I assume to be Precursors, walking among the lesser beings of the planet. The urn has five sides—

Side One: Precursor in the center, other beings arrayed around. They are all smaller, but clear racial signifiers can be seen such as horns, pointed ears, etc. The main body of the lesser forms seems to be elven, with a few dwarves and goblins mixed in. Light comes from the Precursor's hands. The other races dance, a celebration.

Side Two: The Precursor comes to a valley where he finds a large group of dragons. (Wings, tail, crown of fire— clear elven iconography for draconic beings.) Light comes from the Precursor's hands, but the dragons do not dance. Their faces are all teeth.

Side Three: Two dragons prominent, one silver and one gold. The Precursor in the center. The other dragons seem to split—

Ach, is this a mustard stain? Xenon took a careful whiff and then nodded. *Spicy mustard.* It completely obscured the rest of the entry. Silverhammer was a giant in the field, but clearly his habit of journaling while eating was just gross.

Side Four: The Precursor stands on the earth, but the dragons are above, wings wide. They are diving to attack, fire plumes from their jaws. The Precursor looks . . . dejected? Defeated? Arms down, head bowed.

Side Five: The dragons in the air have all been bound in a great circle, inscribed with the sigil for "Will," or izus in the Arkanic tongue. The Precursor's hands are wide, and the light holds the circle aloft. The dragons inside appear terrified. A few cower at the feet of the Precursor as if begging forgiveness. Above it all the night sky is full of stars.

> *Hmm! I must speak with the Grand Wizard about this! I have never heard this story—about some sort of conflict between the Lost and the dragons? They refused to accept the nominal "rule" of the Precursors and attempted a rebellion—then were imprisoned somehow? So many thousands of years have passed that no record survives of this event, and the modern dragons I have encountered have certainly never mentioned such a thing. Not that they would, I suppose—not the sort of thing one brings up over tea and virgins.*
>
> *And still, the sigil for "Shame." Whose sin is depicted? The rebellion of the dragons or the terrible punishment inflicted by the Lost?*

Xenon flipped the page. It was a new dated entry, a few days later. The dwarf had discovered a functioning Arkanic water-saber and had immediately devoted the next score of pages to its function, construction, and utility in the kitchen. She flipped ahead but couldn't spot any further mention of the urn, Shame, or even dragons in general. Her eyes rose and found Enton's dark orbs weighing her.

"Now, do you want to tell me what you found?" He walked back around his desk and sat down, hands resting on the open ledger. "You wouldn't come here unless it was important. And the way you hold yourself—you believe there is danger. Immediate danger. Please tell me."

The goblin carefully closed Silverhammer's journal and tried to compose some sort of response. She wanted to wring her hands and sit down, but she made herself speak calmly and *not* shriek.

"I don't have enough real evidence to support this. The links are tenuous. There's not enough time to do all the groundwork and research on each step of the thesis. I'm sure if I had time to go through it all now, you could punch a hole in it right away and then we'd both feel much better."

"Zee," Enton nearly whispered. "I know you. I know *you*. You've figured something out. And you know it's right. You don't trust your instincts, but I do. Now tell me, please."

Xenon turned, moved toward the door, and then stopped, her back to the desk and the dark eyes of its occupant. "The prison. The prison for dragons. That is Shame. That's what the Precursors called it. And it's going to open. The message I found said that 'Shame will fall'. Wherever they put them—however they did it—someone found out. Someone knows that it's going to break open. Someone who calls himself or herself 'Zero'. A person or a group who—"

"You have to go."

She turned around, surprised. Enton was looking down at his ledger, quill back in his hand.

"Whaa?" she protested.

Without looking back up, Enton sighed. "There are many things that Seafoam Trading Company comes across in its studies of the Arkanic civilization. A very careful, regimented process of intake as that knowledge is sent to the correct department for analysis and development. Individual interest is discouraged. We can't have researchers becoming involved in pet projects and unintentionally activating an Arkanic weapon or stumbling upon an unexpected breakthrough that inspires them to commit larceny and sell the item to one of our competitors."

Xenon put a hand on her hip. "Enton, yes. I know all this. That's why I left the company."

He did not look up but continued to write in his ledger, as if alone in the room. "But there are some items with a special instruction. Any item, any scroll, any tablet, any book, anything of even the smallest significance that mentions the word 'Zero' is to be taken immediately to the home office in Gate City, eyes-only for the president. So even having this conversation I skirt extremely close to an offense worthy of termination. You have to go, Xenon."

His voice was level and not unkind, but she felt as if his words were made of dust. "Thank you for your aid, Enton. Seriously, you really helped."

She opened the door, but he spoke again. Xenon turned awkwardly, one foot already placed to leave.

"If I were in a position where I feared some great calamity might befall and needed to see more clearly"—Enton's voice was quiet—"I would find a high place."

Xenon shut the door and scuttled down the hall, her head full. The glass door slid shut behind her, and she quickly muzzled her sister's questions with a firm palm in her face. The goblin kicked *Tobio* into flight, and magenta energy flared behind her as she pulled her goggles into place. She felt the city and the continent and globe itself unfold beneath her like a map. Her mind spun like a compass, then came down pointing east. *"A high place."* Corinth! *It means "seat of the highest" in the Old Gilean tongue.* Mercury's incessant jabber finally found its way to her ears. "Where are we going, you madbucket?"

Even at top speed it will take over a week, and we'll need to stop for provisions and rest. No WAY am I letting Mercury drive. Xenon eased up on the sky-cycle's throttle and grinned over her shoulder into her sister's thundercloud face. "To the throne of the king, Mercy. We're going to see the Knights of the Nameless God. We're going to Gilead!"

Enton Blake leaned back in his chair, letting his fingertips tap lightly on his forehead as he thought. He did not hear the door open, which was unusual as he had extremely sharp hearing. The first thing he noticed was the cold that was emptying the room, frost forming on the windows and edges of his immaculate desk. It was also unusual for him to notice the cold as he did not suffer from its bite; his heart also did not beat as a matter of form. He looked up through his splayed fingers into the eyes of his employer and president of the Seafoam Trading Company, Jayden Moore.

Jayden Moore had white skin, white as mausoleum marble. Jayden Moore had black hair, long and fine. Jayden Moore was one of the few things in this world that could frighten Enton and make his heart remember beating as a recourse for terror.

He did not let his fear show, something never wise in the presence of a predator. "Mr. Moore. Good evening."

The cold spoke. "She has made a discovery."

Enton nodded. *No purpose in being coy.*

"When Shame falls, Zero will rise. I have prepared for this day. Is there any chance the archaeologist could interfere?"

Enton blessed his dead heart as he did not blink. "No, Mr. Moore."

The president turned and left the room. The cold remained for quite some time, and Enton was shocked to find sweat on his fingertips when he pulled them away from his forehead.

CHAPTER NINE

JONAS & RIME

The *Cormorant* sailed away without a word. They unloaded no cargo, took on no wares. Captain Blackberry dropped the gangplank long enough for Rime and her guardian to cross to the skeletal dock, then pulled it back in as if it were sitting on hot coals. He turned and bellowed orders to his sons; only his daughter's cool gaze met the travelers' for a moment, before she too was gone. The wild mage turned her back on them; it was nothing she wasn't used to.

"So we're here," Jonas said, his voice muffled. He wore his brown hood pulled up to conceal his sheepdog head and a strip of blue fabric wound around the bottom of his face as an impromptu scarf. Rime had torn it from her nice dress with equanimity; the silk garb had gotten too much dirt on it to pass any longer among any form of nobility. She was back in her plain travel tunic, the white half cloak held with her skull-shaped pin. Her guardian's attire was a bit odd, but at the very least it would hide his features until she thought of something better.

"We are." She turned and faced the small port city of Shiloh, a dot on a map in her mind. She glanced around, recording salient data points from the passing crowds and architecture. *Small town. Predominantly human, which is common for Gilean territories. The capital city, Corinth, is landlocked, so any hamlet or village on the coast can slap together a quick dock in a weekend and become a reputable trading hub.* She gave the wooden post closest by a nudge with her boot, and it wobbled in embarrassment. *Maybe in a quick afternoon. It's early morning; these all seem to be sailors and tradesmen. No sign of any knights or anyone associated with the court—chance of anyone recognizing Jonas by more than reputation: 12 percent. Safe to proceed.*

Rime laid a finger over her chin in thought and began to move. Jonas shouldered their satchel and pawed at his sword nervously, but fell into step behind her. *We shouldn't remain in any one place for very long. We'll purchase provisions, gear, and horses and be on our way before noon.* The crowd around them paid only a tiny amount of heed to the two young travelers.

Her boots slapped onto the simple roadstone. *Last night.* She commanded the words to report back to their barracks, but they insolently stood at parade rest on her shoulder, picking their noses. Rime remembered how good it had felt, how right— floating, no, *flying,* and calling down the lightning on her foes. The beasts in her head had howled, and she had howled right along with them. *I need to be more careful. I'm getting out of control. Easier and easier each time.*

"So, what should my name be?" Jonas asked, coming up to her side. "You know I'm no good at coming up with one on the spot. If people ask who I am, what do I tell them? Or you? Your name is going to be hard to hide pretty soon too."

She chuckled despite herself. *I'm losing my grip on sanity, and Jonas keeps having good ideas. Upside down we go.* "A good cover name should be something simple, close to your own name in case you stumble. Do you have another name already? Do they give middle names in Gilead?"

"Nah, just Jonas." His brow furrowed. "Wait, do you have a middle name?"

Rime's mouth went dry and she picked up her pace, nearly shouldering a pair of leather-clad sailors out of the way. She angled for a nearby archway that seemed to lead away from the docks and toward the center of town, the most likely place to find the market. The dawn sun made the archway a black silhouette, half of a dark circle. The mage squinted and could see that it was fashioned from what appeared to be a pair of ancient rib bones, encased in a cunning lattice of brick and mortar. Earthen pots were placed at regular intervals along the top, and bright-yellow flowers bloomed despite the advance of fall. *I wonder if someone waters them; do they have a ladder nearby that they use for maintenance?*

"Oh man. It must be *terrible*." Her guardian practically salivated as he trotted to catch up. "You've got to tell me."

Rime turned back, arms crossed. "No. Not going to happen. And this is not one of those times where someone says that a thing will never occur to build up your anticipation or even an opening for some passing deity to prepare some sort of ironic comeuppance. This is not a thing that you will know, ever."

Jonas grinned. "Yeah, well, we'll see."

"No, we will not *see*."

The squire laughed. "Aww, come on. What could be more complicated or strange sounding than—"

"*Doma* Rime Korvanus," a voice came from the archway of brick and bone.

The two travelers spun, the squire's hand already on his sword. Standing in the shadowed circle, outlined by the rising sun was a ghost. The hunter, Linus, had already drawn his white sword and held it out before him as if in benediction. His dented iron armor was the same, the white spiral sigil on his chest was the same, and his cool blue eyes were the same. The same as the last time, on the beach. The few citizens of Shiloh coming through the archway eyeballed the situation with curiosity but kept moving around the knight and his white sword. *It's so odd, that fucking sword. People think it's a staff or a cane or some-weird-thing, and off they go with their business.*

"You are dead." Rime's panic was slathered over with a thick coating of bruised propriety. It was just so *rude.* "I killed you myself. I made sure."

The beach, the sand, the seer's blonde hair in the wind as Rime tore her apart, Jonas's lackluster duel with Sideways, and their harried gambit that had tricked the hunter, flinging away his white sword into the waves, leaving him naked before her power, helpless before the final, exhausted thrust of her dagger, that she buried in his neck to make certain that Linus would never rise to follow her again. It all flashed through her mind with quicksilver venom.

"Yes," Linus agreed. "But our business is not complete."

"Get behind me, Rime." Jonas stepped forward, eyes on the other swordsman. The squire dropped their satchel and began to draw his own steel to match the white blade in front of him.

"Have a care," the older man instructed. "The Law of the King is held here, as in all lands of Gilead. Naked blades in the streets— the guards will come, questions asked. Your lady cannot risk such an entanglement. Nor do I think would she wish to reveal her *nature* in this crowd of gentlefolk."

Rime snarled in frustration and found the old man's blue eyes locked with her own.

"Use your head, *Doma,*" Linus said. "Weigh the risks—the cost in innocent life—if you are not too far gone yet."

"What should we do, Rime?" Jonas turned, his eyes wide.

She made her mind go faster. *Fight?* There were currently eighty-seven people within a two-hundred-foot radius of her position. Little room to maneuver without precise use of her magic. The white sword ruined most of her options. When she had faced it in the past, it had proven anathema to her magic; it canceled out anything she could throw at it. It possessed the ability to undo any magical effect it came into contact with. It was her bane. It was the sword that would kill her, unless she was extremely clever immediately. *Escape?* She could grab Jonas and fly them out of there, but it was impossible for that to go unnoticed. Her exact flying distance was untested, but it would be sufficient to get them out of Shiloh—but then Linus would of course raise pursuit and they would be caught in open ground without any horses or provisions. *Parley?* She knew much of the Hunt, the wild mage killers, but not enough of this man called Linus the Blue. He had pursued her before with implacable intent and merciless execution. *He will kill me the moment he has the chance, without preamble or warning. Delay?* Jonas could at least keep the ironclad knight busy for a few moments, enough time for her to attempt something, look for some other variable to enter the equation, but that seemed a long shot at best. *Variable. Variable!*

"Tell your sellsword to come out where I can see him," Rime demanded, pointing up at the archway.

Linus chuckled, then nodded as if in salute. The devilkin rogue, Sideways, rolled up from his hiding place. He had been hanging out of sight on the far side of the arch; she had only spotted the barest edge of his orange fingers when she had looked for them. The assassin's horned face beamed down at her in a good-natured fashion, his gray short sword held lazily in his left hand.

"Hey, girl." Sideways waved.

"Hey!" Jonas waved back, then lowered his hand in shame.

The rogue saluted Jonas, two fingers to his eyebrow.

"Now that we've all made our pleasantries"—Linus pulled the white sword's hilt to his breastbone and leaned on it as if it were a staff—"will you answer me with fire or ice, *Doma*?"

Think, damn you, think! "What do you propose then, Linus the Blue?" she took a quick look at the crowd; they were still essentially ignoring the strange group's interaction.

"I asked you once to surrender to me. I will not ask it again." The old man looked weary as he spoke. "I chose our battleground more carefully this time. I believe you have not fallen . . . yet. I believe you are still sane. That you are not ready to take the lives of strangers. We are at an impasse. I must kill you, and you do not wish to die. Even now you prepare yourself to flee—the angle of your shoulders, the turn of your chin, it's written all over you. The white sword can unravel whatever magic you weave, but it cannot fly faster than you. I do not know what has brought you to this land, but it must be of great importance for you to move with such haste. This, then, is what I propose. A lesson."

The old man brought the white sword up again, quicker than his age should have allowed, and then swung it in a clean arc at the closest person walking by. It was a woman, red hair shot through with gray, white tunic stained by long use, a basket crammed full of wriggling fish in her arms. The white sword cleaved through the basket and her arms like so much wheat, bright-red blood spurted down her tunic and she screamed. Rime noticed a tattoo on her neck as she fell, a blue shield.

It happened so fast. Even Sideways looked shocked. The woman was down and screaming. The hunter, Linus, turned and shouted to the populace. "Monster! Abomination! Wild mage in our midst! The girl! The girl with the white in her hair! She must be stopped!"

The good people of Shiloh turned and saw an old knight with his sword high in defense and a fisherwoman's heartblood leaking out onto the road among a dozen wriggling fish. And a few feet away, a girl with white hair whose eyes blazed with red light. Later, some would mention that they *thought* they saw the knight attack Gratha, but even so he must've fallen under the wild mage's spell.

"Rime, your eyes!" Jonas had time to say before the sudden clamor of shouting, angry voices filled the street.

Rime howled and grabbed their satchel and threw it into the squire's arms. Without waiting for anything else to go wrong, she enveloped them both in a globe of orange light, shot through with angry red lightning bolts of frustration. The shouting people fell back in terror, and she gritted her teeth. *Just further and further into the hunter's snare.*

She forced herself to take one last look into Linus's eyes and raise a hand in salute. For better or for worse the old man was a worthy opponent, and she would be damned if she would flee without some scrap of dignity.

Her ball of light launched into the air, and she turned her concentration to moving as far and as swiftly as possible before her magic ran out.

Sideways hopped down from his perch and crouched down next to the dead woman. His employer was surrounded by terrified people, and he was dispensing instructions and comfort with a calm voice and careful hand. The rogue saw one old woman kiss Linus's gauntlet in thanks.

Stay paid. The dead woman was cold to the touch, and the fish that surrounded her had all but stopped flopping, only a few still working their gills or closing and opening their mouths in defiance of the inevitable. Sideways picked up one and tossed it out to sea. It made him feel somewhat better.

He could guess what was next: Linus would speak with the town mayor or headman, then the local guard, then they would "feed" the mage-hound, Nora, and head off on their quarry's trail again. *But now with a small regiment at least at our backs. Smart old man. I'll bet he even has a good source of "logs" for Nora all ready to explain to these people he's here to save.*

Stay paid, Sideways counseled himself and found a devilkin-shaped shadow nearby where he could wait for his employer's next instruction.

Rime flew for nearly an hour before her head started to spin. She sat them down in a copse of old oaks, then let the Magic Wild slip away. The mage leaned against a nearby tree and fought back unconsciousness. *I can do it. I can stay awake. We need to make plans, keep moving. It's too dangerous for me to pass out right now, even with Jonas to carry me.*

"What the hell was that, Rime?" Jonas asked. "I mean, why did he do that?"

Oh good, questions now. The squire had kept his peace during the flight, not wanting to distract her, probably. He had stared out at the clouds whipping by with his mouth wide. Rime turned slowly and then flopped down to sit with her back against the tree.

"It was a lesson, as he said."

"A lesson? What kind of lesson was that?" The squire shuddered.

"He was telling us that he knows we don't want to hurt people. And that he will. He was telling me that he's going to keep coming, alerting everyone he passes to my name and location. He knows that we can't run forever. The lesson is this: He's going to keep burning the grass until we have nowhere to wriggle. And then he's going to cut off our heads." Rime covered her face with her palms, exhaustion creeping over her.

"He can't do that, Rime." Jonas kneeled down next to her. "I mean, yeah, he can do that, but we're going to stop him, somehow. And he also made a very good point."

"What good point?"

"The Law of the King. It holds everywhere in Gilead, but nowhere more strongly than in Corinth. If we can make it there, it will prevent him. He can't just walk up to us again in the street and murder us." The squire pounded his fist into his other hand.

Rime smiled crookedly. "Is this the same law that wants to hang you as a deserter and a murderer?"

"Yeah." Jonas nodded.

"Oh, so, good."

"Rime, I'm just saying it will give us some breathing room—maybe. And we're going there anyway, so . . ."

"I get it, I get it." Rime sighed. "Any idea where the closest town is, oh, son of Gilead?"

Jonas squinted around. "I'm pretty sure I saw Mount Cahill while we were flying; it shouldn't be more than a day's walk to Zebulon."

"Okay." She sighed again and forced herself up. "Let's get walking."

The two travelers picked their slow way out of the oak tree copse and out into the open country of Gilead, green grassland shot through with occasional plateaus of granite and small strips of trees.

After about an hour, Jonas piped up. "How about Rumble?"

Rime rolled her eyes, too tired to argue. "Fine. And you can be Josh."

FIRST INTERMISSION

The Demon spoke, alone onstage:

"Grove of green, leaf and bough,
path entangled that bars me now.
Somewhere within, the gleam of water
cleansing blood and dreams of slaughter.
The hunger bites, hour by hour,
so easy to call my bloodred power.
But I must hold and I must stand
lest I be lost and never mend.
Faithless, friendless, pernicious I.
Who sheds a tear when Evil dies?
Knee-bend courtesy and lickspittle shame,
I cannot yield my hammer-stone name.
I'll find the fountain, sacred, pure,
or tear out my heart with claws obdure.
And dying fall on careless earth,
love's forgotten, I care not its dearth."

CHAPTER TEN

THE HUNT

The doorframe was simple wood, hand crafted. It did not show any great eye for beauty, but it served its purpose ably enough. Edge to edge, each beam square. Linus did not know why it caught his attention as he debated whether to burn Zebulon to the ground.

The hunter stood on the porch of the tavern and laid an iron hand on the door. He allowed himself to let a little bit of his weight shift and rest against the banal wood. His eyes flicked to the preposterous sign that hung out into the dusty street—some bumpkin's best attempt at the fierce talon of a dragon. *Have I been here before? Leaned in this same place, stared at this same doorframe? Sneered at this same sign?* It was possible. Linus had joined the Hunt when he was twelve, mother's blood still fresh in his hair. Decades of the chase, the weight of his armor, the quiet nothing of the white sword at his side. Sleeping in barns and castles and crude ditches in the earth. Cobblestone roads and chewed goat trails leading nowhere—anywhere and everywhere his prey fled. Linus looked around again.

Zebulon was a cattle town. A few wooden buildings, surrounded by ranches that sprawled across the grasslands. Other
than the Three-Toed Claw, the largest building in town was the
stockyard where bovine flesh was bought and sold, orders filled
and plans laid for transport to the larger metropolises beyond:
Pice, Gate City, Corinth. Linus crossed his arms, cold clink of
metal on metal as his gauntlets met, and watched two young
women ride past on tall black stallions, both laughing as they
tossed a garish red hoop back and forth. *The wild mage was here,
left just after dawn. She sent her boy to do all the talking, waited on
the outskirts of town. They bought a pair of horses: a gray quarter
horse and a white mare. Simple provisions: food, water, two or three
pots of black ink.* The old man let a grin spread as he enjoyed his
prey's craft. *A fine move,* Doma. *You understood my lesson quite
well, and you are thinking as a hunter would. How will I track you?
What words will I put in every ear, in every bard's cup? Quite wise
to dunk your head in ink, Snowlock.*

Linus pursed his lips. He wasn't entirely pleased with the
name he'd chosen for his demon of Shiloh. It had done its work,
setting the eyes of the people wide and their mouths fluttering.
Every traveler coming or going from the tumbledown dock
would know of the demon girl with the white hair. The magistrate
had nearly begged him to take the entire garrison with him in
pursuit and any able-bodied folk the hunter wished to arm. Linus
had thanked him and insisted on only taking twenty guards—the
youngest and most fit, the best suited to guide him on the trail.
And the best suited to feed his hound if the trail went cold again.

Nora stood close at hand, her glass chest glowing cerulean
certainty, her muzzle pointed east. A thin cord of white silk was
wound around her neck; the other end fashioned into a long lead
terminated in the hand of the devilkin Sideways. The assassin was
leaning against the outside of the inn's porch, doing his best to
appear nonchalant while keeping a maximum extension on the

mage-hound's leash. Linus stepped forward, rapping the wooden sign absently with his knuckles. Nora's leash was artifice, as was much of the Hunt's public face. The leash calmed his new conscripts from Shiloh, even as his false words about the terrors of the demon Snowlock inflamed their valor. Keeping their attention on the demon without prevented them from questioning too closely the methods within—or noticing the "scout" that he had dispatched with a message back to Shiloh had met his end between the mage-hound's jaws, feeding her torch.

"Okay, I gotta ask." Sideways scratched his nose.

Linus took the last few steps down to the dusty street and laid an affectionate gauntlet on Nora's head. "Yes?"

"Why are we stopping here at all? If we can track Skinny Girl anywhere with the vampire pooch, why not just press on?"

The hunter straightened his blue cloak and gave the mage-hound one last fond pat. "One. Information. We know how much food they purchased enough for three days' travel. Their final destination is close. Also, the trick of the ink is another scent we can follow. Nora is the ultimate tracker for our prey, but it would be foolish to leave any scent or spoor uncollected or unconsidered. Two . . ."

The devilkin had leaned in as his employer's pause drew out. "Yes? Two?"

Linus's faded blue eyes watched a pair of Shiloh guards approach. He saluted them, gave the two some quick instructions about preparing for their departure. The senior, an older woman, requested permission to conscript some additional arrows from the local blacksmith, which he authorized. The hunter made note of her; she seemed more solid than most of her compatriots. Only when the two guards walked well out of earshot did he continue his explanation. "Two. These guards we carry are fuel for Nora, and perhaps a momentary distraction for the wild mage. Our true goal is to assemble a far greater army, an invisible one, made of air and fear."

The assassin nodded. "You want people to be scared shitless of her. Wherever she's going, she'll find no friends, only enemies."

"Precisely. As fast as we ride, terrible tales have a thousand wings. Nora's light guides us east; I believe *Doma* Korvanus makes for Corinth. Why, I know not. But I intend to poison that city for her. She will find no aid, no bastion. It was my intention to burn this town to ashes as another harbinger of her coming."

Sideways's mouth dropped, ever so slightly, but then he angled his orange face in a studied manner of indifference. Linus kept his own face blank and continued. "What do you think of this plan, assassin?"

The devilkin scratched his nose again, then began to twirl the end of Nora's silk leash. "I mean, it won't really make sense, will it? All the Shiloh folk will know that when we left it was fine, that she wasn't here when it was burned."

Linus looked down the dusty streets of Zebulon to where the two young women were looping around on their horses, still playing the game with the ring. Now both were standing up in their stirrups, hooting with glee as each tried to outdo the other for outlandish ways to toss the ring or to catch it. One young woman had long red hair, the other short-cropped blonde. A small crowd had gathered to cheer on the local riders' game. The hunter spoke quietly. "We ride out of here within the hour. You slip away from the column, unnoticed in the shadows, as is your training. You come back here, just after sunset, with a fistful of torches. You fling them into that hay barn there, into the back of this inn, into every window that you pass. Then you cut the rope on the well and let the bucket fall down far below. I will look back at the sudden flame that will appear on the western horizon, and I will say, 'By the gods, the demon moves in shadow like the wind itself. She has set fire to Zebulon, to punish them for aiding us.' And the good folk of Shiloh that ride with us will see the flame in the dark and they will believe. I will dispatch a handful of them as heralds—to ride out to every small town between here and Corinth, bearing the tale of the slaughter in their home, of the razing of Zebulon. You will arrive back, unnoticed in the shadows. We will then ride on, and the night will be alive with our invisible army growing larger and larger by the moment."

Sideways met the hunter's eyes. "Are those my orders?"

The cry of the crowd surged; the short-haired rider had fallen from her stallion into a nearby pile of crates. The onlookers were converging, laughing while pulling the groaning and bruised rider free from the shattered wood. Linus felt the weight of his armor. *I think I have been here before.*

"Not an order. A choice. A boon, if you will," Linus said. "If you wish it, you can save the all-but-unknown city of Zebulon. If you say so, we will ride away and leave it unmolested. And we will burn the next small city we come upon."

"Why . . ." The devilkin swallowed, orange skin taut. "Why would you give me the option?"

Linus laid an iron hand on the assassin's shoulder. "Because this is not my first Hunt, but it is yours. I know there can be comfort found in choices like these. Rider of Zebulon, what is your name?"

The still-mounted rider was trotting past, red circle in her teeth, and long hair like eager fire. She spat it out into her left hand and waved a greeting to the knight and his companion. "Veronica, grandfather!"

The horse's hooves thudded past. Linus turned his attention back to the assassin. "Veronica of Zebulon. You saved her. If you wish it."

The leather-clad rogue's face was empty as a stone's mercy. Sideways tapped the side of his nose with a long orange finger and turned aside uncomfortably.

"I wish it," he said.

"Then let us be gone from this place." The hunter took the leash from his hands.

CHAPTER ELEVEN

⸱ RUMBLE & JOSH

Jonas took a long breath of crisp fall air. The shadows were lengthening from the few oak trees they passed; it would be time to make camp soon. The squire patted the side of his horse's neck and wondered if he should be more concerned about how close they were to Corinth. He *was* wanted for murder and he *did* have years of unresolved emotional turmoil pent up in his return, *but* he had also discovered that morning that Rime had never ridden a horse and was positively terrible at it.

"The horse is going left again," the mage complained, holding both reins up at nearly her eye level.

"I just don't get it. You've driven a wagon before; that was a whole team of horses. Hell, you've even driven a freaking wyvern a time or two." Jonas chortled.

"I think this horse you bought is defective." Rime leaned over and shot a murderous glare into the eyes of her placid mare. "Did the man laugh behind his hands as you walked away?"

"No. I know about horses, way more than you do." The squire assured her again. "There's nothing wrong with your horse. You're just weird, and she can sense that you're uncomfortable. Just relax and ease up on the reins."

The mage grumbled something but then settled back into the fragmented silence that had been her shield most of the day. She would erupt a few times an hour with complaints, odd questions, or pointed insults, but it was clear that her mind was occupied with their predicament. Jonas had learned to recognize the signs and kept his attention on the road ahead.

They had encountered only a few other travelers during the day. Both Jonas and Rime kept their hoods up, limited conversation to easy pleasantries, and did not linger to speak with the tanner or the family of potters or the absurdly dressed clown with the trumpet. Speed was their main concern, and they would soon be in Corinth where the chance of being recognized increased tenfold—better to stick to the main roads and travel swiftly.

"Why is the horse slowing down again?" Rime sputtered.

Mostly swiftly. Jonas grinned and slowed his gray quarter horse down until he and his companion were traveling side by side. The mage had wanted to start out at a gallop immediately; he was proud of himself for convincing her of the foolishness of that plan. *A great horse can gallop for an hour or walk for ten. Most often we are given okay horses that can gallop for ten minutes or walk for two hours. Better to save however much gallop they have for when it is truly needed.* The squire felt a hot place behind his eyes. *Master's words. Again. I hear him more and more the closer we get, it's almost like he's right next to me.*

As plain as pyrite, Jonas saw Sir Pocket riding before him. His giant roan, Pasadena, hooves flashing with the silver-studded horseshoes that his master has insisted upon. The squire had never been sure what he had spent more time on—polishing his master's gear or brushing Pasadena's coat and mane. The vision charged ahead, shield slung over his shoulder, gleaming with the three blue swords of Gilead bound in a circle of white.

Held high, the silver sword Hecate burned as bright as moonlight. Jonas blinked and the vision was gone. He brought his horse to a halt and reached out absently to grab Rime's reins as her white mare kept steadily walking along.

"What? What?" Rime waved an imperial hand at him. "Why are we stopping?"

"I've been here before," Jonas answered, keeping his eyes away, just in case they were wet. "There's an old campsite over that hill, beneath those three apple trees. I stayed there once with my master. It's out of the way; we should set up camp."

The mage shrugged and slid out of her saddle. "Fine, whatever."

Jonas got out of the saddle as well, taking both horses by the reins to lead them. He followed the mage, who walked unknowing in the hoofprints of the Past.

An hour later, Jonas stirred his new cauldron and tried to think of nothing. He had set up camp, tended to the horses, and built the fire; he had even checked the trees for late-season apples, but they were bare. Finally, he had set to making the evening meal without a word. A slight glow of acquisitional pride came over him at the solid little cauldron that he had bought in Zebulon. The man at the stockyards had found it crammed into one of the saddlebags that he was selling the squire, and had shrugged and thrown it in as a bonus. It was nice, thick iron, well cured. The ham shank he'd bought in town, with some flour and water, would turn into a fine stew—with the help of the carrots, potatoes, and fresh green onion he'd snagged from the farmer's cart. The squire spooned up a generous portion with his new wooden spoon and gave it a frank taste. He abruptly realized two things: being sent unsupervised to shop was enormously fun and he was entirely too good at filling his brain with nothing.

Rime hissed softly from across the fire, where she sat with a bowl containing the three vials of ink they had purchased. With deliberate care she was portioning out small dollops of the black ink and straining her hair through it—first the signature white, then the mundane brown to match. Jonas went back to stirring the stew; it needed just a few more minutes.

"So, why don't you just change your hair color with magic?"

The mage cursed with customary venom and continued dyeing her hair. "It doesn't work that way. I can't permanently affect the properties of an object unless I'm destroying it. I could change the color, but I would need to constantly keep a slow trickle of my magic going to keep the illusion operational. Wasteful use of resources, so the ink."

The squire scrunched his forehead up in thought. "But why? I've heard of plenty of wizards that could do a simple spell like changing the color of something. Or complicated stuff like changing a person into a frog or lead into gold. And I've seen you do some really crazy things, really powerful things . . ."

"Look, can we just leave it? You don't remotely have the vocabulary to understand." Rime dragged her fingers around the bowl, wanting to use every bit of the ink. "Think of it like this. Most wizards are putting magic into a preexisting shape. That's all a spell is really, just a shape for magic. It's like a glass—a glass of water. They coax a tiny trickle of water into the glass, so the water takes the shape of its container. Now, imagine that, instead of a trickle of water, you were trying to fill a glass with a river, with a waterfall, with an entire ocean at once."

"Oh, it won't fit in the glass?"

"It breaks the glass." Rime's eyes flickered, and the ink in the bowl and on her hands danced free and hung in the air like black pearls. "Stuff like this is about the finest control I have—very small physical interactions. I understand the mechanics of most spells, but my magic just burns them out too fast—I have to really concentrate to keep something complicated together. And that makes me pass out faster. I can make shapes, objects, elements, light. But it all requires my active concentration."

The mage gestured, and the tiny droplets flew through the air and began to orbit her finger like black moons.

"Maybe your magic just likes showing off," Jonas suggested as he spooned some stew into a bowl for his companion.

"Maybe," Rime said, and the ink-moons each took on a different shape: a black sword, a leering face, a rocking chair, a cat's silhouette, a broken guitar.

"Do you want to talk about the boat?" Jonas heard himself ask, but he kept his eyes down on the simmering cauldron.

"It's getting worse. My magic. It feels . . . it feels right. It feels wonderful. I think there's a day coming when I can't stop. I think I'm going to go insane soon." Rime's voice was barely audible over the crackle of the fire.

"What's in Corinth? Something that can help?" The squire made his hand and voice stay steady as he passed the bowl of stew.

Rime took her bowl and held it in her lap. "I don't know. The Gray Witch told me. That time, that time we met her in the marsh. She said my answer was in Gilead, at the throne of the king. I have to get in there somehow—someway. It's that or die out here. Either when that old man's white sword lops my head off or when everything in my head explodes."

The mage flung the shifting ink off out into the darkness around the campfire and pressed her knuckles into her eyes. Jonas made himself stay calm, mechanically spooning brown warmth into his mouth. *The Gray Witch!* He himself had talked to the strange woman—and more times than Rime knew of. She appeared when it suited her to challenge and question him. The Gray Witch was one of the things he was *most* proud of not thinking about. She spoke in quarter riddles, and the squire was terrified of her. He opened his mouth to speak, but a sudden itch in his lips prevented him. Jonas rubbed the itch hard with his hand as Rime continued, letting her fingers spread across her face and fall quietly into her lap next to the untouched bowl of stew.

"Tactics. Resources. Options." The ink-haired girl shuddered at the last word. "We are pursued and in great haste. We do not have time to slowly infiltrate the city, gather information, or seek out any sort of allies or aid. Corinth is the home of the Iron Legion. The full might of the army of Gilead stands between the king's throne and us. Anyone who recognizes you or me will instantly set up an alarm that will result in an armed, well-trained response. Possible outcomes: capture, defeat, death. Easy enough to flee such an encounter, but then all chance of us moving about the city unrestricted is removed permanently from the board."

Jonas smiled and went back to slurping up stew. He waved his spoon between bites to get his companion's attention. "Like I said, this is my hometown, I've been here before. I do know a couple of ways in and out of the city. Unless things have changed a whole lot, they won't be interrogating us at the Shield Gates or anything. We can walk right down Providence Road to the gates of the Keep. But the Knights of the Sword at the crossing aren't going to let us in without introducing ourselves at the very least. Have you thought of a reason why Mistress Rumble and her manservant, Josh, should be admitted to see the king? Immediately?"

Rime raised a finger, eyes light. Then she crooked it in thought. Then her eyebrows fell and she turned her attention to her own spoon and bowl of stew.

The squire coughed a short laugh, but he felt his chest go tight. "Come on, Rime. You've been brooding about this all day. I know. I figured out how we get to see the king, so there's no way you didn't think of it hours ago. You can say it."

"Shut your face, Jonas."

"Mistress Rumble marches right up to the knights on watch and pulls back the hood of her traveling companion. 'Here he is, Jonas of Gilead. Come to answer for his crimes.' They'll swoop right down and take us both inside the castle. I'll be headed down to the dungeon, but you'll be taken right to the king's chambers, to thank you for your service and question you about how you crossed paths with me." Jonas set to scraping the few tasty remnants in the cauldron into his bowl.

"I don't want to do that," Rime said.

"You have to." The squire eased back to the ground with his refilled bowl. "It's not just to get you into the throne room, it's to protect you from Blue Linus and Sideways—I can't protect you, but the Law of the King can."

"I don't want to do that," Rime repeated, as if convincing herself. "You'll be put to death, and for some stupid honor-trap that your master put you in."

"Rime—" Jonas began.

"No. That old man *used* you. I said so on the boat. There has to be another way. You don't need to answer to any stupid law."

"But I want to," the squire said. "It's time. I can't run forever from this, and—"

"Yes, you can! You can in fact run forever," the mage seethed without much conviction and pushed black hair out of her face.

Jonas tossed his bowl into the cauldron. It would be easy enough to carry together down to the stream along with Rime's bowl for cleaning later. He stretched both arms, freed his sword from its scabbard, and laid it across his knees. From the nearby satchel he snagged his whetstone and cloth, and for a time the campsite was silent except for the mutter of the fire and the clean scrape of his stone on the blade.

Without looking up from his task, Jonas spoke again. "Neither of us is going to pretend. There are things you do. Things you are. Things you find in your blood. And there's always a cost and a time you have to pay out for them. Doesn't matter if you meant it, or if you were born to it, or if you stacked up a pile of good deeds on your platter hoping they'd lessen the bill. Your magic is burning you up. I've got white blood on my hands. Tomorrow let's ride to Corinth and settle up."

The mage stared at him across the fire as if he were a stranger. Jonas kept his mind empty as he finished his bowl of stew and did not think about his master, or the Gray Witch, or the swift, cold bite of the sword that lay across his knees. There was another sword waiting for him in Corinth, waiting to fall on his neck once and for all. He looked down for a moment, feeling the air of the headsman's swing—then looked up into Rime's eyes. She was kneeling down right next to him, her hands on top of his, the blade beneath.

We've been holding hands a lot lately. The thought flew by like an arrow.

Rime looked into his eyes, as if choosing a cut of pork at the butcher's block. She wrinkled her nose and shrugged. "Fine. We'll do it your way. But once I've seen the throne, I'm breaking you out."

The squire's mouth dropped. "Rime! No, you can't do that. You can't break me out of the king's dungeon, the Knights of the Scroll would—the Law would, my word as a soldier of Gilead; it's just wrong!"

Rime stood up and smacked him on the top of the head. "Yeah, yeah, the Law. If all the stories you told are true, there's no way you can have a worse reputation around here. And just because all the fancy knights in your hometown make you feel a need for some sort of poetic justice out of a bard's saga doesn't mean I have to coddle that kind of nonsense. I'm used to you now; I'm not starting over with another guardian. So deal."

"Nonsense!" Jonas sputtered. "The Knights of Gilead are the greatest heroes this planet has ever known. Do you know how many fell before the Red Wizard? Or battling the Vampire Dread? Or putting down the wyrm Melgatoth?"

The mage considered for a moment. "Reports vary. Between three hundred and fifty and four hundred ten fell during the Dragoon War proper, and a few score more at Korthan Zul's tower. Thirty-seven were turned by the vampire lord's touch, but nine were saved by various divine intermediaries—so twenty-eight net were lost. Twelve knights exactly fell fighting the dragon, a thirteenth survived a full month after the battle before succumbing to the beast's psychic venom at last. Sir Basil, Knight of the Wand."

Jonas groaned. *Never argue with a library.*

Rime sauntered away to her bedroll and laid down with her back to him. The squire finished sharpening his good steel and watched the campfire whisper itself down to embers. The White Moon was full, the Red Moon a crescent, and the Black Moon all but invisible in the night sky—Jonas covered the white moon with his thumb and then rolled up in his brown cloak for sleep.

We have a plan at least, he told the moons, and his dead master, and the Gray Witch too, if she were listening. "Good night, Rime," he whispered.

"Call me Rumble," she said testily.

RIME'S DREAM #3

In a garden, she found a well.

The garden was green, but the plants were dead.

In the well there was a bucket and a rope and a crank.

She turned the crank and lowered the rope and heard the splash.

She turned the crank and pulled up the bucket.

There was water in the bucket, but something else.

She reached in and the water was cold, but her hand was hot and the water was cold and her hand closed on the something else.

It beat in her hand, a heart. A heart, a heart, a heart.

She was singing a song and pulling the heart out of the water.

Tears on her face, the song on her lips, the heart in her hand.

The heart beat. The heart beat. The heart beat.

The heart did not. The heart did not. The heart did not.

Her hand was hot, and the heart was cold, and the water was cold, but her hand was hot.

Her hand was hot, and she was singing, and her hand was hot, and she was singing, and her hand was hot, and she was screaming, and she was screaming, and she was screaming, and she was screaming, and she was.

CHAPTER TWELVE

XENON

The sky-cycle cut through the clouds, and Xenon laughed as a sudden updraft blew the hem of her square-cloak right over her head. She pulled the fabric free with one hand while keeping her other hand steady on the throttle. Mercury grabbed the flapping cloak's hem and jammed it down into the edge of her piloting sister's belt—it had become a tediously common occurrence during their days of flight. They would be humming along, magenta light spooling out behind them, goblin eyes wide at the vast and beautiful landscape beneath them, then whop—faceful of cloak. Xenon snickered as her younger sister grumbled—her cloak was perfect for travel and investigating clammy ruins or burning sands—but it patently was not intended for the air speeds that *Tobio* could reach.

"Take off the cloak!" Mercury spat in her ear.

"Nope!" Xenon laughed and straightened her goggles. Something about the way it flapped against her shoulders felt proper and just—plus the wind's bite and the high altitude made the skies a fierce torrent of cold.

The last silver-white vestiges of the cloudbank parted and the city of Corinth lay before them, like a child's plaything. The surrounding grassland green, broken occasionally by outcroppings of sheer granite and thin copse of oak and elm, smashed up against the gray-stone walls of the city like a verdant wave. Xenon took a long breath of cold fall air and wished she could make her eyes go wider, or pause their descent a moment so she could sketch it all in her journal. The city walls were vast slabs of granite, surely quarried from the surrounding countryside—but each slab showed a hundred scars. Scorch marks, cracks wide enough for a goblin to stick his hand in, a pockmarked graveyard of abandoned steel rusting away in the walls, arrowheads, lances, halberds, and glaives—all flung by the champions of evil come to lay siege to the crown city of Gilead. Time itself seemed to be the greatest beast savaging the high walls; the simple erosion of rain and sun had widened the gaps between slabs to the point where industrious soldiers were working now to construct wooden palisades and gates in between the dwindling granite. Corinth was a city that had known the hammer and the breaking of stones, and every shattered line of building or errant cobblestone street carried the memory of the days when darkness had beaten down her defenders and made vicious festival in the home of the righteous.

And yet the sun shone down on Gilead's capitol as if it could not remember Night. From every tower, every high place, the brave blue flags flew and snapped in the wind. *Blue for the sky, where the priests of the Nameless God teach that all valor is recognized. A white circle, for the will of the heart that cannot be broken. Inside the circle, three blue swords crossed. Rage, Fear, Despair—all bound by Faith.* Xenon turned the sky-cycle into a slow banking arc across the northern face of the city, information running through her head. Gilead had never been her specialty, but there were things that any scholar worth their salt knew by heart. The small country, really a city-state with allied territories across a small corner of the continent of Eridia, had managed to involve itself in far more than its proper share of history. *The Dragoon War. The MNO Incident. The Sandwich Rebellion, where Carroway broke free of the domination of the Dwarven empire. The Swords of the Faith, found in every major conflict for hundreds of years. Always on the side of Good.* The goblin's academic brain quivered at this last thought, a shallow mealymouthed platitude. It was the sort of statement put in children's history texts, not the thing a true researcher would accept at face value. *Tobio* flew lower across the spine of the city, and she shrugged off her quibble. *Of course it's hard to assign such gross qualifiers as "Good" and "Evil" to historic events—but I think it's a reasonably safe approximation to assign "Evil" to the Red Wizard and his armies. And "Good" to the Knights of the Nameless. The Knights of Gilead have always answered the call of any other country in peril and nearly lost their own country many times. This is the place where I'll find help with Shame.*

The interior of the city showed a veritable maze of cobblestone streets, old architecture next to new in haphazard reconstruction. The three largest structures that caught her eye were the vast Temple of the Nameless in the center of town, the Academy where the soldiers and knights of the Legion were trained, and the grand castle of the king pushed forward through the granite walls of the city facing the empty plains. Any approaching army would fall upon the walls of the Keep first, like a shield thrust out through the granite. Many researchers had remarked how unusual it was for royalty to place its seat in the location of greatest danger. *An example or an error?* Xenon wondered.

"Hey!" Mercury's sharp fist banged her ribs. "Where are we going to park?"

Xenon shook her head to clear it and peered down below. "Uhh. I don't really know?"

The vast warren of gray-and-black streets wound beneath them. Her sister stood up on the back of the cycle, using Xenon's shoulder as a brace. "There!" the young goblin pointed down toward a wide, flat area adjacent to the Academy. It was a large field with short-cropped grass, with a few other small airships docked, their anchor lines swaying in the breeze. *Of course. The knights would want to keep an eye on any travelers arriving via air. High-profile merchants, diplomatic envoys, and archaeologists bearing vague warnings about uncertain danger from over a thousand years ago.* Xenon grinned but felt a spike of anxiety in her stomach. It was the sixth of Towerspan, still over a month before the Precursor's dragon prison would open and . . . *what? What happens then, scholar?* She laid on the throttle and tried to outrun her confusion and concern. *I have time. Still have time. It doesn't matter what happens when it opens; something here can help me stop it from happening.*

Her cloak came unstuck and flopped into her face again.

Mercury howled in frustration, pulled the fabric free, and held it out of the way, her sharp teeth grinding loud enough to be heard over the wind. *Tobio* rolled slightly as Xenon adjusted to the movement, making their landing slightly more dramatic than she would have liked, missing the prow of a crimson-stained sloop by inches. She did her best to ignore the angry shouts from the sloop's Dwarven captain as her fingers ran along the sky-cycle's console. As the cycle settled onto the grass, she slipped the metal bangle free from its customary place around the handlebars and locked it into place on her wrist. The command-circle resonated with the aerolith that powered *Tobio*—it meant that no one could activate or fly the sky-cycle without it being present, a useful deterrent against theft. Her sister was already off the cycle, stalking around the perimeter of their landing area and yelling back at the sloop's captain with one hand on her dagger. Xenon shouldered her travel bag and slid down to the ground, hoping to stave off any immediate bloodshed.

"You can't be thundermad about a thing that didn't even happen, stonefoot." Mercury wagged her head, red bone-clips clattering. The dwarf shook his fist and bellowed a response, to which the goblin sneered. "Eh, punch water and die on an ant bed!"

"Mercy, you really can't talk that way," Xenon moaned, then noticed a figure trotting across the green field toward them, a scroll-board in hand.

It was a tall young woman with straight yellow hair that fell to her waist, contrasting with her dark skin and black tunic. She wore a simple breastplate held on with leather straps that bore the three crossed swords of Gilead etched in the metal, an unadorned rapier at her side. "Hail and . . ." she began, then stopped to blow out her cheeks and catch her breath. "Sorry, you caught me by surprise, and it was quite a sprint to this end of the landing field. I am Ganalie Cadet, Sparrow Unit. Welcome to Corinth and the land of Gilead, travelers. Who are you and what business have you here?"

Ganalie turned her attention to the scroll-board in her hand and plucked a chunk of glasschalk from a cunning slot recessed into the bottom of the board. She raised the writing instrument expectantly.

Xenon took a breath, then abruptly spun to clap her hands over her younger sister's mouth. Mercury's eyes exploded with wrath at being denied an opportunity to further embarrass her sister and complicate their journey. Sharp goblin teeth gnawed on her fingers, but Xenon did not release her grip, only with as much gravity as possible ignored the ravening beast between her palms and politely answered the cadet's questions.

"My name is Xenon, and this is my sister, Mercury. We are from Pice. I'm a scholar, here to do some research and also to request assistance from . . . OW." Her sister's canines had found purchase in her right palm.

"She has *no idea* who to request assistance from, strawmane." Mercury swaggered up to the cadet and eyed Ganalie's rapier with open admiration. "She found out about some thing, some bad dragon thing that's going to happen."

Ganalie had been filling out the docking form and nodding, but on "bad dragon thing" her eyes had slowly risen, and now she was looking at the two goblins with a mix of concern and confusion. "I could take you to my unit commander or maybe even to one of the knight instructors?"

Is that what I want? Xenon ran a bleeding hand down her face and pushed her goggles up. "No, thank you, Cadet. There is no need to—" *What? Go get an adult wearing lots of steel to come figure this out for me?*

In the days of flight, the archaeologist had sifted her predicament most carefully, trying to separate the sand of delay from the few shards of fossil-possibility. She was sure that Enton's clue was solid; Corinth was the place to be to find some aid, or the next piece of the puzzle. *But what do I do? I could turn this over to the knights, but it would take a great deal of luck to convince them of the severity of the danger. I have a few scrolls, my journal, and a report of a Precursor urn that I cannot even show to them.* The spike of anxiety in her gut became a spear, and Xenon felt the weight of the clock on her shoulder. Time was passing and the Precursor's dragon prison was returning, and every moment she blinked in the concerned face of the cadet was another moment she could never reclaim on her quest.

"No need to take us to them so abruptly, Cadet. I have some research that I would wish to share, but it is not complete. What would be the proper method to seek audience with the Legion, if my work bears fruit?" *Good! Collected, polite, leaves the door open for later.* Xenon congratulated herself. Mercury spat on the green turf.

Ganalie ran a finger along her forehead, guiding a long shower of blonde hair to a better position out of her eyes, then cocked her head in thought. "Any citizen of Gilead can visit the Academy and ask to speak to one of the knight instructors, or the commandant. But, as you are an outsider, it might take some time before you were heard, and your words might take even longer to reach their hearts. I could help you, though—my mentor is Sir Dryden, a Knight of the Scroll. Come find me in the cadet barracks, Sparrow Unit, and I'll invite you up to tea with him. Knights of the Scroll are the spy masters of our order, and Sir Dryden would be both more interested and more likely to aid you. He's a . . . outsider, like you."

The cadet looked away at these last words and Xenon's eyes widened. *Outsider. That must be the colloquial, semipolite way of saying "not human."* Unlike most major city-states on the continent, Gilead's population was almost completely human. *Ah, those qualifiers are already beginning to show cracks under close observation. Racism! Not unexpected in an isolated geographic location with a monolithic faith and governmental structure.* Xenon felt a little of her mother's iron enter her spine. *But "outsider"?!? Don't they know that goblins are one of the three native races of this planet? Humans are the outsiders; most experts in the field place their arrival at approximately a thousand years after the Precursors arrived. We were here before all of them! "Goblins for might, and elves for grace, and dragons for will" as the Pondiver Doggerel goes.* She made herself smile and nod to the slender cadet; the tall human was offering to help them after all.

"Why are you being so accommodating, suntower?" Mercury crossed her arms with naked suspicion.

Ganalie looked confused, then repeated her elegant hair adjustment. "Why wouldn't I be helpful? It is my duty to aid the new arrivals, and also part of my oath as a cadet. My sword is ready for any noble deed."

The younger goblin squinted up at Ganalie, then slowly backed away, never taking her eyes off the cadet. Xenon slipped in between her sister's field of vision and waved her hands apologetically. "Thank you for your help, Ganalie. Is there any fee for leaving our vehicle parked for a few days? Could you suggest lodging that is—err—reasonably priced?" She tried very hard not to clutch at the extremely lean coin purse at her side.

"Your vessel can remain here as long as needed; you are a guest of Corinth. I have your name and business here, so we will find you in the city if we need to adjust the landing area if a larger ship arrives." Ganalie's voice became businesslike as she returned to the rote passages of her duty. "If your stay will extend beyond a fortnight, we do require that you return to the landing field to check in with the flight squire. No departures after sundown, except in case of emergency."

Xenon surreptitiously stroked her coin purse in relief. She and her sister had eaten lean on the way to Corinth, but she had no idea how long her vanishing store would need to sustain them.

"As for lodging . . ." Ganalie seemed slightly embarrassed again. "You may want to avoid the inns on Cooper's Row as they do not welcome outsiders. The Weary Titan next to the northern Shield Wall would be best."

Xenon gritted her teeth in irritation and turned to gaze off toward the sagging granite wall that the cadet indicated. *Easy enough to find. And well away from all these fine humans.*

"Also, a warning to be on your guard. A wild mage has been savaging several small towns in the vicinity. It is reported to have the form of a young girl, with a swath of hair as white as snow. If you see it, please sound the alarm immediately and bring it to the attention of the closest soldier of the Legion."

A wild mage? The archaeologist turned back in alarm. "Really? How reliable are these reports? One hasn't been seen in decades."

Ganalie nodded. "We've had survivors from the burned towns and reliable witnesses from the slaughter it brought to Shiloh. It might not be a wild mage, it could be some other form of mad demon or dark spirit, but there is definitely something out there and it is incredibly dangerous. Our instructors were very clear."

"Shiloh! Wow, we almost stopped in Shiloh," Xenon looked across the back of the sky-cycle to where her sister was gathering the rest of their paltry gear. Mercury shrugged, nonplussed by their near miss with unbelievable danger.

Xenon's mind started to flip through all the information she had on wild mages, but she made herself stop. *There's a whole army worrying about that problem, and you are the only one trying to unravel Shame.* "Thank you for the warning, cadet, and the assistance. I suppose we'll be off." The goblin took one step forward, only to find it immediately mirrored by Ganalie with her scroll-board between them like a shield.

"There's one last thing. Could I say the blessing of the Nameless for you?" the cadet implored.

Xenon looked down at her sister. Mercury looked back, then shrugged. Their family kept the gods as distant neighbors. You were aware of their presence, and were not above borrowing a cup of sugar when needed, but they were not regular guests underneath their roof. Taking their silence as assent, Ganalie pressed her scroll-board to her chest and closed her eyes. She spoke with simple, unaffected faith.

"Time and wave, sun and wind, night and fire, moons and stone. We walk through the world Only Once. Only one life is given by the Nameless. It is a gift, a burden. A challenge, a duty. To not waste it. To serve the Highest. To the end of the Path, with our honor intact."

When she finished, Ganalie smiled with relief, as if she had forced a thick cloak on them as they stepped out into winter's chill. Xenon and Mercury looked at each other again, then made their way off the landing field and into the twisted cobblestone streets of Corinth.

◦

"I believe that winter is an abstraction." Bolander raised the fine porcelain cup to his black-furred lips and took a long sniff, allowing the tea's careful aroma to fill each nostril.

His cohort, Munch, scratched behind his left horn but said nothing. He was a younger Minotaur and gave way to his senior, quietly focusing his attention less on the conversation and more on the pile of cucumber sandwiches in the center of the table.

"Yes, yes. Is it a function of cold? A permutation of the calendar? When does Winter truly begin, or end? Ask each man or woman on the street and receive a different tale. If we cannot proscribe the limits of a concept, we must concede that it is purely a fictive construct—a trick of language bereft of Truth." The black-furred Minotaur took the most petite of sips from his tea.

"No," the third Minotaur at the table, a wide-shouldered, red-furred beast, intoned.

"Oh ho, a challenge from the Axis of Spirit." Bolander chuckled, setting his teacup down on its matching saucer. "What fairy wings will you sprinkle upon us today, friend Pembleton?"

Pembleton was very still, but then could not resist the bait. He turned so his broken horn was facing his opponent, and took an atom-sip of his own tea. "Winter is a reality. It is a bone-deep knowledge, primal and sure. Every mouse, every grub, every leaf on every bough knows Winter's scythe. Plotted in every hair of our pelt is the watchword of Death that nature has prepared us for. You can bandy about the nomenclature and the calendar and the regional definition all you want, but Winter is real. The quiet hush of cold that pulls us down, that prepares the world for slumber."

Munch bit down on another cucumber sandwich, his eyes rocketing between his comrades.

"Poetry! Poetry and piffle!" the older Minotaur bellowed. "No Truth here, just the limited worldview of a culturally bound observer. What about worlds where there is no change to the season? Or creatures that thrive in vicious cold, such as the ice serpents, frost weasels, blizzard whelps, and no-molecular-motion molemen?!?"

"Why waste an argument upon premises that are so outlandish as to be absurd?" Pembleton countered.

The red-and-black Minotaurs locked eyes, and the silence grew fraught. Pembleton and Bolander each took slow, glacial sips from their tea without ever breaking eye contact. Munch ducked down below their ocular entanglement to reach the teapot and freshen his own cup—he shook a horn in Xenon's direction. "Take a cucumber sandwich, miss?"

Xenon held a cooling porcelain teacup between her fingertips and waved a polite dissent. The Weary Titan was as advertised: reasonably priced and welcoming to goblins and demi-humans of all sorts. Mercury had flopped upon the narrow bed that the sisters would share and fallen immediately into snoring oblivion. The innkeeper, a short Gilean man with iron-gray hair had warned her that the Minotaurs came each week on this day to have tea and discuss philosophical matters. "It can get rowdy in there, miss!" he had warned with a twinkle in his eye.

She sat at the far end of the common room table, watching the Minotaurs' tea party and trying not to panic. When at last the silence broke and Pembleton embarked on a blistering monologue about the teachings of the northern barbarians and their attitudes about the cold, she would have liked to focus on it—the vicious tribes of Malgor were a culture that she had not sufficiently studied. But the spear of anxiety in her stomach had

become a lance, and she felt pinned to the seat like a botany specimen, watching her tea cool.

Something about checking into the inn, and sitting down in
the common room, had pushed her over the edge. The days of
flight on *Tobio*'s back had been ones of simple exhilaration. The
sky-cycle was a wonder, and she'd had a clear destination and a
clear goal. Now that she was here, she had no road map. She didn't
have the first idea of where to start, other than throwing herself at
the Legion or the king and praying that they would be willing to
listen, capable of understanding, and able to help. As she pushed
the three criteria around in her head, she couldn't convince herself that any of them were all that likely.

The tea cooled. The heat escaped. Time marched forward.
Time she would never have again to find a solution. Xenon
wanted to scream.

The goblin sat in the common room of the Weary Titan and
distracted herself with the spirited debate, and at the youngest
Minotaur's insistence, finally a cucumber sandwich.

Then, out of nowhere, a perfect idea appeared in her head.
Xenon laughed with relief and threw back her tea with relish.

Unfortunately, that perfect idea soon fell apart under further
inspection. She had four more perfect ideas while sitting in the
common room that lived short but happy lives before her ravenous anxiety fell upon them and ate them whole. Xenon spun the
drained cup slowly between her hands and tried not to look down
at the empty circle that could have been a zero.

CHAPTER THIRTEEN

RUMBLE & JOSH

A black-haired girl and a boy with a brown hood pulled up high made their way through the streets of Corinth. Rime elbowed her companion again as she saw his head begin to swivel back and forth, taking in the buildings, the people they passed, even the blue sky above.

"Sorry, R-Rumble," Jonas said, his voice muffled by his impromptu silk scarf again.

"It's all about not attracting attention. Head down, look straight ahead. Quit flashing your stupid flat face around for your auntie or Academy bunkmate to recognize," she hissed.

"Oh, my aunt doesn't live in Corinth. She moved to Caleron when I was ten, married a merchant of some kind? At least that's my aunt on my mother's side. My father's sister ran off with a band of thieves when she was fifteen; I never met her—but every so often we'd get letters from Flenelle." The squire chattered on cheerfully. "And my bunkmate! Well, she—"

"I don't care. I don't care. No one has ever cared." Rime took the squire's elbow firmly and navigated them down a side alley.

They had passed through the west gate without incident; Jonas's memory about the guards had proved true. They were not questioned or stopped, but the Legion guards at the gate had been warning travelers about the wild mage "Snowlock." Rime had gritted her teeth at the speed and effectiveness of her hunter's tactic but had grudgingly agreed with her guardian that it *was* a pretty cool name.

"I'm sorry, Rumble," Jonas said, pulling his blue scarf down slightly. "I just honestly never thought I'd come back; it's like wandering through a memory. It doesn't feel real."

He leaned out over her, eyes hungry, toward the busy cobblestone street. Where Carroway had seemed a city of business in their short stay—everyone's eyes on their purse, quick march from delivery to market to home to inn—Corinth seemed like a city of families. People spoke long to each other, laughing with ease. Most wore simple brown or gray garments, but even Rime could spot the bright splashes of color that seemed to mark the bonds of home. A mother and daughter with the same proud nose, sky-blue scarves keeping their hair in check—a noble's son stopping to aid a tottering peasant, red buckles on each belt denoting some military service—a crowd of red-haired children in yellow caps screeching as they sang a hymn to the Nameless God. *This is a place where you could be proud to belong.* Rime kept that thought in her head as she pushed Jonas back away from the street again.

"Okay. Fine. *Josh*," she said. "Now, we need to make a quick stop on the way to the Keep; it's much easier to be taken seriously when you aren't wearing rags. I could also probably stand to invest in a hat."

She ran her fingers through her ink-stained hair with chagrin. The ink had proved sufficient to cover the telltale white, but it had shown its cheap manufacture in the morning light. By firelight it had looked a dramatic shade of ebony black—in the morning sun it proved to be more of a demi-purple. The ink also appeared to be reacting oddly with her scalp, leaving a faint green discoloration no matter how hard she scrubbed with sand and water in the camp-side stream.

Jonas squinted at her hair for a moment. "I mean, it is sort of eggplanty."

"Hilarious. Now where would be a clothing shop for a young woman of means, traveling, from out of town?"

The squire just blinked at her a moment, so she prodded him with a quick jab to the sternum. "Not really something I would ever know anything about." He skipped out of the way and pulled his scarf back into place to cover his face. "But I expect if we head up to Cooper's Row, there will be something—lots of fancy shops there!"

Rime took his arm, the better to monitor his distraction at homecoming, and piloted their way back out into the busy streets.

Most of the people they passed paid them little notice, other than the occasional nod or hand touch to brim of cap at their passing. A pair of armored knights approached, brilliant white surcoats crossed with three blue swords, and she could feel Jonas growing ever more wooden as they drew near. She dug her nails into his arm and led them to the opposite side of a convenient pumpkin cart until the knights had clanked on by.

"I think I knew him. The tall one. He was a few years older than me; he passed his trials when I was a second-year cadet," Jonas whispered.

They were coming to the center of Corinth, where the dozens of ramshackle roads all seemed to originate like idle streams from a mountain spring. There were four wide plazas circling a massive stone building. It was the most depressing building that Rime had ever seen—all black stone and jutting spires.

"The Temple of the Nameless," the squire said and knelt.

"GET. UP." Rime hauled on his arm until he started moving again. "You'll have plenty of time to pray if the plan works; now come away from the awful black brick."

"Awful?" Jonas looked down at her. "No, no—you just have to see it the right way. Come on, this will only take a second."

The squire took her by the hand and led her around the plaza to the western face of the Temple. He did take care to keep his hood in place and his face toward the cobblestones, using his shoulder to push through the midmorning crowds. He pointed up toward the Temple, but Rime could already see what he wanted to show her—half the people milling around this part of the plaza were all looking at the same thing. A massive circular window, nearly a hundred feet across—filled with a riot of stained glass. At this moment, with the sun rising behind the opposite side of the temple, it burned with a fierce rainbow light. *There must be a similar window on the opposite side to allow the sun through at midmorning and late afternoon.* She had seen this style of window before, but in other places it had been used to depict a specific iconography—a scene from a deity's mythos or an important symbol of the faith. Here it was just a thousand shards of light, every color that could be imagined, all burning with the glory of the sun. Rime opened her mouth to speak, but then checked herself as she saw the simple hurt in her companion's face—surrounded by the proud serenity of the other worshippers that filled the plaza.

"Okay, it's nice," she said.

"Nice? Just nice?" Jonas complained, then his voice grew soft. "I thought about that window a lot. When it would rain, or when it was dark on the road, or when I was drunk and sprawled under a log. It was nice to know there was something like this, something beautiful shining at home, even if I could never see it again."

"It is beautiful. It's not what I expected," Rime said, and was a little surprised that she had.

"Oh, well! I'm glad," the squire replied, uncertain of his conversational footing.

Rime rolled her eyes and took her guardian's arm again. "Come on. New clothes for me, then jail for you."

Rime looked at herself in the mirror. *This will serve.* She threw a few gold pieces to the gibbering tailor. He had thought she was some lordling's simpering child who needed to be told and advised and smothered and swaddled like a doll. A few sharp words had put an end to that, but he had delivered what she'd asked for, so she would pay accordingly.

She now wore a pair of snug breeches and fine leather boots that came up past her knee. A simple shirt, and a cunning longcoat of brilliant red with silver buckles shaped like half-moons pleased her greatly—and she had spent a few moments seriously considering a wide-brimmed hat with a magnificent plume, but had at last settled on a simple black skullcap to mask her hair. The mage ran an appreciative hand down her new coat as she stepped back out into the foyer of the clothes shop. *No one's looking at my hair while I've got this jacket on.*

Jonas rose from the stool in the corner he had languished upon and fell into step behind her. The tailor did not even bother to throw a few empty pleasantries after them as they departed, simply picked up his money and kept his eyes on the floor. Rime made a note that this was how she would like to end all such encounters with tailors and tradesmen—with them well paid and cursing her name.

She stuffed her old clothes into their satchel and fished out her favorite pin, a large, leering skull fit for a puppet show. It only took half a moment to affix it to her cap and enhance her swagger enormously. *This is how Rumble dresses. I could get used to it.*

Jonas chuckled and swung their satchel back over his shoulder, where it nestled companionably with his battered leather scabbard. She prepared herself for an insult or thick comment of some sort, but the squire said nothing, just kept in step behind her. Cooper's Row ended and gave way to a wide thoroughfare that led directly to the gates of the castle, studded with sharp-sided stone obelisks like the spines on a lizard's back. More and more armored knights could be seen, but with only a few thousand paces remaining, Rime decided the time for being coy was past. They were here to be captured, after all.

"Providence Road," Jonas said and pulled his hood forward as far as it would go.

"What are these pillars?" Rime pointed at the ten-foot obelisks set at regular intervals down the center of the lane. *I need you calm at the gates, no second thoughts.*

The squire squinted, then smiled down at her. "Something you don't know? They're vampire wards. King Alain built them after the Dread. They're supposed to shine a bright-yellow light if a vampire comes within a thousand feet, but I've never seen them work."

"Over a hundred years have passed since then." She nodded, and then her magic *bristled.*

"Rime, what's wrong?" Jonas's voice was distant, like he was calling down a well.

She did not respond. The mage looked carefully in every direction—no one in the crowd was paying them any attention. They were in a completely uninteresting portion of the road, halfway between two of the stone pillars. Rime bit back her instinct to pull hard on her power and make her eyes see farther, demand every sense strain to the utmost. *No, no—too public, calm down!* The feeling was already fading, but it was unlike anything she had ever felt before. Like coming upon a cold spot in a wide river or the sun hitting your closed eyes for half a moment before vanishing behind clouds again. She turned in a slow circle, ignoring her guardian's chirping concern. *What was that?* The mage captured every stone, every line of the street and sky in her mind. She would *remember* this place.

"Rime—Rumble . . . Rime!" Jonas grabbed her by the shoulders. "What the hell is going on? Are you okay?"

"Yes." She nodded. "It was probably nothing. Just a weird moment that we don't have time to look into. Come on."

"Are you sure? You look like someone took a bite out of your heart."

"Let's go," she insisted and continued on toward the castle. *Is this how it starts? Is this how the magic takes you? Just decides to wake up, all by itself, and make you dance?* A line of sweat ran down her spine despite the fall chill. The squire fell into step beside her and took her elbow; she did not dissuade him, which was disconcerting all by itself.

The drawbridge of the Keep was down, square wood timbers thick with pitch so they were almost black in the afternoon sun. Rime straightened her cap again and gave her silver buttons a quick polish with her cuffs. *Worries for another day.* The mage and her guardian marched directly up to the first guard on the left, a thin-faced man wearing full plate armor and a ceremonial helm fashioned in the shape of a gryphon's head.

"Good day, Sir Knight. My name is Rumble, and this is my companion, Josh. I have a matter of urgency concerning criminal activity. Could you escort me to your ranking officer or the proper authority to discuss the issue?"

The thin-faced knight's brows met in consternation, but after a few more questions he led the two travelers through the gate and into the Keep of King Tamar the Dream Walker, daughter of Alain the Just. King Tamar the Fargazer, the Glory-Gold. Tamar the Lantern, Tamar the Surprisingly Nimble, the Truth Binder.

King Tamar the Evil's Bane, King Tamar the Thrice-Cursed. King Tamar the Beloved.

"... and the Beloved," Jonas finished reading from the small pamphlet they had been provided. "Wow, she's gotten some new ones since I've been gone."

Rime looked up through splayed fingers and just *hissed*.

They had been sitting in the tiny antechamber for about four hours. The mage was splayed on a couch the color of overripe limes, while Jonas sat almost primly on a hard-backed wooden chair nearby.

The gryphon-helm knight had led them there after making them repeat their names a few times and their business. A half hour later a servant had brought water and a basket of bread for them. Then absolutely nothing had happened except Jonas reading the complimentary pamphlet *Welcome to Gilead!: The Balm Is Here and So Are You* out loud. Twice. The second time with copious comments, one-sided arguments, and hand waving. Rime understood that the squire was justifiably nervous, but her never-substantial store of patience had been completely exhausted. "How about we just open that door"—she pointed—"and yell, 'Jonas of Gilead is in here' really, really loud?"

Jonas rubbed his face, having long since dispensed with the hood and scarf. "I mean, it would probably, uh, expedite matters."

"No!" The mage sighed. "I don't want any hero in ham-iron to decide to take vengeance for the lost Sir Pocket in the heat of discovery. Quickly and quietly to jail with you, with as many delays as possible before your proper, lengthy trial. Time for me to visit the throne room, then spring you."

"Oh, about that." The squire began to fold his pamphlet into uneven rectangles. "If you can't spring me, I want to say that it's okay. I've made my peace with it."

"Lame. And dumb. You're not dying in this castle, not on my watch." She yawned.

"Oh, and whenever the lord or whoever gets here, you should probably—"

A brief knock came at the door, followed immediately by the entrance of a very short man with a tuft of astonishingly green hair. Rime blinked and recognized that the man was actually a gnome. *Strange, what's a gnome doing so far from Pice? And wearing the sigil of Gilead?*

The gnome straightened his spectacles, wide circles of steel inset with an almost invisible glass. "Yes. Well. She was right, it seems, something out of the ordinary in the fourth hall antechamber. She's usually right."

Rime stood up and smoothed the sitting-crease out of her red coat. "Whom do we have the pleasure of addressing?"

The gnome flapped a hand at her but craned his neck and peered at Jonas. He closed one eye, then the other, in rapid succession. "Sir Graham. Knight of the Wand. Do I know this one?"

The mage blinked. *Knight of the Wand. Specialized orders within the Gilean military. The Wand are wizards. Tread carefully.* "Perhaps. It is actually this man that brings us here today—"

"Yes, eh?" Sir Graham kept squinting at Jonas, finally pulling his spectacles off and swabbing them with a frilly pink doily he produced from inside his tunic.

"Yes." Rime stifled her irritation. This twiddling gnome wasn't going to rattle her prepared tale. "He has served me as a bodyguard for several weeks, quite honorably and well, I might add. After some time I gained his confidence, and he entrusted me with his dark secret."

"Mmm, dark, yes." The gnome began to nibble delicately on his steel glasses.

"He committed a crime some time ago, here in Gilead. I convinced him to come back and throw himself upon the mercy of the king. It is our hope that he can receive both justice and some degree of amelioration by turning himself in. If you have not recognized him, he is—"

Sir Graham took a bite out of his spectacles as if they were a market cookie, and the sharp crack of the glass seemed overloud in the small room. "Jonas of Gilead, of course—the murderer of Sir Matthew Pocket. But who are you, my lady?"

Rime blinked twice in surprise, then fought to keep her tone even. "My name is Rumb—"

"Rime Korvanus of Valeria," Jonas blurted, his hands already moving into defensive posture. "I should have said this before now! I'm sorry, we talked about it, and your road-name is super good, but I want you protected by the Law, and you won't be if you begin with a lie."

"Are you insane?" she demanded.

Jonas crossed his arms and met her anger with his square face. She crossed the few steps between them to immediately exact retribution when two things stopped them both in their tracks. The first being that Sir Graham, still happily munching on his spectacles, vanished before their eyes. The second being that the folded pamphlet still clutched in the squire's sweaty hand started laughing. Jonas dropped it on the floor like a snake.

"Oh, you two are *fun*." The pamphlet chuckled as it slowly unfolded itself. "Interesting to see the power dynamic between the pair of you, also a worthy thing that our tarnished squire still seems to have some vestiges of his honor rattling about."

"What. Why is the pamphlet talking, Rime?" The squire backed away.

"I . . ." *Magic, powerful magic. Transmutation, mind control, what?* Rime instinctively moved away as well, but could not decide whether to flee, attack, or hold. *If Linus's whispers have already reached the palace with my name, then I need to fight—but then I give up any chance of seeing the throne. What is the right move?*

The pamphlet unfolded itself all the way, then began to grow. It took the outline of a paper gnome with green hair, then popped into full dimension all at once. It was Sir Graham, as before— but this one seemed older, shrewder. *The first was an illusion, to bait us! He's been in here with us the whole time, listening!* Rime wound her mind back; she had barely spoken, and not a word had passed the squire's chattering lips about her magic. *Maybe I'm safe. Maybe.*

Sir Graham snapped his fingers and new spectacles appeared, dark wood rimmed with pearl. He placed them on the bridge of his nose and folded his hands politely. "Now. Here is what will happen. Our young squire errant will be escorted to the cells below immediately, ten knights wait outside, and unlike you their training and honor is not remotely in question. I can have you stripped and searched, or you can simply peel down to your tunic and leggings now—everything else you leave behind."

Jonas blinked a few times, still amazed at the irrational turn of events—but swiftly complied. He stuffed his cloak and boots down into their battered satchel as best he could, the poor container was already crammed with Rime's discarded travel garb. He laid it on the nearby divan but seemed uncertain about his sword. He padded over in his bare feet and held out the ratty scabbard and blade to Rime. "Take care of it for me?"

Rime shrugged but noticed the note of panic in his voice, and she took it with careful solemnity, letting the red cord rest on her shoulder. She also kept her face toward the gnome and the door. *He heard our plan; he knows I want to free Jonas, even if he doesn't know I have the power to do it. There's another shoe to drop.* "I will," was all she said to her guardian.

Jonas turned to Sir Graham and nodded, then made his way to the door—raising his tunic carefully to show that he had no concealed weapons. The gnome nodded back and rapped on the door with his knuckles. A pair of stout knights grabbed Jonas by either arm and almost bodily pulled him from the room. Rime felt a tiny flower of concern begin to bloom but crushed it under her boot. *Steel and stone is all they have; they can't keep him if I decide to take him.*

Sir Graham closed the door and turned back to her with a smile. *Not just steel,* she amended.

"Now, Mistress Korvanus. I have had lodgings prepared for you here in the castle; I'm sure you will want to keep tabs on your manservant's plight." Sir Graham tapped his spectacles, as if recalling a bit of lost lore. "Or do you prefer the old style of address, *Doma* Korvanus?"

"Either is fine. Thank you, Sir Graham." Rime felt the flash of steel, as if she were dueling the gnome. *A worthy foe. Shit. I had hoped everyone in Gilead was as stupid as Jonas.*

"It grows late in the day, but I am sure the king will wish to speak with you on the morrow about the honor-thief, Jonas of Gilead. Please let me walk you to your quarters." The gnome's green hair bobbed with energy, and he pushed the door open and said cheerfully over his shoulder, "You must tell me of your travels. Did you encounter any wild beasts on your journey? The king does her best to keep the roads safe in Gilead, but one can never be sure what strange things will wander in out of the dark places of the world."

Shit. Shit. Shit. Rime smiled, picked up her satchel and Jonas's sword, and followed the gnome out of the room. *Jonas in the dungeons below, me in a cell above—or as good as. This throne room better be freaking amazing.*

PROBABLY NOTHING

Down below
the cobblestone,
down below
your feet
a seed
grows darkly.
Patient, sure,
slow time
unwinding roots
unbinding rhyme.
We knew.
We didn't.
You know.
You forget.
Remember then,
remember well.
Green bone
slow time

seed grows
Forever lies.
The Fall
begins here.
The Fall
was always
over.

—*Found in the notes of Radd Plateglass,*
    after the sack of Gate City 1179

CHAPTER FOURTEEN

XENON

X enon was adjacent to drunk. Three drained glasses sat in front of her, housing only tiny slivers of ice and bright-red limes. The Weary Titan's bartender had offered to clear them, but she had insisted on keeping them lined up in front of her, tiny glass sentinels of shame. The fourth glass was cool in her hand, and she thumped her quill idly on the open page in front of her. It was an ink-spattered morass of attempts, avenues, and aborted ideas, a crosshatched record of her first three days in Gilead:

Temple of the Nameless
—Library on-site restricted to faithful.
Academy Research Library
—Primarily concerned with tactics and strategy, war
*   historicals—nothing esoteric or related to Arkanic*
*   civilization.*
Knights of the Wand—???

—Message left with Sir Fold, dubious. Said he would add to "incoming reports" and I could follow up in a few days.

Corinth Observations: I refuse to call it "wandering," which of course is all that Mercury will call it. In between my admittedly weak attempts to find information or aid, we've surveyed the city. Corinth is a marvel from an archaeological perspective—so much has happened here, so much history crammed into these few square miles! There are buildings here that predate the Vardeman Accords if I'm not mistaken, and many remnants of the various invasions that the city has suffered. They still have vampire wards from the time of King Alain! I wouldn't have the heart to tell anyone that the Sarmadi enchantments laid upon them have long since worn off if I was asked, but still it is remarkable to find them so well preserved. I caught a contingent of squires from the Academy scrubbing them down with salt and coriander; I wonder how that odd scrap of lore made its way here? That's a Dwarven mixture for preserving limestone sculptures, First Mountain sect. Regardless, it has preserved the physical state of the wards admirably, if not their delicate enchantments.

Xenon took a measured sip of her fourth drink, a scarlet hare, as it was known in Gilead. She had known the same drink by other names in other parts of the world: a crimson sundown in Pice, a bloody eyeball in Gate City. Perhaps one day she could devote some study to the ebb and flow of cocktails across the globe, morphing and changing nomenclature and salient ingredients as they met new cultures. The Minotaur Pembleton had bought the first after finding her moping at the bar, and she had bought the next round, a tall mug of ale for him. The next two had been on her own out of pure anxiety and a desire to both further empty her vanishing purse and annoy her phantom mother. The goblin finished reading her latest entry in the journal:

The institutional racism of Gilead is very carefully concealed behind custom and language. Overly formal reactions from shop-keepers, swift attention from the knights and city officials I've approached. The trademark irony of certain highly placed "outsid-ers" in the Legion and city affairs—the defining of the Acceptable Other, while beyond these selected, nonhuman households are kept to the outermost fringes of the city. Would the officials I've spoken to at the Temple and the Academy and the Knights of the Wand be more helpful if I were human? Yes.

The last word had been underlined a few times.

She sat her glass down and chewed on the end of her quill. *If only I could have better evidence of the threat!* she thought. *A crack of thunder, an army on the horizon. Something I could point to and say, "THAT! That's about to happen!" Why did Enton send me here? Am I missing something? Or was this just something to get me out of the way, to keep me in a harmless corner of the world for a while?* Her fingers groped around her purse and clasped the few coins that remained. *Two more days, maybe three. Then a long, hungry ride back to beg Mother's forgiveness.*

Xenon shuddered and pulled the quill free from her mouth. She put the nib down on paper and began to add to her journal. She would not give up; she would not despair. She would not have that fifth drink . . . yet . . .

At least Mercury has had a good time on this expedition. She's acted as my bodyguard, snarling at a pair of children today she thought were pickpockets.

There was a slight movement at the entrance to the Weary Titan, but she paid it little attention. Some traveler arriving, look-ing for a room or a drink.

We actually haven't fought hardly at all! I think she plans to blame this entire thing on me when we get back, so there's no point in being a terror at the moment.

The traveler slid onto the barstool next to her and dropped a small bundle and short sword at his feet. She glanced up. He was orange, like a carrot. Two misshapen horns blossomed from his brow, and he wore a brown vest with black buttons, with no shirt beneath. "Hey," he said and raised a hand to get the bartender's attention.

She's upstairs right now, sleeping. Or at least I hope she's sleeping. For all I really know she's out in the back alley throwing black dice and spinning blood coins. I hope she's winning. Maybe she could help pay for our way back to Pice.

The orange-skinned devilkin received his own glass, filled to the brim with some black concoction. Xenon's nose wrinkled at the acrid stench bubbling up from the glass—which appeared to be melting slightly at the base—and happened to look a moment longer at the traveler.

Oh no. No. I don't. No.

Her pen moved as smooth as glass, and she riveted her attention to the page. There are many strange gifts that goblins inherit in their blood: a finger that can always point north, a tongue to taste the lie in the air, eyes that only see purple except on the skin of the pure hearted. Xenon's gift was inherited from her mother, and it was a convenient if simplistic one. Sometimes she would look at people and *know* they had something for her. A kiss, a song, a ring of gold, a story, a season, a lie in the rain. When she had met Enton she had *known* that he had a very quiet, dark song for her, and she had taken the time to listen. She wasn't always sure exactly what the person had for her, but she could always see the space like a box with a lid hovering above their brow.

I do not have time for this carrot person. Ancient dragons wake from a prison forged by Precursor lore, and there's only a few weeks remaining—

Her pen scratched out a long gouge and set to whirling as she followed the thought into the pit of emerald anxiety that waited for her. *I don't know how to move forward, and I don't know enough about what's coming.* With precise control, Xenon stopped her frantic writing and planted her quill into one of the empty glasses of scarlet hare. With martial vigor she turned and faced the devilkin, who was blankly staring down into his decanter of oily ichor. *I don't know what to do about Shame. But I could do something about this. And . . . why not?*

"So. Hello. My name is Xenon," she said.

The carrot looked up. "Uh . . . okay. Hello. Sideways."

The goblin blinked. *Is that an instruction?* "Oh, your name is Sideways."

"Yep."

Why are people so hard? A slab covered with cuneiform, a scroll written with elf blood, a half-forgotten limerick inscribed in light on the reflective mica of a cavern—these were things she could translate. "This is the awkward lobby," the goblin nodded and took another measured sip from her drink, letting the ice rattle.

"The awkward lobby?" Sideways turned more to face her.

"Yes. I don't know you. You don't know me. It's like this really terrible lobby that conversations have to wander through. There is nowhere to hang your coat. There is no snack bar. It's not easy to figure out exactly which way to go. No bellhop." Xenon pretended to ding an imaginary bell between them.

"So . . . I should . . ." The devilkin raised his eyebrows expectantly.

"Help with the luggage."

Sideways smiled. "What brings you to town, Xenon?"

"Oh, I'm a scholar and I've discovered a secret dragon prison that's going to open up in a few weeks and unleash untold havoc on an unsuspecting world. You?"

"I . . . I'm a guardian of sorts. I work for an old knight, he's hunting for a dangerous . . . criminal. We've tracked her to town, made all sorts of ruckus, gathered a fair band—but the minute we got here, he told me to make myself scarce. I guess he doesn't want me spoiling his image or something," the devilkin groused.

Xenon tossed the last of her drink back and sucked on the bright-red lime. "Mine is way better," she said as she pulled the lime free and dropped it back into the glass. "Lots of dragons. Whole world in danger."

"Uh, sure. Our criminal . . . well, she's pretty dangerous too." Sideways drummed his orange fingers on the bar.

"You wouldn't happen to know anything about a dragon prison or Precursor relics or something strange called Zero?" Xenon retrieved her quill from the empty glass and stowed it in her pouch, then closed her journal and bound it shut with its leather thong.

"Nope."

"Well, I can cross you off in my journal later." The goblin straightened the goggles she still wore perched high on her head. *What am I doing?*

"Are you . . . flirting with me?" Sideways asked. "I mean, you're doing a good job, and you have nice ears and all that, but—I don't know. Your heart doesn't really seem to be in it?"

"My ears?" Xenon's hands covered both in alarm.

"You have a problem with the dragons or whatever. It totally makes sense to look for distraction. And I can be that if you want." The devilkin nodded, looking down into his malformed glass. "Yeah, I can be that."

She took another quick glance at the closed box above his head. No telling quite what Sideways had for her, not something as simple as a kiss surely. Her eyes came down and saw the crow's feet at the corner of his eyes, the easy, comfortable strain in the sharp lines of his face. She sighed and put a coin down on the bar to pay for her bill. Sideways nodded again without looking up.

"Yeah, probably the better choice," he said.

"Do you want to go look at some *necro-mori* specimens with me—err, gravestones? I noticed some old Gilean tombs have a similar shape to Arkanic memory cairns. It's probably a complete coincidence, but I thought it might be worth recording in my journal for later study." Xenon studiously did not look at the devilkin as she spoke. *Don't want to see even a peek under the lid.*

Sideways lifted his odious black goo and took a methodical bite from the side of the glass. "Yeah, okay."

The goblin and the carrot walked out of the Weary Titan together, she with her journal and he with his sword and an unopened box hovering in the air between.

Several score miles north of the city of Corinth, in an unremarkable stretch of ocean, a large sea vessel dropped anchor. The black-coated sailors went about their business on deck without any banter or foolishness; they all knew that the president was on board. Scarves and thick gloves were issued to every man, even though the fall chill was yet mild. None had to be reminded to bundle up and watch their tongue when veins of frost crept along every seam of the steel plates of the deck and a sailor's spit could bounce in the unearthly cold emanating from Mr. Moore's stateroom.

Enton Blake stood near one railing, looking south. It had been a long time since he had been this close to Gilead. He thought about his father—or at least the man he honored as such. A sudden chill crept between his shoulder blades. *Thoughts for another time.* He turned to greet his current master, Jayden Moore.

The president was wearing an immaculate tunic of soft pearl, leaving both arms bare. An amulet engraved with the crashing wave sigil of the company hung loose from his neck. "Is all prepared?"

"Yes, Mr. President. We are positioning signal buoys at regular intervals around our location; the airships and cargo vessels will have no trouble tracking us."

"Good. We must be ready when Zero rises. I will oversee the excavation personally."

"And, sir—" Enton bowed ever so slightly. "Shame? What of it?"

"Dragons are not my concern." The president turned to depart.

"The impact will be very significant." Enton kept his voice neutral. "And of course the . . . aftereffects. We have offices and ships in most major cities; we could prepare people, evacuate—"

"Mr. Blake."

"Thank you, Mr. President." Enton bowed again and said no more.

Enton Blake turned back to the south and looked out across the water. Down below the dark water, Zero waited. A city forged with stolen lore and technology from the Precursors, built by human hands at the direction of dragons malevolent; he had read much of them from the president's files. They had risen once in the first dark years of the Precursor's disappearance—and they would soon rise again, as the best funded research on the planet could be trusted. Zero: a cult, a city, a name, and a promise. The promise of destruction and the stolen power of the Lost.

"'The hour comes around . . .'" he sang, the old verse blood-fresh in his head, a whisper above the waves. "'Around and around, the hour comes around again.'"

CHAPTER FIFTEEN

JOSH

Jonas somehow heard the kick before he felt it—the intake of mad breath, the rush of air—or maybe it was just the loud voice screaming, "Blood-dog!" He was awoken most clearly by the pain, the thick yellow-worm wriggle of nausea and bile in his stomach as the boot landed. The squire did his best to cover up and pull himself into some sort of a defensive crouch, but the next kicks landed moments later. *Three of them today, I think?* his brain offered muzzily in between violet stars and dagger-teeth of pain.

He had been in the cells for four days. And most mornings began this way—and some evenings ended this way—and some midnights soured this way: the surprise addition of other prisoners to his cell and the conspicuous absence of the jail's wardens for ten minutes, twenty minutes, nearly an hour the second day.

The squire pushed himself up. He wasn't surprised. Gilead was a place of the Law, a place for justice—but it was also a place for warriors, for hard punchers, for white-teeth lions. And when lions are turned loose on a jackal, mercy is a joke. Jonas got his shoulder down and managed to bull-rush one of his attackers a few paces back, but the other two grabbed him bodily and began to claw at his face and eyes.

"I knew Sir Pocket, you breakfaith," the sallow man hissed, knobby fingers working at Jonas's cheekbones, trying to find purchase in the soft flesh beyond. "I'll tear you apart, I will!"

"We're all getting extra rations for this, but I don't even want 'em. Throw that right back on the pile, I said, I'll clean this clock on the cheap," his companion snarled. The third was already back on his feet and pulled the squire up from the clutches of the other two and slammed Jonas's head down into the stone floor hard enough to rattle teeth.

Jonas feebly tried to grab the larger man's arm, to wriggle free—but the other two were immediately on his legs, pinning him like millstones. The heavy man on top began to lean on the squire's chest, and Jonas gasped in panic. The room began to grow dark, and only the very distant clatter of steel on cell bars caused the men to release their grip and step away.

"Oh my, what is this commotion?" The jail warden pursed her full lips and artfully held a hand up to her ear for the benefit of her companion. "It appears that the prisoners have had a small squabble."

"Yes! That does seem to be the case," her companion, a tall knight with a thin black beard, replied, grinning. "Oh no! It seems that we've put the wrong prisoners in this cell by mistake!"

"Ack, paperwork, you know. It's so easy to get them mixed up." She smiled as she opened the cell. Jonas blinked at her and wondered how such an attractive woman could be so vicious. "Out you three go, let's get you away from this miserable, murdering scum. It's not safe for you in there!"

"Yes, Lady," the three visitors to his cell replied, voices joining like a child's chorus. They followed her partner off, but not before taking time to deliver some parting kicks and choice spittle on Jonas's aching form.

The warden entered his cell with a sarcastic tsk of concern; she knelt at his side and uncovered the bowl she carried. It was a simple clay bowl, and the rag that covered it was at best a scrap left over from a dirty bedsheet, but within a thick gel glowed fire-fly green. "Lie still, blood-dog," she instructed and began to liber-ally apply the paste to his face, arms, and chest.

The squire obeyed. *Century balm.* As the green substance spread, the light faded as it soaked into his skin, taking the bruises and pain with it. Jonas looked up into the warden's blue eyes. "This costs a fortune. My dad had a tiny, tiny bottle that we only used—"

"We passed the hat. And we'll keep passing the hat. Pleasure to do it." The warden slapped the last tiny bit onto a cut above his eye, then stood and smiled down at him. "Got to keep you unmarked for your day before the king. Keep you nice and squeaky shiny for the headsman's axe."

"Okay." Jonas nodded and began to push himself up off the floor, bracing for pain that was already fading away.

The warden gave a desultory kick to his side, doubling him back over as the pain rushed back. "Everywhere that shows, at least." She smirked.

The cell door rattled shut, and the bolt swung home. The vicious warden walked away, calling over her shoulder, "You've got a visitor, a proper one. Hard to believe, but pull yourself up, blood-dog. Wipe the tears and snot off your face. Show a little pride. You were a man of Gilead, once."

Her voice vanished, and the squire slowly uncurled and worked his way up to standing. All of the other cells on this wing of the jail were empty, no other voices to jeer him except the ones in his head. "Only Once," the squire said and clenched his fists against the memory-pain. *Who would come visit me? Not Rime. Unless she's breaking me out?* No one else had been to see him, except the changing of the guards and the other guest-prisoners and their thick fists. He leaned against the cell bars and let his forehead press against the cool metal as he tried to see down the hallway.

The jingle of chain mail and the clean tap of boot heel on stone heralded his guest, and he backed away from the bars so he didn't look even more like a crazed murderer to whomever was coming. The boot falls stopped for a moment, just out of sight, then continued, and a slender young woman stepped into view, her black tunic pressed and a hand on the hilt of her sheathed rapier in a classic First Matthew position. *Firm but light, ready to strike.*

"Ganalie?" Jonas said in shock.

"Greetings, Jonas Squire." She stood at attention and directed her gaze immediately into his own eyes, a habit that he had never gotten comfortable with during their Academy days.

The name took a moment to register. "Jonas . . . Squire? You still would call me by correct Legion rank? Down here, in the king's dungeon?" He found himself grinning.

"Of course. You are accused of many things, but until the king passes sentence, you are still a citizen of Corinth, a soldier of the Legion, and my comrade," she said, primrose proper.

"Well, uh, thanks, Ganalie . . ." He glanced at the single blue circle of chalk at her collar, "Cadet? Why are you still a cadet? You were only a class behind me."

"I . . ." She considered. "I was not willing to judge your tale until I heard it from your own lips."

She didn't join the world in cursing my name. She didn't think I did it. Jonas groaned and covered his face for a moment. *And they punished her, set her back. Another thing that's my fault.* He looked up and saw Ganalie's slim face waiting patiently.

"And that's why you're here?" He sighed.

"Yes."

"I . . ." *I did it.*

"Your family moved. People stopped buying your father's bread, for obvious reasons. There were also some incidents of vandalism. The king ordered a Legion patrol to keep watch over them. It slowed the damage, but it didn't make people buy bread. None of them were harmed, but they took a ship for Flenelle. Months ago," Ganalie reported.

"Ganalie . . ."

"They say that no child of Gilead will ever bear the name 'Jonas' again. Hard, because it used to be so common. They're burning you in front of the Temple, have been once or twice a day since the word went out that you'd returned. Must've been a few spares left over from when you left," the cadet continued, her eyes never leaving his.

"Ganalie, you were my best friend—" Jonas said, breaking her gaze in misery. *Give me a hundred days of being beaten in this cell; anything would be better than this.*

"Yes. Our bond remains."

"Until I tell you my tale, right?" Jonas sighed. "That's what you want to say."

"Jonas." Ganalie had dropped her rigid posture and now stood with one hand through the bars. He took it in relief, but her clear gaze met his again like the point of a sword. "Did you kill Sir Matthew Pocket?"

Easier the second time? "Yes."

"Why?"

Jonas let his head fall forward. *I just can't look at her anymore.* "Because he asked me to, Gan. There's more to the tale, but that's the heart of it. He was the greatest man I ever knew, and he asked a nothing like me to serve him. So when he asked it, I took his life."

Ganalie let out a long breath, her hand's grip steady in his. "Then we are still comrades. And you are still Jonas Squire. And my sword is yours."

Jonas's head jerked up in surprise. Ganalie let go of his hand. She smiled, her face at last breaking as far as it ever could from its severity. The squire was overwhelmed, but somehow he couldn't hold the relief in his head—it just melted away and he found himself grinning back at his friend.

"Shit, Gan." He crossed his arms. "Shit."

"I will be there tomorrow when you appear before the king. I do not know how she will judge you, but know at least that I am there for you." The cadet touched her rapier's hilt grimly. "And if she calls for the axe, there will be one to light a candle for you in the Temple of the Nameless."

"Yeah, not super comforting, Ganalie." Jonas found himself laughing, snickering, really.

"Why are you laughing?" she said, confusion and annoyance appearing on her face. "I will write letters to your family and make sure they know of your death, and the truth of your account."

"Oh man." The squire continued to chortle and slid down to the floor. Ganalie peered over at him like a confused stork.

"Your memory will not be one totally tarnished in bloodshed and dishonor!" she shouted over his manic belly laughs.

Jonas let the chuckles subside and wiped the tears from his face. He rolled up again and stuck his hand through the bars. "Seriously, Ganalie Cadet. You honor me, okay? Right down to the floor."

Ganalie shook his hand once more and then turned to go. He called after her. "But don't make a big fuss this time, okay? You're too good a fighter to keep in the Academy a whole 'nother year."

"I will make as significant a size fuss as my honor dictates, Jonas Squire." And she tossed him a regal salute as she walked away.

Jonas sat down on the floor of his cell and smiled. Having a friend's understanding was a stout roof in the rain. *Now all I have to do is convince the king, the Legion, the entire country . . .*

In the distance, he heard the sound of the vicious warden jangling her keys. Also, in a passing alto voice she began to sing:

". . . in steel, they die in stone,

Children of Gilead sing alone.

Black sea, white sand, the lives they fall,

from broken horns still sound the call.

Where Night and Beast dare wear the crown,

Knights of Gilead will throw them down."

She laughed at the end of the last line, then repeated it louder. Her voice was almost loud enough to mask the sound of other cells being flung open and hungry boots heading his way. Almost.

Jonas sighed and stood up. *It's going to be a long night.*

CHAPTER SIXTEEN

RUMBLE

The high-backed chair was overstuffed, comfortable, and bright mauve. Rime hated it.

She also hated the gnome sitting across from her, the chess set made of simple wood, the four walls of the elegant but simple room she had been deposited in. Four days where every moment awake was chaperoned by Sir Graham, every step outside the room shadowed by four grim-faced knights. Her room had no windows, nothing she could easily slip through. She flopped in bed each night and ran her fingers through her magic, dreaming about how easy it would be to rip a hole right through the ceiling. *Just keep punching through walls until I get to the throne room.* Caution kept her furious and ruminating in bed, caution and lack of information.

"Ah, an Oblate Bishop Reversal, interesting," Sir Graham tapped his spectacles, eyes on the board. "You must tell me who taught you the game; your tactics are quite unorthodox."

I taught myself, you squab. Every day, turn and riposte with the Knight of the Wand. He kept up a boundless font of empty conversation but would remain quiet whenever she did, patient and kind. He probed every part of her shadow tale carefully, never quite revealing whether he believed her. Her attempts to pry any information of her own from the knight were all but fruitless. Jonas waited in the cells below and was in good spirits and health. The king would sit in judgment when it suited her. Her tiny question jabs about the hunter Linus were met with effortless parries. *"A knight with a white sword, a traveler you saw on the road, you say? I have no word of such a man in the city, perhaps if you could recall his name?"* She had hid her concern well, or at least she prayed she had. She knew in her bones that Sir Graham could call her a wild mage at his whim, but for some reason did not. Or did not yet. She had not even been able to discern what sort of wizard the gnome was, though a master of illusion magic was her best guess. She had spent part of the third day conversing with him only to have his *actual* self join them a half hour later. Rime was stuck, caught in a game of manners and patience—two occupations that were like persimmon on her tongue.

The only relief from the boredom and terror was the wooden board and the hand-carved chessmen. The gnome had brought it with him on the first day; it folded up upon itself into a tidy box with the pieces inside. Rime had won every single game. Gingerly at first, feeling out her opponent, then as frustration and boredom grew, savagely and recklessly, as quickly and totally as possible. The gnome was clever, and in the king's castle he had her in check—but on the wooden board he was no match for her intellect. She grunted into her knuckles, eyes down on the game as she captured his bishop.

"Such fascinating strategies," Sir Graham continued as if she had responded. "It pains me that this will be our final game."

"Final game?" Rime's head jerked up.

"Yes." The gnome pushed over his queen mildly, even though Rime was still several moves from clinching the victory. "You have been summoned before the king at sundown. You and your erstwhile companion."

A burst of adrenaline spattered against the inside of her skull. Rime made herself nod sedately. "I should prepare myself for the audience." *For my answer.* "Would you excuse me?"

"Of course." Sir Graham nodded and slipped down from his chair. "I will come to escort you to the throne room a quarter glass before sundown."

Not long to compose myself, make plans. Hell—what plans are there to make? She gave a small bow to the knight, then gestured to the chess pieces. "Your board. Best not leave it behind, if there is to be no rematch."

The green-haired gnome stopped a pace from the door. "Ah, that board is not mine. It once belonged to a far greater knight than I. You keep it, as a token of our time."

A greater knight. Her mind unbolted the words and reduced them to their component bits. *Sir Pocket! Jonas's master; he even told me about this stupid board.* Rime resisted the urge to slap her forehead and bowed again. "I will treasure it."

"Not as much as I will treasure our time." Sir Graham nodded again, his spectacles catching the candlelight, and then he was gone. The clank of armor in the corridor confirmed that her guards were still firmly in place.

She walked over to the board, tapping it idly, then set the chess pieces back to their starting position. *Sir Pocket. The supposed hero that Jonas killed. It all comes back to him in this place. What's that broccoli hair gnome trying to get at with this "gift"?* She ran an idle thumb over the white knight piece. *Jonas would love to have this.* Rime pushed it into the pocket of her coat and flopped back onto the bed.

She stared at the ceiling; the uneven candlelight flickered in ghost circles. It was a few hours before sundown; she had plenty of time to plan, consider, revise, but nothing came to mind. This was the end of her road; she had gambled everything on a witch's riddle to get into the room she would finally see in just a few hours. After that—just a blank. Other than smash and grab her guardian if things went awry. *"To the throne of the king, there you will find your answer."* *Isn't that what she said?* The mage let her fist fall on the bed in frustration. In times gone by she could have slipped inside her own mind, into the library of her memories. Everything she had ever said, did—every book she had ever read, every song she ever heard—preserved perfectly on tidy shelves. But it had been getting darker and darker in there, the cry of the Magic Wild, the beasts in the dark howling louder and louder. She would never admit to anyone that she was afraid to visit her own head.

But she was. But she was. So she would have to make do with paltry, normal-person recollection, as near useless and shifting as it was.

What do I do if Jonas is sentenced to death? Easy. Grab and run. What do I do if there's no answer waiting for me? Easy. Grab and run and go mad and die.

Rime stared up at the candle flicker wobbling on the ceiling.

RIME'S DREAM #4

Her in a box, her in a house, the house was small, and the box was smallest. The box had no hinges, no seams to gather, just rude clapboard wood bound tight with chain and rose vine. She pried with two fingers and could hold the box open just enough to see out.

The house was on fire; now it was ash. There was a rainstorm, but now puddles soured.

There was someone sitting in front of embers, their back to her. She could call for help but didn't. The someone was something, and golden light dripped from the edges of the thing's cloak like burning honey.

She let the box fall shut and sat alone in the dark. The dark was made of bricks, and she was ash.

There was a knock on the box.

There was a knock on the door.

Rime sits up, sleep sweat hot on her neck. Most of the candles had guttered out.

"Lady Korvanus?" Sir Graham's wire-rimmed voice came through the door. "Are you ready?"

"Yes! Just a moment!" she yelled, flopping forward, scrabbling for her tall boots. She was already wearing her long red coat and breeches. Surely a vicious crease must run along the back from where she slept, but Rime was beyond caring. She spared a quick glance for her satchel and Jonas's sword—nothing there she could possibly need. The mage threw open her door, nodded to the gnome, and ignored the clanking retinue that surrounded her.

Sir Graham fell into companionable silence beside her. *Is it worth asking him anything? Any sort of straight answer would be a miracle.* "Is this to be a trial, then?"

"Of sorts. More of a military tribunal, as your companion was a member of the Legion when he fled the country. Twelve true knights to hear his words and the king to pass final judgment. The king would not be required for a normal transgression on the battlefield, of course—but a transgression of such renown requires a more authoritative response." The gnome guided her toward a wide staircase that led up. Most of the Keep was the same almost-black granite as the rest of the city, held together with dingy-brown mortar.

Normal martial tradition. Similar to other chivalric legacies like the Dragoons and the Order of the Key in Caleron. At least my memory's not total garbage. Rime called to mind as much as she could about those traditions, any bit of insight could be crucial in Jonas's trial. She smiled. *Huh. I'm actually worried about him. Beyond my Answer and all of that.* She frowned and pulled up her sharp chin. *No one can ever know.*

The stairs continued upward. "Throne room is near the top of the Keep?" she inquired blandly.

"The Alabaster Throne is open to the sky, that the Nameless may better keep watch on his chosen champions," Sir Graham recited, then laid a finger to his nose as if telling a joke.

Like Jonas on the ship. Rime frowned. "What happens when it rains? Just no 'kinging' that day?"

"It never rains when the king holds court," the gnome replied seriously. "Not once, in all recorded history of Gilead."

The mage screwed up her face in disgust at this blatant fable. "So, what if it's already raining, and the king decides to hold court—does it just stop?"

The gnome and the mage turned the last bend of the stair, with the four guards close behind. They were on a simple landing with a high dome; a few knights milled around. The jangle of chain mail and the clamor of voices echoed in the small space, voices filled with red anger at the criminal they had come to convict. Two broad doors made of white stone were a sudden contrast in the black granite walls, and she concluded immediately that they led out to the throne itself. Rime processed this all very quickly in the half second before her gaze fell on an older knight wearing a long blue cloak, standing in front of the doors. At his side was a white sword, too long for his height—unusual in that blade, cross guard, hilt, and pommel were all one unbroken piece. She felt her feet slow, then stop as Linus the Blue turned and raised a hand in greeting. None of the other knights around appeared to be paying the least attention.

"*Doma* Korvanus," Linus said.

Speak, girl! "Linus." Rime even made herself lower her head politely. *He's bound. By the Law, right? Like Jonas had said. He can't just chop your head off right here, or he would've done it. RIGHT?!?*

"Ah, there you are Master Hunter." Sir Graham took the knight's hand. "Such a pleasure to have you visiting us again; it has been quite some time."

Quite some time. He's been here before. Of course he's been here before; the Hunt was everywhere. "Hunter"—*the gnome knows his function. And is clearly taking great pleasure in having us at bay in his hall, like two caged hounds that cannot bark or bite.* "Such a surprise to see you here, Linus. What business do you have with the king?" *I can play it cool. Where is his assassin?*

She tried to keep her eyes wide, looking in every shadowed corner for the orange devilkin, but found no sign of him.

"Ah, I have a request to make of King Tamar. Old treaties to be upheld, promises kept." Linus's faded blue eyes seemed distant. "Her people cry out that a great danger is at her gates. I would remove that danger."

"Fuck you, old man," Rime said, tired of dancing. She pulled up the collar of her bright-red coat because that is what one does in such situations. "You want me, I'm right here."

"I will not be goaded, *Doma*." The hunter actually seemed disappointed. "I am patient, if nothing else. We will speak soon."

Rime turned away, her face flaming the same color as her coat. She moved toward the white doors, then stopped. "Can I go in and wait; I assume I'll be sitting in the gallery?" she addressed Sir Graham without looking back.

"Of course, Lady Rime." Sir Graham came to her side. "Your companion knights and I will guide you to your seat."

He pushed the doors open and led her through. Rime could feel the hunter's eyes on her back, but she refused to sweat. *He's been hunting me for days, weeks. He came back from the dead to hunt me. Let him stare; I need to get used to his eyes on my back.*

The sun was still a few golden minutes from setting, casting red-and-orange majesty upon the wide landing. The roof of the Keep beneath her feet was the same dark granite, but here white marble had been brought to craft tall pillars holding up a roof of sky. Simple wooden benches were set at regular intervals on either side of an enforced aisle leading up to the throne itself. A few servants bustled about straightening bunting and checking the alignment of the benches with a cord marked in severe knots. Closer to the throne was a large square drawn on the stone floor in careful blue chalk; Rime guessed that was where the knight tribunal would stand in judgment. Behind the throne two tall flagstaffs stood, blue flags of Gilead whipping in the wind.

The throne itself seemed to rise out of the black granite, a white coracle on a wine-dark sea. She noticed absently that a large, fluffy pink pillow had been placed on the seat to enhance royal comfort.

Rime walked down the center aisle, the gnome and his knights just behind, her mind whirling with questions and perils and not a little wonder. And then her magic bristled again, as it had days before outside the gates of the Keep. But where before it had been a quiet tremor, a shifting—this was a hurricane in a handbasket; adrenaline poured down her veins howling, and her mind sprouted gryphon wings and spread wide. She looked down at her hands, half expecting to see them coated in fire, in ice, in the pure force of the Magic Wild. The mage looked behind her and saw that Sir Graham, the guards that trailed him, the servants that bustled, all were as still as an oil painting.

She looked ahead and saw a tear, a rip in the face of the world. It peeled back like dead skin, and through the tear she saw another throne room. The same throne room, but broken and foul. Here the golden sun still shone; there a foul mist filled the air and the white columns were torn off like jagged bones and covered with the dark letters of End. Shadows flickered at the corner of the room, spinning and whirling—a battle. Too fast to catch, a flurry of steel and spell, bright lights struggling to not be swallowed by the Night. Only one thing could she see clearly, one image through this hole in Forever. A circle of steel, spinning like a top as it stutters and begins to fall. Inside the circle she saw two people, a woman with white hair and a man in a brown cloak. The woman seemed to be supporting the man; dark blood ran down his arms and covered his face. Rime blinked and the tear began to close. Her heart pounded and she tried to cry out. *The woman. The woman is me. The man is Jonas! But we are older. When is this? What am I seeing? What am I seeing?!?*

She ran forward, but the air held her back. The tear slid shut, leaving only a single glimpse of the steel circle as its revolution crawled to a halt. Sunlight danced across the Alabaster Throne and the moment was gone.

Sir Graham came up behind her, still blithely conversing. "It is a beautiful sight indeed. Come, my lady, let us show you to your seat. I believe the king shall be joining us shortly."

Rime could only manage a frail nod. She sat at the offered bench on the front row without question.

Was that my Answer? she thought with horror. *Was that it?* The strange feeling of her magic resonating on its own was gone, and she was left with a crater where her brain should be. Rime looked up blankly as the knights began to enter. *I have no idea what any of that meant.*

She touched her face absently and was shocked to discover that her fingers were wet with tears. *Whose?* she wondered.

CHAPTER SEVENTEEN

THE HUNT

L inus entered the throne room with measured steps and stood at the back of the last row of wooden benches, his iron gauntlet resting on the pommel of the white sword. The *white sword, never* his *white sword.* The old man smiled at the odd, grim thought. The room was full to the brim with whispering courtiers, red-faced merchants, sour servants, and prim-waisted lords wearing their most venomous scowls. The knight tribunal stood in the rectangle at the right side of the throne, drawn in the ceremonial blue chalk. His prey sat with head bowed, stained hair barely visible above the high collar of her absurd red coat. She was flanked on either side by guardsmen, with Sir Graham the Liar at her elbow. *A dangerous game you play, old friend. To keep the abomination at bay with simple tricks and shadows.* The gnome had succeeded thus far; even the hunter had to admit that the wild image girl seemed completely bowled over by the pomp and proceedings around her. *I do not know why you did not turn her over to me at once, what advantage you see—but the king will hear my words and obey the Need of the Hunt.*

There was a sudden burst of angry voices and shifting steel as the boy, Jonas, was led out onto the wide landing. He wore a simple gray tunic and showed no bruises or cuts, but his eyes were dull and scraped clean. No manacles on his hands or feet, just a length of cotton rope wound around his brow dyed an angry tulip red. A knight with warden's bars marked on her breastplate followed him, a cruel smile on her lips. The gathered crowd bubbled like a kettle, many forgetting propriety and decorum as their emotions burned to the skin. Linus heard the names they called the boy—"Cutthroat," "Blood-dog," "Murderer," "Deserter"—and felt pity. *You are in the twist now, young man.* Again he wondered, what could have prompted the wild mage's journey to Corinth? What was worth risking the life and freedom of her guardian? *Not that she's showed much concern for those baubles before.*

The boy was escorted to an empty space opposite the knight tribunal, with the Alabaster Throne between. Linus could almost hear the tightening of leather straps and the scrape of armor plates as the gathered knights inflated with wrath. *Not a sympathetic jury.* He watched as Jonas scanned the crowd and caught the wild mage's eye. They shared a small nod, and some light came back to the squire's eyes. *Ah—an escape route, then. Not while I am in attendance.* His gauntlet tapped on the white sword's pommel. Jonas noticed another face in the crowd that didn't curse his name, and Linus saw his face relax visibly into almost a smile. *A friend. Good for you, boy. Terrible to meet judgment before a court of daggers.*

The clamor was rising, murmuring like a hungry beast jealous for blood, when at last the trumpet sounded. The talk ceased and the people of Gilead stood as their king came into her throne room.

She was old, her hair a long tangle of gray, gold, and brown. Her robes were simple white, but buckled over them as ever was her boiled leather cuirass patched and cobbled together with the ravels of each battle until not one hue matched another in a riot of hide. She leaned, ever so slightly, on the haft of her glaive. King Tamar walked slowly, but without any other aid. Her crown was a simple circle of steel, naked and unadorned. *The King of Gilead, ready for battle as ever,* Linus thought fondly.

The gathered throng stood in silent attention, broken only when a small child slipped free from his parents and ran squealing toward the king. Tamar chuckled and scooped up the child with her free arm without pausing. "Now, Benjamin, your grandmother is trying very hard to look imposing right now, do you think you can go back with your fathers?"

The child giggled happily and tugged on a free lock of the king's hair. Tamar made a brief stop to hand off the boy and went back on her way toward her throne, but not before delivering a blistering gaze of rebuke to Benjamin's parents that could have melted lead.

At last, King Tamar took her place on the Alabaster Throne, settling in comfortably on her wide, fuzzy pillow. She leaned her glaive across her knees and gazed out across the assembled faces of her people. She nodded to the knight tribunal and to the green-haired gnome. As Sir Graham stood, the rest of the gathered citizens took their seats in anticipation. Linus kept his feet, his eyes trained on the wild mage.

"We stand here under the sky to hear the words of an accused murderer: Jonas Squire, deserter from the Legion. He will be judged by the wisdom of twelve true knights and sentenced by the hand of the king herself." The gnome bowed toward the throne. "The charges are simple. Sir Matthew Pocket, a true knight and Hero of the Realm, was murdered by you. Do you wish to contest these charges?"

The boy had been staring openmouthed at every moment of the king's approach, and continued to stare up at the white throne. *He's never seen her before. Not this close, at least.* Linus shook his head. Jonas jerked his head back around to the gnome's question, then set his jaw.

"I don't," the squire said.

"WHAT?" a sharp voice came but was quickly squelched by the murmurs and gasps of the crowd.

If Sir Graham was surprised, he did not betray it. "Then I suppose that makes the normal deliberations and examinations of our tribunal ephemeral. The accused has admitted guilt, is there a recommendation for the sentence?"

There was a comical series of pings and clangs as the knights quickly conferred, but then a bald knight with a thick black beard raised a fist and they all nodded in agreement. "Death. Immediate and sure," he said, then bowed to the throne.

King Tamar looked at Jonas with vague puzzlement, then raised her eyebrows. She opened her mouth to speak when a young woman in a preposterous red coat stormed out before the throne. Linus sighed.

"What the hell are you doing?" Rime demanded, thumping Jonas in the chest with both fists. "Why aren't you telling them your story? Why not explain how that terrible old man manipulated you?"

Linus couldn't hear the squire's response over the angry exclamations of the crowd, but the defeated hang of his head was answer enough. The hunter moved down a few aisles, his grip tightening on the white sword. *What is your play,* Doma?

"You must remain calm, Lady Korvanus," Sir Graham was saying. "This is the exercise of justice. Your companion has admitted guilt of his own free will; there is no other recourse. There is nothing left but to accept the king's sentence."

"Accept? Accept? I'm not going to accept this flower pageant you've all worked so hard on. Jonas says he does not contend the charges. Well . . . well, I do. I contend the charges," the wild mage sputtered.

The squire came forward, desperately whispering in the mage's ear—shoulders racked with embarrassment. Linus moved forward two more rows. Rime shook the squire off in disgust. "Honor is stupid, and so are you."

A silence spread from the throne as King Tamar stood up, the last light of sundown shining on her blade. "Who are you?" she spoke, a low voice that carried to every edge of the landing.

"Rime Korvanus." The mage didn't even pretend to bow. "And this fool is my servant, my guardian—my squire. I guess that makes *me* his knight."

A torrent of angry laughter came from the blue chalk rectangle, but the king held her hand up for silence. "A knight, you say? That is not something just anyone can claim."

"Doesn't seem that complicated." Rime sneered. "Just some stupid rules and a bit of metal on your back. Do you want to bring a horse in for me to tie ribbons in its hair? Or do I need a flag to wave?"

The bearded knight took a furious step outside of the blue chalk line, his hand going to the hilt of his sword. Tamar's eyes met his and he knelt instantly in shame. The other knights took their cue and kept still, mounting fury in their eyes. Linus held his place, a few short paces from the front row of benches, listening.

"None of these things are what makes a knight, Rime Korvanus." The king nodded toward Jonas. "I think perhaps he could explain it better for your ears, but I will try. A true knight's duty is sacrifice. Her pledge is justice. Her song is glory. It is not something you can seize like a leaf falling through the air; it is a weight that you carry like a stone."

"You're not killing my friend today, King of Gilead," Rime warned. "You say I am no true knight? Then prove it. Prove it in the old way."

The mage turned toward the crowd, and the old hunter had to resist an urge to applaud. *Oh, you are a fine beast indeed, Rime Korvanus, Snowlock Demon.*

"I say to you, you gathered nobles and knights of Gilead, my name is Rime Korvanus and my blood is as old as any that has spilled here in the halls of Corinth. I lay claim as Knight of the *Wild* to this idiot here." She pointed toward Jonas. "I will prove my worth and prove his innocence in the only fair test that any child of Gilead should require. Trial by combat."

With those words, her eyes flared and a nimbus of magenta light surrounded her, beating back the evening shadows that filled the landing. Her ink-blotched hair flew up and then burned clean, revealing the bone-white hair underneath. Her red long-coat had become an immaculate breastplate of crimson steel, molded and fitted to every curve. In her right hand a shield of green fire, in her left a sword of lightning.

"Now, who would answer my challenge?" she demanded, facing the knight tribunal. "Any trueborn knight of Gilead may answer and stand champion, if you dare. If the blood of Gilead is thicker than piss or stronger than milk, step forward."

There was a moment of stillness, the wild mage with her light-ning bolt weapon leveled at the tribunal, her companion behind her, his eyes wide with shock. The king held her glaive forward protectively, and the knights were already pinging and clanging together in consternation.

A fine bluff, Doma, Linus thought, pulling free the white sword. It seemed to breathe in the evening air. *At the very least it buys you time, confusion, a chance to escape. But not this day. You have seen your last sunset, my beast.* And he stepped into the place that was waiting for him, the white sword outstretched, his back to the knights. The hunter and his prey, framing the Alabaster Throne like sentinels.

Rime's face went white. "You? Is this how Gilead answers? Letting some crazed wanderer from the road step forward to fight her battles?"

"I'm afraid you have a small problem, wild mage." Linus enjoyed the scramble of onlookers struggling to get away from their duel. "You spoke the terms. 'Any trueborn knight of Gilead,' was it? A clever choice, hoping to prevent Sir Graham from being your opponent, I imagine. Well, unlike your philosophical position on chivalry, I am a knight. And I was born not ten miles from this place. Is that not so, Your Majesty?"

King Tamar nodded, a sadness in her eyes. "It is so, Linus the Blue. Though long it has been since you have stood your homeland's champion."

"I have come for this creature, King Tamar. And I will take her life." The old man carefully settled his grip on the white sword's hilt. "If this trial is your command."

"Don't do this," Jonas pleaded. "I mean, holy crap, your armor is amazing, but it's Linus. You *know* what his sword does to you. He'll tear you apart. Rime, please, just walk away from this."

"Never." Rime raised her lightning bolt in salute. "I've got nowhere to be. This is the closest I'll ever get to a fair fight with the old man."

"Then, so be it." King Tamar sighed. "Let the matter be settled by sword and spell, by skill and might, as it was in the old days."

Linus raised the white sword in salute as well. His beast's eyes locked on his, and he prepared himself for the slightest move. This was not the best battleground he could have selected, but he had her off balance, surprised. He shifted his grip slightly, then lunged—the white sword leapt out like a snake.

"What the heck is that?!?" Jonas pointed suddenly toward the early evening sky.

A weak ruse at best, Linus thought, but then he saw the terrified faces of the surrounding crowd and the widening eyes of the wild mage as she too looked into the heavens. King Tamar pointed with her glaive and his gaze followed her direction.

A new moon had appeared in the sky. The three moons that were customary, red, black, and white, were not yet risen, and this new moon burned bright and hot, like a mimic-sun. Linus blinked. *Is that moon . . . getting closer?*

The wild mage looked up and bent her lightning sword into a pair of binoculars, as quickly as thought. She put the lenses to her eyes and stared, the clamor of flustered voices and broken questions filling the night air like a restless sea. Rime pulled down the binoculars. "I don't know what it is—but it's definitely coming closer. Quick. Its trajectory has it landing about one hundred forty miles north of here, in the sea. I'll need to observe longer to be sure, but I would calculate its time of impact to be two hours before dawn—approximately seven hours from now."

Some trick. Some distraction. Linus's mind reeled, and he gazed at the illusion shaper Graham with suspicion. But a sick surety found his heart as he watched King Tamar turn back to her people with her eyes dripping blood.

"*Shame . . . shame . . . shame falls . . .*" the old woman whispered. "*Shame . . .*"

King Tamar toppled forward, and the ball of fire in the heavens shone like a forge door thrown wide.

Sideways held the thick, waxy paper taut over the gravestone and fought back a yawn. The sun was only just now setting; it was early yet, but the frantic ride across the Gilean countryside with the extra trips for burning had worn him thin. The goblin's clever hands moved quickly across the paper, rubbing a stubby black rock of some sort across it, leaving behind an impression of the carvings underneath. The devilkin scratched his nose on his shoulder and grinned. Xenon had been so preoccupied with the last two tombs that she had forgotten to speak to him.

"Yes, yes—this seems like an early form of the Gilean House sigil, the 'Spreading Lily,' as it was known. But look at the line work, so similar to Arkanic . . ." Her voice submerged back into her thoughts, never looking up at him.

I'd like to work for Xenon better than Linus. Other than the fact that the goblin clearly didn't have remotely enough money to hire him, the thought had a great deal of appeal. He started to visualize long days of carrying her books around and stacking up specimen jars and bringing her cheese sandwiches on a blue plate when she was too caught up in whatever dead people she was pestering that week. *She likes learning about dead people, instead of making dead people. Could be nice.*

Sideways took another moment to admire the elegant curve of Xenon's avocado ears, the way they flared up to the sharp points at the tip. He blinked—had someone lit a torch, off beyond her ear? He looked past her and saw that the light was actually coming from up in the sky, just over the jagged square horizon of the city walls.

It looked like the tip of a red-hot poker, jabbed in the flesh of night. "What do you think that is?" He pointed up.

Xenon kept rubbing mechanically on the gravestone as her eyes rose. She blinked three times, then jumped up with manic lightning in every inch of her frame.

"That. That. That!" The archaeologist pointed. "THAT. That's about to happen! And . . . and I know what's going on. I have to tell someone. And, and . . . oh no. Why is it here now? This is weeks too early? I must've miscalculated?!?"

Sideways grimaced up at the blazing bright spot and grunted. *Of course. I'm having a nice time and the heavens fall.*

Xenon stormed down from the gravestone and grabbed the front of his vest. "Hey! Can you get me into the castle?"

"Uh, yeah? I suppose I could. Why?"

"I need to speak to the king, five minutes ago!"

"Hell-shard yes!" a penny-bright voice called from the top of a nearby obelisk, where suddenly a short goblin uncoiled. "Let's go to the castle top, Zee! Enough of you making moon-face at the devil boy."

"Mercury!" Xenon screeched, then paused. Then screeched again. "MERCURY."

The smaller goblin cackled and did a nice forward roll off the top of the stone. Sideways noted the family resemblance. The assassin was more than a little impressed that he hadn't spotted her earlier. He offered a hand in greeting to Xenon's sister. "Yo."

"Nice grip, blade man."

"Enough! Stop being friends. Stop it this instant. Okay, we don't have time to unscramble all of this. We have to get my research to the most powerful authority figure in the area—that means the king, so can you get us in there or not?"

The devilkin squinted up at the ball of fire again. *Is that thing closer now, or did I move closer to it?* He snagged Xenon's archaeologist kit and his own rucksack with the gray blade, Chet, sticking out. "Yeah, let's mosey along up to the castle. I have a feeling it's an 'everybody grab a bucket' kind of fire."

SECOND INTERMISSION

The Demon flung his arms wide, laughing. The Sage and the Paladin recoiled, rebuked by his words.

"I care not for Darkness, care not for your tale,
care not for your sermons and your bright steel's pale.
I am me, made of fire and smoke
and the forgotten days when Glory spoke.
Let the shadows fall, let the frost glass quake,
I am nothing if not my own Mistake.
Broken Heaven, empty Hell,
hollow Earth, Sorrow's well.
I stand in the shadow but burn like the sun,
hard-hearted vandal of black wire spun.
Spare me your riddles, and burn all your lies,
Demon's blood wakes when the first Hero dies."

CHAPTER EIGHTEEN

JONAS

No pickles." Mercury pulled the offending item off her sandwich and flicked it onto the table.

"Mercury." Xenon folded her hands over her eyes in despair. "You . . . you can't throw pickles on the king's table. Not the pickles from the turkey sandwich that the king's servants *also* brought you. You just can't. Not in front of the *actual* king."

Jonas took a sip from his pink lemonade. *This is not how I expected this evening to go.* The hastily assembled platters before them were piled high with thick sandwiches, fresh-cut cheese, even some apples and grapes, but he had not found his appetite yet. The goblin scholar, Xenon, had not had time to take even a bite between her florid explanations and frenzied diving into her pack again and again for the scraps of evidence she had found. No one needed convincing, her proof was bearing down on them, burning in the sky.

"Could you pass the spicy mustard?" Linus inquired politely, a flat table knife in one hand, a slice of bread in the other.

Rime said nothing, her chin on her breast, eyes pointing at the table like cannons being loaded. She did, however, slide the brown pot in question across the table with her fingertips.

Jonas ran a hand across his face and found himself trying to blink this odd dream away, but it remained fixed before him. He leaned back in his chair to where he could see out one of the wide windows of King Tamar's sitting room. The burning circle was just where it had been half an hour ago; he could almost imagine it bubbling and hissing like hot steel dropped in a trough of water, but the night was quiet, except for the conversation around him. Xenon had named the strange thing in the sky an "asteroid." *Something that looks like a star but isn't.*

Pandemonium had surged around the Alabaster Throne as the king fell to her knees. Knights rushing to her aid, servants screaming in terror, lords leaping mostly in place. Rime had instantly placed herself between him and the frenzy, eldritch sword and shield held high, but they had been ignored. Then an—*air rocket bike?*—had appeared bearing two goblin sisters and the devilkin assassin, Sideways. Only the slow rise of King Tamar from the black granite and her fist in the air saved the landing from turning into a complete slide into panic.

She sat, just a few paces away. Her head was bowed as Sir Graham tied a thick piece of white cloth around her head, bones showing in each knuckle tight on the haft of her glaive. Gilead was a place that was no stranger to battle and crisis, a few short orders from the king had dispersed the gentry, dispatched many knights to calm the city, and delegated others to bring the hunter, wild mage, scholar, and various companions to her sitting room. King Tamar's eyes had continued to weep red as she gave her commands and even as she demanded answers from the archaeologist Xenon, who was all too eager to provide them.

"Convenience is the footprint of peril, Tamar," Sir Graham had interjected into the goblin's report. "Should we not view with doubt this scholar arriving at the very moment of our needing her intelligence?"

"No." The king had smiled, bloodlines leaking down her face. "I have Seen. But I thank you for your care, Sir Graham."

Jonas had pretty much lost the thread of the story after the dragons fell asleep in the rock and some Precursor wizard kicked them into space.

The gnome's fingers tightened the last knot, and Tamar's head rose. The white cloth covered both her eyes, but the squire could see the bloom of pink at the edges where the blood was already seeping through.

"There, a courtesy for our guests. I thank you, Graham." Tamar smiled.

"Does it pain you, Your Majesty?" Xenon inquired, concern battling with academic curiosity on her face. Rime looked up as well, the battle already won.

"Somewhat, but it is no matter. It has been some time since the Sight has taken me so strongly; the pain it requires is a small burden compared to the boon it grants. A glimpse of the road ahead, a few phrases of the Melody. What is, what was, what may be, the threads of Possibility unspooling before you. The blood, the pain in my eyes? No, it is fleeting, a physical wound— nothing compared to when I have Seen the deaths of loved ones or the triumph of evil souls. Nothing compared to what I have Seen tonight . . ."

The room fell silent as the king trailed off. Sideways leaned in from the shadows behind Linus's chair and snagged an apple. He whipped back into nigh invisibility, emitting only a crisp scrunch as he bit into the fruit.

"You saw it all? The Precursors, the dragons, the prison?" Xenon absently picked up her sister's pickle residue and placed it on her own plate. "And Zero—did you see anything about that?"

Tamar placed two fingers on her temple as if remembering a dream. "I can see the face of the Lost, tears running down his face. I can feel his shame. I can see him crying in a dark room, comforted by a lover. A sapling becomes a tree—years pass. Somewhere far away, I see men—humans with a mark on their hands, faces, backs. It is a circle, a circle cut through by a slash. Zero is a broken circle. They are underwater, in a city made of metal and pain. Around them are . . . broken things, bits of wire and shattered tools of the Lost. They all crowd around a screen—green numbers against black, then an image of the asteroid Shame. They create a circle of shining metal that spins. It spins faster and faster, then vanishes. They run through the zigzag halls of their city in celebration, only to fall on their knees before three dragons. The brotherhood of Zero has succeeded. They offer themselves up to the dragons, weeping with gratitude as jaws crush and blood flows. More time passes—a mountain becomes a hill. The spinning circle appears—somewhere dark. It spins and a thing with no name awakens."

"The Node! You're talking about the Node," Xenon said, pushing her journal and sketch of the device around the table for all to see. "But what do you mean about the 'thing with no name'? How did it make the asteroid come back?"

Rime steepled her hands. "They interfered somehow, that's what really matters. The actual manner is irrelevant, only that they succeeded in the asteroid's return."

"But it did not return swiftly; it did not return even within the lifetime of those dark dragons," Linus agreed. "It is here. Now. Ours to contend with."

"Pretty clockwise too." Mercury slurped from her cup.

Jonas stood up and walked to the window, forcing himself to look at the asteroid again. *Why are we eating turkey sandwiches? Why is everyone being so calm?*

"Have you seen what will happen when it hits?" Sir Graham folded his hands.

"Lands," Rime corrected. "It's moving too slowly to be in free fall. The Precursor orb is moving under its own propulsion. It will still impact with sufficient force to atomize a few miles of seawater, but what happens after that is impossible to predict."

"A cloud of dust will erupt into the sky and we will not see the sun again for months. Plants will wither, people will starve, the creatures of night will thrive, and we will struggle to band together, a savaged, malnourished army to stand against the dragons' revenge." King Tamar's voice was level stone. "This Path is an End, if we falter."

"*An* End?" Rime and Xenon leaned forward simultaneously, the same words on their lips. The goblin shrugged and shook her fingers like a dying spider in awkward apology. The mage pressed on. "So, when you see the future, it can be changed? It is not permanent? It is malleable?"

The blindfolded woman sighed and shifted her grip on her glaive. "Time is not etched in granite. Time is not free as sunlight, nor careless as the wind. Time is not a river or an ocean or a tree with branches. Time is Memory. It shifts and changes as we do, foggy and indistinct here, sharp and bright there. The smell of blood and cedar, the taste of my true love's wine, the song they sing at my bier all muddled and mixed, present and gone as we see them. I have Seen a Possibility, a memory of destruction. I have also Seen a chance to prevent it. Which is the true Memory, only our actions now can decide."

"And now you will tell us what must be done." Linus stood.

"You have broken bread with your enemy, Linus the Blue, a tiny thing but perhaps enough. I know little of you, Rime Korvanus, but your hunter is well known to me. You seem sane, and we have no time to dither. I have need of heroes, but the world has seen fit to send me a wild-magic demon, a goblin with a book, a murderer, and a monster." The king's blank eyes rested on the bent-iron plate of Linus at this last title.

The hunter inclined his head in simple recognition.

"I'm here too," Mercury complained. Sideways leaned back out of the shadows to give her an understanding thumbs-up sign.

"Can you put your battle aside until the asteroid falls?" King Tamar's voice was quiet.

"Of course, my king." Linus bowed.

"I'm not battling anybody, but my calendar is completely clear for the next several hours!" Xenon said, then clapped both hands over her mouth in mortification.

"If I help you and table my grievance with the Hunt"—Rime leaned back in her chair—"I want Jonas freed. Absolved of all charges and a royal proclamation of his innocence."

"Rime, no, you can't—" The squire moved closer, despairing hands plowing through his mane of curly hair.

"No," King Tamar replied. "Our Law shall not be broken, though the Heavens fall. He stood in fair trial; he admitted guilt. There must be a Cost."

"Welp, good luck with the space rock, then." The wild mage stood up and theatrically wiped her hands free of crumbs.

"Rime!" Jonas grabbed her shoulders and fought the urge to shake her. "You have to help. I mean, I would die *anyway* when that thing hits, right?"

"I can fly pretty fast," Rime retorted.

"Banishment," King Tamar said. "His sentence I will not erase, but I can commute. If you survive this night, he will be banished from Gilead until the end of his days. And now you will agree, because we must spend what little time remains to prepare more wisely."

Rime opened her mouth, but the squire bodily dragged her back into her chair. Mercury snickered and earned a piranha glare from the wild mage, to which the young goblin immediately responded with an Adamant Ice Eyebolt glance. Rime squinted, then gave Mercury a grudging nod of respect. Linus sighed and rubbed his brow with the fingertips of his left hand.

King Tamar dabbed again at the underside of her blindfold; the red tide was beginning to break loose. Her voice remained commanding and firm. "The bulk of my knights will remain here to prepare Corinth for the aftermath of impact and, if you fail, the darkness beyond. An airship is being prepared to bear you aloft to contend with this asteroid; a small crew of brave souls will pilot it for you."

"I hope it's a fast ship," Rime complained. "The sooner we can close the distance, the more time we'll have to find a solution."

King Tamar smiled, out of place and young. "My uncle Slade once had a ship that was thought to be the fastest in the world, but he lost it. Crashed it on a very foolish escapade saving my father from an even more foolish adventure when they were old graybeards and should have known better. The *Raven* is not half as swift, but a good ship all the same."

This is crazy. This is crazy. Jonas found his arm rising, as it would again and again in Academy classes when he didn't understand. Mercury hissed at him, "She's wearing a *blindfold*; she can't see that your hand is up, brickhead."

"Speak, Jonas." King Tamar turned her hidden eyes toward him.

Not squire. Not "of Gilead." Just Jonas. He pushed those concerns away, at least until dawn, if there was one. "I'm sorry to interrupt, Glory-Gold. What will we do when we get there? I mean, Linus's sword can eat magic, and Rime can blow up just about anything, and Xenon seems really smart, but that thing, that asteroid . . . it's huge. What can we do? How can we turn it aside?"

"You must be the circle. All of you. The circle that holds even though it wishes to break. Stand in the center and hold, Jonas.

My sight is filled with darkness, but three lights, three memories, have we to find a new Path. A blade of white and a blade of silver held fast against the Night. A scholar's journal flung open on a table of jewels that shine. And you"—the king pointed to Rime unerringly—"your hair, completely white."

The wild mage bit her lip and looked down. Jonas felt sick, his hands clenched on the back of Rime's chair. "A 'blade of silver,' huh? I guess you mean Sir Pocket's sword. You mean Hecate."

"We searched for it for weeks but never found it," Sir Graham spoke up, from where he had remained quiet at his liege's side. "It was thought that you absconded with it, perhaps sold it somewhere to finance your escape."

"No . . . no," he replied with dull grief. "It's here, in Gilead. It's near Sir Pocket's tower . . ."

"We do not have much time; it must be reclaimed quickly. The *Raven* will be ready in half an hour." The gnome gazed at Rime speculatively.

She snorted. "Yes, I can fly—but it wouldn't be a good idea to use that energy up now."

"I can take him!" Xenon stood up, knocking a mostly empty lemonade cup flying. She grappled for it, spilling even more in the process. "On my sky-cycle; it's fast."

Her younger sister mouthed the words *"it's fast"* and poked her sister.

"Uh, okay—yeah, I can show you the way." Jonas nodded gratefully. "You going to be okay with, uh . . . him?"

The squire jerked a thumb at Linus. Rime scratched her chin with studied nonchalance. "Whatever. I'll be fine."

"Go, then," the king commanded. "Bring your master's sword to the flight green at the Academy; I'm sure you remember the way. Your companions will meet you there, and the prayers of Gilead go with you."

Jonas looked at the goblin's vehicle with consternation. It glowed a fierce magenta, and the two goblin sisters were already in the saddle, pulling their flight goggles into place.

"Sorry, we don't have an extra pair for you," Xenon called over the sky-cycle's hum. "Squeeze in behind Mercury; we don't have a moment to spare. You'll need to sit on the posterior housing, but your cloak should protect you from any aerolithic blowback from *Tobio*'s engine."

This is a weird day. The squire vaulted gingerly over the back end of the sky-cycle and settled in, taking care to put as much brown fabric between him and the strange vehicle's not-metal. He grabbed tightly onto the edge of the saddle. Mercury craned her neck backward and leered up at him, the red clips in her hair tumbling in ragged array. "Comfy, sheephill?"

"Yeah, I guess I'm all right. What kind of a name is *Tobioooooooo*—" Xenon slammed on the throttle and the sky-cycle erupted into the night sky.

"It's an old story our dad used to tell us," the archaeologist called back. "It's about a puppet who learns to fly."

"I never heard that one," Jonas called back, but his attention was drawn up to the asteroid hanging in the northern sky. It had been only most of an hour since it had appeared; it already seemed twice the size, bright enough to rival the White Moon when full. *No time for stories.* "Head over the west Shield Wall, then look for a grayscale tower next to a lake; it's not far!"

The goblin thumbed the accelerator further and the darkened streets of Corinth fled beneath them. Jonas caught quick glimpses of torch-bearing knights on horseback moving swiftly through the street, knocking on doors, alerting the populace. The windows flickered alive with light as storm lanterns were lit early, rippling underneath them as they flew. Xenon pulled up hard when they arrived at the Shield Wall, the wind whipping cold against his face. Jonas wished he had some sort of protection but made do by pulling his hood down as far as it would stretch.

Time is Memory. The king's words. Jonas almost had to agree when he saw the familiar shape of his master's tower up ahead. In just a few minutes they had flown backward in time; he half expected to see Sir Pocket himself ride past on his stallion, galloping toward the city in peril as he had a hundred times before. "The well." He pointed down. "Land next to the well."

Tobio came to a perfect stop a few paces from the old well, stones ramshackle and tumbledown. There had been a crude wooden roof over it when he left, but some passing storm had pushed it over. Broken beams and rotten thatch crunched under his boots as he scrambled to the side of the well. *Okay, okay—gotta hurry, gotta hurry. Gotta do this before the sky falls or I remember too much about what happened last time I was here.*

Xenon and Mercury were close at his heels; they flanked him and peered with naked interest down into the well. "So, you tossed it in there? What're you waiting on?" the younger goblin demanded.

Jonas gave a sickly smile. "Ah—just, ah—nothing."

"What is it, Jonas?" Xenon looked at him with concern.

Do NOT start crying in front of these two total strangers right now. The squire made himself smile in a less pained fashion. "The sword, Hecate, is blessed by the moons. In the hands of a true hero, it's a sight to behold. My master used to be able to call it to his hand. When I—left—I threw the sword in here; I don't know why. I was just thinking how nice it would be if I could just call the sword up to me out of the well."

The three looked down into the well, only shadow and the sound of water. Jonas half extended his hand; the two sisters watched with expectation, then slight disappointment.

"Guess I'm not a hero," Jonas said and heaved himself over the stone lip of the well.

The thick blocks were covered with fungus and algae, slippery in his hands. Jonas did his best to brace himself with his legs as he clambered down. The two green faces above watched him silently, not wanting to break his concentration. Xenon pulled a small bull's-eye lantern from her belt and turned the knob until warm yellow light followed him down. It cheered him slightly, but he kept his mind on the climb. He had never known how deep this well was and was not looking forward to climbing back out.

His boot splashed and he shivered. He'd reached the waterline. "I'm going down, shouldn't be more than a few feet until I find the sword." *I hope.*

Jonas took a deep breath and let himself fall.

The cold water wrapped around him and hammered at his chest. He forced himself to remain calm and push down against the sides of the well. Glimmers of lantern light followed, showing him the vague outlines of muck-covered stones and green moss wafting like a drowned corpse's hair. Only a few feet farther, and he felt the edge of the well terminate and go wide. *An underwater cavern! Shit. If there's a current down here, no telling where that damn sword could have wandered.* He swam downward, already feeling the burn of his lungs. All around was darkness, but the faint gleam of the lantern that followed him caught a reflection of silver metal a dozen feet below. *Luck! I hope it's not just an old bucket.*

The squire swam down, hand outstretched against the twilight. His eyes could just discern the outline of the sword, wrapped in black mud and long green grass. He swam harder with relief, reaching for the sword.

Then the mud was not black, but gray. And the grass was not green, but gray. And the sword was not wrapped in muck, but the naked arms of the Gray Witch. She smiled as if she was dreaming, her fingers circled around the silver blade gentle and sure. *Why is she here? Why is she here? Why is she here?* Jonas forgot about the water and the asteroid and time and stared at her like a painting, one that was slowly coming to life. The Gray Witch's eyes opened.

Her brown eyes met his and she smiled. "Hello, *Izus.*"

Jonas's eyes bugged in complete shock. *How is she talking? We are underwater!* She was the same as she ever was. Naked and gray, the color of storm, the color of pockets turned inside out, the color of empty rooms at dawn. Only her eyes, human and brown, reminded. The Gray Witch lay on the floor of this dark cavern among water and dark and mud and grass as easily as a sparrow on the branch of an elm.

"I just wanted to say I'm proud of you." She smiled.

What? Why?

"Home is important. Not to abandon it. To take up your master's blade. When Gilead calls, a true knight will answer." She kept her gaze on him, taking stock. "You are without your lady, sir knight. A pleasant thing to see. Soon I hope to see her button fall off your coat."

What do you want? You always want something.

"Nothing. Nothing this time at all." Her hands closed tighter on the silver metal of Hecate, her brown eyes burned into his. "Except maybe a kiss?"

Uhh. Jonas felt flustered. The faint light from the well's lip above filtered down, but the Gray Witch and the silver blade seemed to shine with an illumination all their own. She rose from the floor, the sword pressed between them, her face an inch from his. The Gray Witch ran a hand along his brow and cheekbone with something akin to tenderness, then pulled his head down with empty fury.

The squire wanted to cough, but somehow he didn't. This was the second kiss he had shared with the Gray Witch; the first had filled him with a feeling of profound strangeness. *Second kiss ever!*

a peapod voice in his head reminded him with derision. This kiss was not strange.

Her eyes never closed but stared into his own. The kiss broke and her voice cut him to the marrow, "You are mine, boy. Rocks in the sky, shadows in the heart, lies between the page—no matter. You have tasted the gray edge of Necessity and neither sunshine stammer nor holocaust howl can shake it from your lips. I am the end of the sentence."

Jonas floated up and found the silver blade in his hands. The Gray Witch slipped back into shadow, leaving only questions in his head and a taste like copper on his lips. *What do you mean? What are you?* His questions were not answered.

The squire floated up toward the lantern's light, and his lungs reminded him that he needed to breathe, most desperately. He flailed and gasped upward until he broke free above the waterline.

"Are you all right?" Xenon called. "Did you get the sword?"

"I . . . I got it," Jonas replied weakly, holding up the sword by its hilt. *This is a weird night,* he thought and reached for the algae-covered stones of the well's walls. At the very least they were real, not prone to kissing him, not likely to chop his head off, and most importantly not about to impact the planet and drop angry dragons on him. He began the awkward climb up, after sliding Hecate in his belt. *It's not even bedtime yet. Sun's only been down an hour or two. This is a weird night . . . that is just getting started.*

CHAPTER NINETEEN

ASTEROID RESPONSE TEAM

The cloudbank parted and Xenon leaned on the throttle; the Academy landing field was below. It was easy to spot their destination, a frenzy of moving bodies and torches circled around a black clipper with thick metal wings folded back along the hull, silver etched into the form of fierce pinions. They were descending at a sharp angle in their haste, but the prow of the ship did seem to be fashioned to resemble the head of a vicious bird. The wings and prow were metal, but the rest of the ship's construction was an unfamiliar black wood. *To cut down on the weight, this design looks familiar—maybe something out of the Flenelle shipyards?* Xenon wondered. The blue banner of Gilead snapped in the night wind from a lance post near the back, there were no other signs of masts or sails. *Some sort of propulsion drive, good, we don't have time for fussing around with rigging.*

"Hey, Xenon?" Jonas called from behind, surprising her. The squire had been all but silent since recovering the silver sword from the well.

"Yeah?" She brought *Tobio* down in an easy spiral, then let the sky-cycle go flat as a board to come in for a soft landing on the *Raven*'s deck.

"Do you know what the word '*izus*' means?"

"Isn't that what the dwarves call cucumbers?" Mercury suggested.

Xenon looked carefully on either side of the sky-cycle as she descended, making sure there were no stray ropes, boxes, or knights on the deck. "Uh—it's actually a word from the Arkanic language, Precursor language. Where did you hear it?"

"Oh, someone called me that one time, and I just thought of it and thought maybe you would know since you're a master scholar." The squire's voice went on, pitched a little too loud to be heard over the hum of *Tobio*'s engine spinning down.

The sky-cycle landed on the deck without even a thump, and the archaeologist nodded with satisfaction. "Arkanic words have a lot of meanings, and they change depending on context, position. And that's just the written language. We have so few samples of their spoken language that it's hard to say exactly, but that word is fairly common, I suppose. Most experts translate it as 'Will' or 'Willpower' or sometimes just 'Power'. It can also mean 'Determination' when used as a personal address, instead of a formal one. I guess whoever called you that was saying you are determined? Or maybe stubborn? Who called you that? Do you spend time with Arkanic scholars often?"

Jonas scooted off the seat, then turned to help Mercury down. Her younger sister snorted at the squire and tumbled backward off the sky-cycle to illustrate her point. The squire shrugged and adjusted the silver blade stuck in his belt. "Oh, not too often. I'm sorry, it was a random thought that popped into my head. I know we have way bigger things on our minds. Well, bigger thing."

He pointed toward the gleaming asteroid Shame that continued to grow larger as it descended. Xenon nodded her agreement.

She looked across the deck, where last-minute flight preparations were concluding and saw the old knight Linus, his guardian, Sideways, and the wild mage Rime all clustered around a large map spread on the *Raven*'s deck. Sir Graham seemed to be leading the discussion, making notes on the map with an inkpot and quill. Xenon grabbed her sister's arm and followed Jonas to the strategy meeting that was clearly in progress.

"Thanks to the interestingly precise calculations provided by Lady Korvanus," the green-haired gnome was saying. "We have a working location for the impact zone as well as an approximate time for the asteroid to hit sea level. The site is a hundred and seventeen miles north of here; impact will be in four and a half hours."

Xenon craned her neck to see the unceremonious circle drawn on the map, a simple line of ink with an X in the center. *Circles, from the Node to now, all circles.* She tightened her grip on her sister's arm, mostly for comfort. Mercury hissed quietly but kept still, a mark of the severity of the situation. A flicker of movement from the nearby shadow cast by a barrel of rainwater lashed to the deck pulled her eyes away from the map for a moment. Sideways's orange hand appeared from the darkness holding a neatly wrapped bundle of wax paper held together by a toothpick. Her stomach gurgled. *A sandwich! He brought me a sandwich!*

"It's not all that approximate," Rime groused, hands bending her skullcap into vague contortions of anxiety. "That's where and when. If this ship takes off in the next fifteen minutes, and can maintain the speed promised, then we should reach the asteroid about three hours before impact."

"Captain Chalk is very skilled; he would not have been chosen for this duty if he were not. The *Raven* will carry us swiftly, worry not." Sir Graham's eyes flicked to the older knight's.

"Now for our plan, such as it is. I apologize that we made decisions while you were absent, Scholar Xenon, but time is not our ally." Linus looked up from where he knelt at the western edge of the map. "We have based our battle strategy on surmise and conjecture, but it is a framework only. We will have to adapt to the situation as it evolves. For the moment, we have accepted *Doma* Korvanus's conjecture as valid: the Precursor's prison is not falling but *landing*. It is not a rock falling from a wall but a ship making for port."

"Somehow the Precursor's technology is propelling that tremendous amount of mass—they set a trajectory and now it has been steered back here. By some sort of dragon cultists, if the king's visions are true." Rime took the reins of the conversation and pointed up emphatically at the roaring ball of fire above their heads. "If that thing is a vessel, then it stands to reason that it has some sort of helm, some sort of control panel, something. We fly up there as quick as we can and then we have to find the helm and steer the fucking thing back out into space."

"That's pretty thin, Rime," Jonas said dubiously. "Just climb in and yank the wheel the other way?"

"It will probably be more complicated than that." Rime stood up. "But fortunately we have an expert in the Arkanic civilization in tow."

"Yes, of course." Xenon nodded. "I have a couple of reference books in my pack, of course, and my journal. I'll do anything I can to help."

Mercury looked up at her sister, eyes bright, hand tight on her dagger.

"We will split into two groups." Linus slowly began to rise from the deck, his face showing the strain, if not his voice. "I and my associate will accompany Scholar Xenon on her sky-cycle to find the asteroid's controls. You two will remain on the *Raven* along with Mercury—"

"Why?" Jonas could not hide the concern and suspicion in his voice. "I mean, what good can we do out here?"

"Idiot." The wild mage rolled her eyes. "We already talked about this. It's fine. There's no telling how long it will take Xenon and the old man to find the control, and no way to predict how long it will take them to make anything useful happen—especially in three hours. I'm the fail-safe. Once Shame gets below a mile above sea level, then I play catch. You and Mercury are here to watch my back."

"Catch?" The squire's voice squeaked.

"Not like anyone else can do this." Rime's eyes glittered.

Jonas's brow furrowed with extreme concern. Xenon felt sympathy as she watched the young man struggle to put into words his unease. The goblin sniffed the air. *Is someone burning coffee nearby?*

"Ah, may I suggest one revision to your strategy?" Sir Graham began to roll up the map. "Do not forget the words of the king. 'A blade of white and a blade of silver held fast against the Night.' Jonas should be at the Blue's side until dawn, until the truth of this vision is revealed."

"Absolutely not!" The squire growled. "I'm Rime's guardian; I'm not leaving her alone when she—when we are about to do a thing like this. Plus, she said the thing about the sword, nothing about me using it. Let Sideways take up Hecate; he's a better swordsman than me anyway."

A dark chuckle came from the nearby shadows. "I'll be fine with Chet; no hero's sword for me, thanks."

"I'm no hero, either!" Jonas complained. "When I touch Sir Pocket's sword . . . it's just dead metal to me. I won't be any good."

"That remains to be seen." Linus's eyes were blank slates.

"And it's cursed. *Proper* cursed."

"Jonas." Rime pulled her skullcap on, hiding her distinctive white hair. "Go."

"But . . ." He turned, but her hand was already landing briskly on his sternum in rebuke.

"No time, okay? Prophecy is a puppet show for gods and drunkards, but I'll hedge every bet we make tonight."

The square-faced young man stared down at his companion, misery and confusion plain on his face. She passed him a satchel and a sheathed long sword that she had been using as an impromptu cushion during the council of war. "There, now you got two swords." She smiled. "Don't lose any of my stuff."

"Sir Graham!" a fierce voice called from the arched bridge of the *Raven*. It was two dozen paces back from where they stood in the heart of the deck surrounded by thick metal shields, each etched with the three-sword sigil of Gilead. "We're ready to lift off at your command!"

"The command is given, Captain Chalk! Full speed ahead!" The gnome walked toward the bridge, followed by the hunter, Linus. Xenon watched them go. The carrot-skinned devil Sideways remained in the shadows and the wild mage and her companion walked to the edge of the railing to speak in private. Jonas seemed to recognize someone across the landing field and waved excitedly as the *Raven*'s engines spooled up, earning him a fond but acidic glare from the mage. Xenon felt ill-fed questions wander around her mind, searching for something to gnaw on—as if there wasn't already enough for her to ponder in the skies above. *What will history remember of this night? What will they call us? The Defenders of Corinth? The Unlikely Shield? The Grab-Bag Guardians?*

She looked up into the burning face of Shame. *Or will history remember this night at all? Is this one of those dark places where the stories die? Just desert winds and ash for a few hundred years until enough people gather together again to make memories and cities and words and tools? Does the stone turn at this crossroads and all paths end?*

Her grip was still tight on her sister's arm and Mercury was completely quiet. Xenon looked down. Her sister's eyes burned with a fierce light, like two blue coals. *Oh, Mercy, you take after Dad.* "If we die, at least we never have to explain to Mother."

The younger goblin gave a feeble grin, then her face went empty. "I want to go with you."

"No." Xenon lifted her sister bodily until they were eye to eye, and she forced herself not to squint in the glare of her sister's bioluminescent emotion. "If we fail, the safest place to be is on an airship. You are strong and smart; they will need you to guide them. And you will take care of Lady Rime?"

"I hate her." Mercury sighed.

"You just met her!" Xenon said, scandalized.

"She's awful. Just really, really terrible."

"But you'll keep her safe?"

Mercury put her hand back on her dagger and nodded solemnly. Xenon pulled her sister close and kissed her on both cheeks and both eyelids and then blew a laugh into Mercury's giggling mouth. She sat her back down on the deck.

"Come back?" Mercury insisted, the blue fire in her eyes beginning to fade.

"Okay, if you want," Xenon promised.

There was a brisk clack as the *Raven's* steel wings snapped into place, sharp and angled from the line of the bridge. The metal figurehead belched green fire, and the two sisters held hands as the black ship soared up toward the red-white orb that waited for them.

"Sir, the Scryer Corps has picked up a vessel departing Corinth at top speed."

Enton sighed and placed his jade cup down carefully on its matching saucer. "And they are heading for Shame?"

"Their course would suggest it; they'll be passing directly overhead in thirty minutes on their way to intercept. Should I alert the president?"

"No. He has prepared for this. A city of lions will always come to roar at the whirlwind. Send the order to the fleet."

"The order, sir?"

"Shoot them down." Enton picked up his cup.

The black-beamed ship howled through the night, while Rime leaned against the railing and stared forward at the approaching asteroid in anticipation. Flying directly toward the red-white circle that now filled half her field of vision had filled most of the crew with a thinly veiled panic. She found herself calm, keeping her mind occupied with the problem at hand. *It's just so much mass and inertia. I'll need to compensate with an equal force to even get a grip on it, maybe a modification of the trick with the lightning bolts? Pull ambient energy from the surrounding atmosphere, so I'm not just burning my own fuel the whole time.*

She squinted. The closer they came, small variations and details could be seen on the surface of the asteroid. Regular lines that appeared to be canals or grooves, splitting the orb into smaller sections. The mage blinked and had to look away for a moment, a bloodred circle imprinted on her retinas.

That was when the metal ball slammed into the deck, inches from the tips of her new boots. She hopped back in alarm. The ball smoked and spat as it attempted to sear through the dark planks of the deck. Rime could make out runes etched in bright yellow. *Crude, just a simple incantation for "Fire" machine-stamped over and over into the metal. Activated by any wizard of rudimentary skill, then loaded into a cannon.* Her ears caught the quiet report, almost hidden by the infernal roar of the *Raven's* engines. She dashed to the prow and leaned out over the metal figurehead, bellowing behind her, "Get that old man out here NOW."

The mage gazed down below. They were out over the ocean now, but the illumination cast by Shame had turned the night into an uncertain twilight, every moment winding the clock back toward noon. Five swift-moving cutters were pacing the *Raven*, about a quarter mile below, three on one side, two on the other. They were slowly rising to a parallel course—the first cannonball had just been to check range, she quickly surmised. As if to applaud her deduction, four of the cutters fired at once sending saffron bullets of light arcing up toward her and the Gilean ship.

"Who would be this stupid? Who would try to stop a ship flying *toward* the giant ball of fire that's about to liquefy a good portion of the planet?" Rime demanded.

"Fools. Zealots. Men who hope to profit, does it matter?" Linus's voice was cool as he stepped into place a few feet behind her. "They stand before us. They must fall."

The white sword slid from his belt, silent and sure. Rime's face twisted. Just being this close to the weapon made her temples ache and her skin itch. Linus tapped the still-burning ball with the tip of the sword and its light was extinguished, like a candle snuffed by a hurricane. He settled himself into an archaic-looking stance and held the white sword high. "You must save your strength for the asteroid. I am the lightning rod. Those that come too close deflect to me."

Rime cursed under her breath, impressed despite herself. She looked back down at the blazing yellow bullets. *Two will miss, one a glancing blow off the wing, but the last . . .*

She held out her hands and forced herself to take only a tiny trickle of her magic, a simple net of force, to pull the metal ball in a lazy arc away from the bridge and hurtling toward the old knight's back.

Without a word, he spun, the white sword moving effortlessly as a water current and sliced the metal ball in half. The yellow runes went dark, and the metal itself clattered and crumbled against the deck. *Ah, they aren't iron—some lighter metal. The destructive payload is in the incantation; they are relatively harmless when disenchanted.*

Linus settled back into his stance and waited, giving her only a quick nod.

This could be fun. Rime glanced back down, eager for the next salvo. *Maybe I* accidentally *put too much spin on one of these.*

"Don't be petty, *Doma*," the knight said as if reading her thoughts. "We have far greater matters tonight with which to contend."

Don't lecture me, old man. I know what happens the instant the danger is past. Your pretty white sword on my neck. "Just stay loose, Linus. Five this time, two will miss, but the other three are on the mark. Ready?"

"Ever." The white sword waited.

"Okay, how do we make the ship go faster? Like a lot faster?" Jonas shifted nervously from foot to foot.

His question was met with stony silence and a muttered curse from a squat-nosed knight nearby. The bridge was manned by six other Knights of the Sword, dressed in bright chain mail. Captain Chalk, a tall man with a brutal scar running horizontally across his forehead, kept a firm grip on the *Raven*'s wheel and his attention on their course and the strange game of shuttlecock the wild mage and hunter played on the deck. Only the gnome, Sir Graham, gave any notice that the squire had spoken. Xenon and

her sister appeared from belowdecks, followed closely by the devilkin Sideways, just in time to hear him tactfully rephrase Jonas's
query.

"Is this our top speed, Captain?" The gnome drummed on the
brass housing that surrounded the base of the pilot's wheel with
his knuckles. "The *Raven's* engines are whispered to be exceed-
ingly potent."

"The *engine* can put out more propulsion, but the ship's frame
can only withstand the burst for a few moments. It's enough to
give us a head start, but not enough to lose those cutters. I recognize the frames, even though they've blacked out their bow shield.
Those are Seafoam Trading Company raiders, all with top-of-the-
line Arkanic reactors. They can match our cruising speed easily,
and they're three times as maneuverable." Captain Chalk held up
a gauntlet to shield his eyes from a sudden burst of cannonball
shrapnel flying off the hunter's white sword.

"So, we need to destroy the other ships before we reach the
asteroid? Is that what you're saying?" Xenon asked.

"That, or if we had some way to force them to break off pursuit." The captain grimaced. "They are traders. Do any of you have
a substantial pile of gold you want to throw over the side?"

"A distraction, then." Sir Graham nodded, then cocked his
head to one side. "Young Mistress Mercury. Jonas. You have swift
legs—run to the engine room below and instruct them to activate
top velocity when they hear the captain's bell."

"What do you have in mind, Liar?" Captain Chalk demanded.
"And why send the scrat and the blood-dog? I have good men that
can act as runner."

"No." The gnome sat down calmly on the deck as the report of
cannon fire came again. "Or at least not as many as you thought."

Four of the knights stepped away from their posts: even-
shouldered, bright-eyed sons and daughters of Gilead. Sir Graham
pulled four glass vials from his pouch and snapped them one by

one. As he did, each of the knights popped like a soap bubble. This left only two knights of flesh and blood—the squat-nosed one that had cursed Jonas before and a thin woman who carried a massive half blade. The captain closed his eyes in disgust and spat on the deck. "Illusions," he cursed.

"Just helping with morale, Captain. Now—you two, run to the engine room!" Sir Graham fished around in his pocket and pulled free a large glass jar of smoked blue, something Jonas thought suitable for containing bread and butter pickles or perhaps blackberry jam.

"Let's foot it, crashface." Mercury tugged on his sleeve until they both were running down below the deck.

A blur of wooden stairs and bobbing steel glow-globes bolted into the walls, surrounded by the echoes of more cannon fire. *Amazing that Rime and Linus have kept them off our back so far*—the thick clang of a bullet landing against the nearby wing gave extra speed to his steps. The ship only had two levels, and important stations were marked in white paint in broad letters at every turn. The *Raven* was a warship, no need for any soldier to pull out their reading glasses to find the mess hall. The squire and goblin burst through the wide metal door marked "Engine" and skidded to a halt.

Jonas had been expecting something different. Perhaps a large iron bellows like a forge or some sort of gleaming contraption all brass and light. The engine of the *Raven* was neither. The room was wide, dark wooden beams triple reinforced with steel bolts and braces. In the center of the room was a tree. The tree was a sickly pink, with veins of darker purple—the leaves nearly white. Hanging from the tree—*impaled upon the tree!*—was a demon. Or at least that was the closest word the squire's mind supplied for the horrible eggplant-skinned thing that hung from the branches, its head bowed and the long claws on its feet and hands buried in the bark of the red tree. Even Mercury took a step back when the demon took a long, shuddering breath.

"Can I help you, children?" A kind voice gently grabbed their attention.

"What is that?!?" Mercury demanded.

The voice's owner stepped into view, from behind a trim desk set into the corner of the room, just next to the door. She was an older woman, her hair iron gray and her shoulders slightly stooped. Her black tunic was immaculate, and the three blue swords on her chest were bright as if the thread were newly spun.

"That's the engine," she said.

Mercury stared again, mind transfixed by the horrible sight. Jonas blinked and focused on his orders. "Captain needs maximum speed when he rings the bell."

"Oh my." The priest sighed. "You hear that, Candle?"

"Yes, Alice." The thing in the tree sighed, a weary bass note.

Alice turned to her desk and picked up a strange tool. For a second Jonas thought it was a mace of some sort, but it was too thin and fine to bear much weight. The tool was covered in cruel barbs, and as the priest brought it closer to the tree and its occupant, it began to shine with a pearl light.

"Message received, children. Now report back to the captain. You do not want to be in here when the engine is stoked. Now go." Alice stood at the ready, the vicious implement in her hands shining.

"Now hold on a clockwise snap." The goblin crossed her arms, eyes wild. "What is all—"

"Mercury. We gotta go, we gotta go now. Your sister might need help," Jonas said desperately. He had seen some terrible things in his travels, but he had no desire to add whatever was about to transpire to his store—nor did he want to start Mercury's catalog of horror.

The squire opened the door, and after a brief moment of hesitation, the goblin followed.

"Look at me this time, Alice. Look me in the eye." Jonas desperately prayed he did *not* hear the demon say that as the door shut behind them.

"You missed that one on purpose," Rime snarled as she flung a dagger of ice to impale the rogue cannonball and fling it flying away from the ship.

"I am . . . not . . ." Linus took a few quick breaths. "I am not as young as you, *Doma*. I cannot keep up this pace without error."

"Yeah, well—" The mage took a quick glance at their pursuers. "I don't think we have much choice. Here comes the next round."

Her face was running with sweat, despite the winter's bite in the air. She was still in control; the tiny slivers of her power she was using were not putting her in danger, but it was tiring, and it was not getting the job done. The five cutters were now on an even plane with the *Raven*. Every volley of cannonballs would mean at least four hits, if not five, that she would have to scoop and fling for the white sword to catch and dismantle. She burned with impatience. It would be so easy to rip those five ships out of the sky, instead of skimming the surface of the magic; with her fingertips she could pull it out by the fistful. *The old man is getting tired. It would only take a moment.*

Rime took a deep breath and her eyes began to glow as she reached for more power. Then the *Raven* exploded.

The black wood splintered and fell in large chunks through the air. The metal wings buckled and screeched in mineral agony. The night air filled with screams, and the shadows of the wreckage fell into the sea, dark shapes against the burning light of the approaching asteroid.

There was a hurricane of wind, the stars themselves seemed to blur, and Shame's fire wrapped from horizon to horizon. Rime found herself facedown on the deck of the ship, picking herself up and meeting the confused gaze of Linus as he too pushed himself up from the black wood. She growled in pain, her hands and knees smarting, and made herself stand and look over the edge of the rail.

Far behind them, like tiny dots on the southern horizon, were the five cutters. They flew in frantic circles like hornets but made no move to pursue. "What the hell just happened?" The mage mopped the sweat off her face.

"I spoke the Truth into this jar, Lady Korvanus." The green-haired gnome stepped down from the bridge, where the captain, his knights, and the others could be seen looking around with equal confusion. The gnome held up a dark-blue jar, sealed tight with a wide cork and a bit of steel wire. "The *Raven* was hit. The ship exploded. We are all dead."

"An illusion." Linus sheathed his sword.

"If you wish," Sir Graham replied.

Jonas and Mercury came stumbling up out from belowdecks. The squire opened his mouth to speak, relief clear on his face, but was cut off by Captain Chalk's brisk report.

"Pursuit is broken off. We will be within rendezvous distance of that giant fireball in ten minutes. We'll be keeping pace with it while you go investigate, the Nameless help you. And if you succeed, we'll be waiting to pick you up." The scarred man adjusted course with a fraction turn of the wheel. "Make yourself ready."

Sideways craned his head toward the waiting sky-cycle. "Don't suppose I get to drive?"

CHAPTER TWENTY

ASTEROID RESPONSE TEAM

Okay, so Linus can squeeze in behind me, and then Jonas can sit kind of on the back housing, like before." Xenon pulled on her lip. "Then, I guess, Sideways, you can, uh, brace yourself against that left strut and kind of bend over the saddle. Jonas, you'll need to probably hold on to his waist, just to be safe."

"Moments of great magnitude, undercut by who rides side-car." Rime snickered. "It's a good thing there aren't any bards around."

"Can your vehicle support this much weight, Scholar Xenon?" Linus asked, eyeing *Tobio*.

"*Tobio*'s strong, kettleman." Mercury sneered from where she sat balanced on the airship's rail.

The devilkin scratched his chin, then stepped a few feet away, gesturing for Xenon to follow. "I think me sitting that way will throw off your balance, make it harder to steer, right?"

"Well, not too bad." The goblin considered. "But it could be an issue if we have to move really fast or do some tight maneuvers."

"Okay," he said, and she was surprised to see a slight color in the swordsman's cheeks. Sideways turned back to face the others and raised his hand high to gather their attention. "Okay, there's no easy way to say this, so I'm just going to say it. I can turn into a bat."

"Uh, what?" Jonas looked up from where he was fussing with his sword belt, trying to comfortably situate the mundane blade over his shoulder, with the silver sword Hecate at his hip.

Linus placed a single finger over the small smile forming on his lips.

Sideways plowed ahead. "It's super cute. It's a furry, little orange bat. It even has cute little horns. It is adorable."

The devilkin covered his eyes with his right hand. "Okay, let's get this over with."

Sideways raised his other hand and shouted, "Changify!"

There was a puff of purple smoke, then flapping indignantly in midair was a shockingly adorable Sidebat.

"SQUEAL!" Mercury leaped forward in excitement and Jonas doubled over, choking with laughter. Rime simply rolled her eyes.

Do not laugh. He is super sensitive about this bat situation, do not laugh, Xenon! The goblin put on one of her mother's best Polished Granite Reserve expressions and moved toward the Sidebat with her hands cupped. He flapped into her hands with a clear expression of gratitude, which unfortunately gave her a close-up view of his two perfect little horns. *Why are his bat horns perfect when his normal horns are all squished?* She bit down hard on her cheek and dumped the orange bat into the folds of her hood, where his tiny claws took a firm grip.

"Let us begin," Linus said simply and pulled himself into place on the back of the sky-cycle.

Xenon scooped up her sister for one last squeeze, then swung into her place at the controls. She looked carefully over at Jonas and Rime. She had only known them a matter of hours, but the bond they shared and the tension at parting was clear.

Jonas's face was etched with concern. "Remember what I said, Rime. About the magic."

Rime shrugged with desperado nonchalance and straightened the cuffs of her red long-coat. "Just do your job right and it won't be an issue."

"Okay, okay—just . . ."

The mage took a step back and reached into her pocket, then her eyes widened in surprise. She pulled a small object free and tossed it to the squire. "For luck, I guess?" Rime smiled.

Jonas caught whatever it was and stared at it in the palm of his hand. Xenon waved again to her sister and shook her neck to make sure Sidebat was secure. She activated the sky-cycle and the unlikely defenders of the planet lifted off the pitch-black deck and flung themselves into the burning face of the asteroid.

Xenon thumbed the clock on *Tobio's* dashboard. *Two and a half hours until impact . . .*

Linus shaded his eyes against the glow of the Precursor's prison. It was not blinding, but it did make it difficult to discern any features on the orb's surface. The goblin had made three long passes along the central equator of the asteroid, moving systematically through each hemisphere. It required an investment of time, but he approved of the scholarly diligence. *We play against the hourglass, every move echoes forward and destroys later strategies—we must be careful, we need more information.* From his best estimation, Shame was at least three miles across at its widest point. If the sun were out, much of Corinth would fit neatly inside the orb's shadow. Certainly some of the impact would be absorbed by the sleeping ocean below, but the king's words of devastation hung heavy in his heart.

The boy behind him craned his head left and right, but Linus doubted he would be of much aid. "What are we looking for?" Jonas yelled, confirming the knight's conviction.

"We don't know!" Xenon replied, her own goggles moving tirelessly across the surface. "I can see what appear to be canals that cross the surface, but as far as I can tell they don't meet at any particular point. They aren't symmetrical across both hemispheres and they don't follow any regular pattern."

Linus felt the slow burn of exhaustion spread through his bones. The "game" on the deck had tired him greatly, and the light and heat roaring off the asteroid were not helping the matter. *Think, Linus the Blue. They are younger and their eyes are sharper. If you are to be of use, it is with a brain that knows how to operate properly.*

"The urn, the one you told us of." He closed his eyes to concentrate. "You said there were two main sigils, correct?"

"Yes." The goblin turned the sky-cycle in a slow arc to make another pass over the burning orb. "One for 'Shame' or 'Guilt,' and the other for 'Will'—*izus. Izus!*"

"What are you saying, what is that—" Linus had to grab onto the side of the saddle hard as Xenon suddenly pulled up on the controls, sending the sky-cycle farther away from the asteroid.

"Something Jonas said earlier, that word, *'izus.'* We're looking too close!" the goblin panted, then spun the sky-cycle around sharply. "The canals—they aren't random, they're Arkanic *sigils*! But huge! There!"

She pointed with excitement. "I don't know all of those sigils, and I haven't spotted the one for 'Shame'. But there's the one for 'Will'—but it can also mean 'Power'! I know it's a stretch, but if we're looking for the place that controls the asteroid, or the place where the Lost set the binding of the dragons, then that's our best shot."

Linus looked across the open air. He could make out the symbol she indicated, even wreathed in heat and flame. "Then let us move closer; we must begin somewhere."

"Good thing you mentioned that word out of the blue, Jonas," Xenon crowed, moving the sky-cycle carefully closer to the burning asteroid.

"Yeah," Jonas said.

Linus admired the skill with which the goblin brought them closer, even as he felt the heat of the flames grow. As they came within a few dozen feet, Xenon ceased their advance—matching the asteroid's fall with their own speed. In the center of the massive sigil, Linus spotted a square landing, then he blinked as his eyes grew dry from the heat.

"I think I see a door!" Jonas exclaimed.

"Uh, the flames don't appear natural. They aren't coming from friction or anything actually burning, but they do seem to cover the ten feet immediately above the asteroid's surface." Xenon wiped sweat off her chin.

Linus stood up carefully. "Help me stay balanced," he instructed the boy and felt thick hands grabbing the sides of his armor firmly. The knight pulled the white sword free and then held it out toward the asteroid, the blade's length extending past the nose of the sky-cycle like a small lance. "Forward. Slowly."

Xenon hunched over the console and gave the throttle the tiniest of gestures with her thumb. The three riders and the adorable bat all braced themselves for the onslaught of fire.

The tip of the white sword pierced the flame and ate it like a hungry whirlpool. Xenon gasped, but Linus kept the weapon steady. The white sword opened a channel of empty air before them, a wound in the skin of fire that surrounded Shame. The uniform pool of fire and heat turned to eddies of swirling energy absorbed and deleted by the white sword. The goblin risked a little more speed, and they were soon coming to rest on the square landing near the door that Jonas had spotted.

Linus stepped off *Tobio*, the white sword still free, and he scoured the last vestiges of magical flame from the area. He looked out to gauge whether the flame would rush back in to fill the gap he had created and was pleased to see that the edges he had cut were continuing to deteriorate, not re-form. *Like a tapestry from which the threads have been cut.* He slid the sword back into his belt.

Xenon stepped off the sky-cycle, openmouthed. "How—how is that even possible? Does your sword absorb all magical energy?"

"Just sucks it up," Jonas offered and made a terrible slurping noise.

"Where was this weapon fashioned? Are there more like it? Does it have a name? How did you come to possess it?" Questions tumbled from the archaeologist's mouth, then she clapped both hands over it in embarrassment.

Linus smiled in genuine delight. "We stand at the doorstep of the most astonishing Precursor relic ever recorded, while it falls from the sky and threatens the lives of untold millions of souls, and you have time for curiosity about another item entirely?"

"I'm so, so sorry," the goblin pleaded. "Habit! Habit and nerves."

"Then I will answer your questions with a quick breath. I know not. I pray not. None that it has shared with me, though I have heard it called 'the Spine of Law.' I do not possess it—too long a tale."

In a sudden flurry of adorable orange wings Sidebat leaped from Xenon's hood and hovered in the air. In a pennywhistle voice he cried, *"Un-Changify!"*

A puff of purple smoke and the devilkin stood before them, studiously not making eye contact and already unsheathing his gray blade. "So, how about this really interesting door over here?"

The four moved close to the archway. The outer surface of the orb, when bereft of flame, appeared to be a mottled bronze. The door was cut into the surface and showed no obvious handle or hinge—only a strange concavity at eye height that was deep enough for Xenon to almost hide her fist inside. She pulled a magnifying lens from her kit and leaned in close, but other than the depression, the door appeared all but featureless.

"Hmm, I don't—" Xenon nearly dropped her glass in alarm. The door had abruptly glowed a mottled green, then stopped almost at once.

"What just happened?" Jonas scratched his head.

"I . . . I'm not sure; maybe it reacted to the glass?" the goblin waved her implement in front of the door a few times, but the strange glow did not return.

"Some kind of lock," Sideways shrugged. "Precursors to now, everybody locks things."

"Yes!" Xenon leaned in close, then gave a sudden sharp-pitched whistle.

The door glowed a bright yellow in response to her tune, then faded quickly when she stopped. Linus sighed and laid a hand on the white sword's hilt.

"Yes, it responds to musical tones! The Lost built their greatest magic with songs; it would only make sense that to protect their prison, they would seal it with a musical key of some sort." The goblin reached into her cloak and pulled out her journal and quill.

"Oh, so—we just have to sing the right song and it'll open?" Jonas's eyes widened. "Neat! What song?"

"I have no idea!" Xenon began to flip through her journal. "Almost none of the Lost's songs have survived to present day, and even if we had them all, it would be pure guesswork on which one was correct. And *then* we would have the problem of the proper tone, pitch, and intonation—you see—"

Linus lunged and buried the tip of the white sword in the seam of the door. There was a brief flicker of rainbow lights across the portal's surface, then a quiet thunk as the door flopped open. An acrid smell like burning leaves filled the landing.

"Cool. White Sword eats magic. Let's roll." Sideways entered first, Chester held low.

Xenon stared at the door in complete horror. Linus sheathed the weapon and whispered an apology as he followed his assassin into the Precursor's prison.

King Tamar sat alone. It drove her mad to be blind while her city, her people, were in peril. They were imperiled by the blazing red-white circle that, by her guard's faltering description, filled half the night sky now. She had given them all tasks, duties to prepare the castle defenses, to prepare the city for the long night that could still fall. *My vision will return. There will be much to do come dawn, either way.*

She had decided the best place for her to be was the Alabaster Throne, where at least she could be a symbol of resolve and comfort to her people. Her heirs were safely on their way, bound for the far city of Caleron. They had fought her decision, but they had bowed to her Sight.

The king raised her head. Someone was there, standing a few feet from the throne, silent and unannounced. She craned her ears, trying to decide if she should rebuke this careless guard, but she could not hear the jingle of chain mail, or the creak of leather straps, or the slight tap of a blade against armor. As best she could tell, the someone was standing in the blue rectangle, recently vacated by the knight's tribunal.

Someone walked closer.

"Could I stay with you a moment?"

King Tamar felt as though she was stepping across a dark pit and wished that she had not left her glaive in the sitting room floors below. "I am sorry, but I do not know you."

A strong hand took hers. "You know me."

"Though we have never met." The king returned the grip, the way she might handle a viper.

"I was curious about something. You had them break bread together. Simple magic, old magic, from the bones of the city. Only the hunter noticed. You wanted to bind together your little band of heroes. But why did you not tell them all that you saw?"

Tamar the Thrice-Cursed smiled, all teeth. "I am a king. I owe answers to no one."

"She will pay with the coin most dear. That is what you saw. Why did you not say it?"

Tamar reached up and methodically pulled the blood-soaked cloth from around her eyes. Blind eyes, dry-rimmed with red, but she wanted her questioner to see the iron. "There is always a Cost. I have paid it many times. My city, my children, the stones I bought with steel and death. If they were Heroes they would pay it gladly, but they are villains all, so I will spend their lives for them. I know what Tomorrow holds for them, all but the goblin. The boy's future is a brown cloak, the girl's is an empty cup. The monster will wither in a teardrop of stone. Is that what you ask? Is that what you want to know from a king?"

A gentle hand ran down the king's face, and she slapped it away.

"I know a king's burden." The hand released her and was gone, but as Someone walked away the voice lingered, coiling around her like a green vine.

Tamar sat alone and thought of the falling sky she could not see and her father who was gone and the battles she had fought, young and bright, scattering memories like flower gems on a broken necklace—falling to break on the floor of her throne room. Then she thought of promises. Promises kept and promises yet to be fulfilled. *This is the last curse. To see with eyes unclouded how utterly empty the Game. Block this cut, stamp out this blaze, rip out the Beast's heart again and again, but still it comes. Only Once— only one chance to stand, to move, to protect, to find the right path. Stone cracks, wind falters, sun fades, even Time erodes. I walk down a tunnel of wind with a fistful of sand. What does it matter if the asteroid falls? Everything ends—everything falls apart.*

"The button falls off the coat," the old woman said, but not even Someone was listening.

CHAPTER TWENTY-ONE

JONAS

The four explorers stepped cautiously out of the tunnel into a waiting dark that hung heavy and patient, suggesting a mammoth empty space within Shame. Jonas blinked his eyes, trying to force them to adjust to the dimmer light.

The mottled brass tunnels had been quiet and clean, smelling faintly of lavender soap. Jonas sniffed the air again, still a bit nose-boggled. *It smells exactly like the soap that Mom used, the rose-shaped ones that I wasn't allowed to touch.* As they had passed through the door on the asteroid's skin the glow and roar of the magical flames had died behind, leaving only the brass tunnel that stretched out before them. Glow-globes were set at regular intervals, providing even illumination; the walls were unadorned and showed neither rivet nor seam. It was more than a little amazing to see the same technology in this unbelievable place that could be found now in every city of the world.

After the first twenty minutes of slow, measured plodding with weapons at the ready, Sideways sheathed his gray blade and turned to the others with a shrug.

"Nothing's bitten us yet, just this hall." The devilkin snorted.

"Shame is miles across, and we entered near the meridian." Xenon was doing her best to walk and sketch a rudimentary map in her journal, "Did you think the controls were going to be right inside the door?"

Sideways shrugged again. Linus leaned against the tunnel wall, his iron gauntlet scraping idly against the brass. "The center, then? You believe that would be the most logical place?"

The goblin looked up, quill dripping a bead of ink. "So far there have been no turns, only this single hallway. Let us continue on with less caution and more haste."

And so they had, until now stepping out into the voluminous empty. Jonas could see the brass floor ahead of them was still illuminated, small footlights bored into the side rail. The path continued on, straight as an arrow, but above he could begin to make out other dim lights—red, blue, green, purple—almost on the edge of vision like the sun's echo but growing more distinct as he and the others moved farther along in the dark.

"They appear to be ovoid pods, translucent—" Xenon spoke feverishly as she continued to scribble. "Source of illumination, unclear—nor the reason for the differentiation between the spectrum. Perhaps some form of—"

"Dragons," Sideways cut her off. "It's the dragons. Sleeping away in glass jars."

Jonas squinted and saw that it was true. Hanging from nearly invisible cables and pipes, the vast glowing firmament of egg-shaped pods swayed gently as if in a breeze. *Dragons. Each one of those jars has a dragon in it. One. Two. Three. Red dragon. Blue dragon. Gold dragon. Four. Five. Six. Seven.* There were too many to count. They were nearly a mile away across the interior dark sky of the asteroid, he could only make out vague outlines and the colors of scales. But it was enough to send his hand flying to the hilt of his sword—then uncertainly to the hilt of the magic blade Hecate at his belt. Jonas thought of Rime for no reason he could name.

"Let us proceed." Linus's winter voice pulled them back into focus. "The path continues, and by my estimation a half mile farther across this bay I believe I can spot a central cluster of some sort. Sideways, do you see it?"

The devilkin stood up on his tiptoes and looked farther down the path. He nodded. "The regular light definitely gets brighter up ahead; looks like a small dome of some sort."

Xenon began to trot past the others, still furiously sketching the oval dragon containers and taking notes, all while calling over her shoulder. "Then let's hurry! We can't be more than an hour before Rime will try to slow the asteroid. The economy of purpose; function is supreme—all hallmarks of many Precursor relics. They built nothing that was not purposeful; they would not leave a door and a single path and a prominent central node that wasn't in some way essential to the operation of Shame."

Because if there's nothing there—Jonas thought, as he was sure the others all did—*we won't have time to run back out and try another door.*

The old hunter sighed and turned to Jonas. Sideways had already begun to lope after the scribbling goblin, studied disinterest in the hundreds of slumbering monsters suspended above them bolted to his orange face. When Linus placed a careful hand on the squire's shoulder, Jonas couldn't help but stiffen. "May I lean on you and try to keep pace?"

The squire grunted and shifted his weight so he could support some of the old knight's. He set a quick march without a word. *Rime would boil me alive if she saw this.*

"Necessity," Linus said with gratitude. "It is an ugly wool shawl that the young spurn, but the old press to their breast without shame or regret."

Jonas did not respond at once, just kept his eyes on the path ahead. Then finally, he could not resist. *When am I going to have this chance again?*

"So, you're still going to try to kill Rime when this is done, right?"

"Yes," the hunter replied, his breathing labored.

"I know that wild mages have a bad reputation, and I know that you probably know a lot more than I know about them," the squire pressed on, "but Rime is trying really hard to find a way to not go crazy."

"They almost always do try," Linus replied. "How does she fare?"

Jonas bit his lip. He thought about the boat and the lightning—and about how eager Rime had been to match her magic against the asteroid.

"I have talked to you about this before," the hunter went on, as if Jonas had responded. "Not you, young squire. But people like you. Friends, lovers, companions of wild mages. They all think that this time it will be different. That their friend can beat it, can find a way out. I told you then, and I tell you now. She cannot beat it. There is no way out. She will go mad, and with the Magic Wild unfettered and screaming in her hands—you of all people have seen what she can do while she is in *control*. Do I need to say the rest . . . again?"

Jonas bowed his head, then shook it. "Well, we'll see. We'll see about that."

Linus smiled, an empty reflex. "I will wear the shawl, young man. You wear whatever cloak suits you as long as you can."

"Jonas! Sir Linus!" Xenon called from a few hundred paces ahead. "Come quickly!"

The knight and the squire trotted on until they joined their companions. Jonas could immediately see the source of the goblin's alarm. A long section of the path ahead, perhaps a hundred feet, was completely dark. After that blank section, the path continued and the dome of the purported control room was a quarter-mile distant.

"What happened to the path lights?" Linus demanded. "Some malfunction?"

"'Fraid not, boss." Sideways was kneeling at the edge of shadows. He activated the belt lantern he carried and pointed it forward.

Long, thick gouges had been torn out of the Arkanic metal, cruel grooves nearly a handspan across. The assassin doused his lantern with alacrity. "Something got loose, I think."

"But this asteroid, the architecture and technology of the Precursors!" Xenon protested. "The unbelievable prowess to create a vessel of this size, suspend the dragons, keep them in some sort of magical slumber—all of it, it's just so perfect."

"All it takes is one nail out of place to throw a horseshoe," Jonas said, and looked down to see his good steel was already in his hand.

Sideways nodded his approval and flipped his own gray blade back out into his hand. The white sword rasped against Linus's breastplate as he drew it free.

The goblin turned to the three swords and jammed her journal under her arm, quill behind her ear. "Okay, let's not panic. Shame has been flying for thousands of years. This could have happened days after it was launched and the dragon died hundreds of years ago from starvation."

The devilkin cocked his head at the archaeologist, then chuckled as he stepped out beyond the path lights. "Yeah, I just don't see us getting through the evening without fighting a dragon. It's just that kind of night."

Jonas and the old hunter followed, keeping Xenon in the space between them. *Sideways will be best hiding in the dark; Linus and I can protect Xenon and keep moving.*

The cavernous dome of the asteroid became all the more oppressive as they navigated the gap between lights. It was easier to see the dragon-planets up above in what Jonas realized he was thinking of as the sky. One seemed almost close enough to touch, pulsing a lambent purple, but the squire knew it was just a trick of perspective.

"Have you ever fought a dragon before?" Jonas asked in a low tone.

"I've seen a couple. Traded Sarmadi prayer-daggers with one. The other was wild, a venom spar down near Seroholm; just saw it from a distance and was able to avoid it." Xenon's voice was a nervous clatter of syllables. The squire spared a glance and saw that she was still attempting to record in her journal, using the carefully hooded light of her own bull's-eye lantern.

Linus said nothing. Jonas began to ask the question again, when the purple dragon-jar caught his attention again. *Is it brighter now? Wait, no darker? Wait—no—!*

With a coruscation of air, the glass pod he watched blazed a fervent honey gold. He had only a moment to register what was happening before the creature was upon them. *It was wrapped around the jar, blocking the light!*

In the river of darkness, between roads of brass and light, the dragon landed before them. A great volume of air, strangely gentle like a breath, and they could see it outlined in the uncertain light coming from the central dome beyond. It was thirty feet high at the shoulder, wings wide and enveloping—half butterfly, half unraveling cloak. Its scales seemed to be a dark purple, and a fierce magenta light burned from its eyes and mouth and along the ridges of its sternum. Jonas opened his mouth to scream but saw the empty stone of Linus's gaze and the startled curiosity in Xenon's, so he gripped his sword's hilt tight until his knuckles popped and did his best to remain calm.

"*Caro don ves,*" the dragon spoke, brightly colored vapor escaping its nostrils.

Linus kept the white sword high and his eyes on the dragon. "Scholar Xenon. I do not speak this tongue, do you?"

"Uh!" Xenon took a stuttered step forward, pushing the fingers of one hand into her temple as if they might force out the lore she needed. "Only three words. Could be related to High Valerian; that's supposed to be a bastardization of the old dragon speech. But it could also maybe be Dwarven? Lots of consonants and monosyllabic structure. I need it to talk more!"

"*Ves par mondat? Ves par Sondenai?*" the dragon breathed again.

Jonas swung back to Xenon, hope growing in his breast.

"No! *Sondenai!* That's Tonic—really archaic Tonic, but I recognize the proper noun! It means 'Sun Child'! It's what they called the Precursors! Okay, okay, okay—" Xenon covered both eyes with her long green fingers as she concentrated. "It's been a long time, but I think I can cobble together a rudimentary sort of conversation. I think it just asked if we are mortal—if we are Precursors? I'll tell it that we are mortal, but not members of the Lost—because that's pretty obvious, I would imagine."

Xenon took a slow step forward, pulling her journal free and pressing it tightly between her hands for comfort. "*Nego Sondenai! Uh—ves par rogollo . . . ?*"

The shadowed dragon breathed out another fume of vapor, this one a bright red. Jonas leaned in closer to the archaeologist. "What did you say?" he whispered.

"I told it we are explorers . . . I think." Xenon frowned, then looked up as a strange sound filled the dark heavens inside the asteroid.

This sound needed no translation. The dragon was laughing. More vapors of dark blues and vicious greens escaped its jaws as it spoke, a long stream of the forgotten language. Xenon did her best to keep up with a translation.

"Uh—it slept, then it dreamed. Then in dreams it heard—something—a horn! The horn of—the dark. It woke but still dreamed? It knelt before the—I think—queen, maybe—of the Dark and swore to serve her. I am the second servant? Or is it messenger? The second servant of the Dark. It traded its name to awake and found itself here, in the Sun Child's prison. It—began to feed—on its brothers and sisters to survive—blech. It saw in dreams—or it dreamed it saw—little men, little mondat—mortals!—like us who would bring the prison back home. Zero! It means Zero! And it has come with a message. *This is it! This is the "thing with no name" that awoke!* The Node woke this dragon and somehow it made the asteroid return!"

Xenon stumbled to a halt, but the dragon had been silent for a long moment. It spoke one final time. "*The Circle will Break. The City will Fall. There is no Power to Prevent, nor Song to Preserve. Kneel before the End.*"

Jonas had just enough time to realize he understood the creature's words before he saw the rainbow vapor ignite and a vast plume of energy come screaming out of the dragon's jaws. He surged forward, hoping to pull Xenon back from the assault, but Linus and his white sword were already there. The hunter stepped in front of her, and the patchwork energies of the dragon's breath were absorbed into the blank metal.

"Scholar Xenon, fall back," Linus commanded. "Squire, you guard my back. I didn't spot a tail on this creature, but it seems agile enough. We will keep its attention firmly fixed on us, understood?"

"Yes!" Jonas stepped into place, keeping one eye on Xenon's retreat as she hurried back toward the lighted pathway behind them.

The dragon howled with a rage that teetered on the edge of delight and breathed more of the ramshackle energy upon them. The white sword again devoured it. "The creature is mad. It's been feeding on the life force of its brethren for who knows how long. Its breath is some bizarre mixture of different elements."

"I'm just glad it breathes something the sword eats," Jonas grunted.

"Yes, well—" Linus shifted his grip on the white sword. "It appears he has grown bored with that tactic. Here he comes!"

"Does your magic sword happen to kill dragons with a single touch?" The squire spun to cover Linus's right flank.

"I don't know. Does yours?" the old man shifted his stance, keeping his elbow high.

Oh yeah. Sir Pocket's sword. Jonas looked down at his belt at the hilt of the silver sword. A small, tender part of his heart had almost hoped to see it blaze like moonlight in his hands when he brought it up from the well, but it had remained lifeless and cold. *Will it even work for me? Did I break the magic when I broke the curse? Or is it that I'm not . . .*

"Move, boy!" Linus's voice cracked like an autumn twig.

The dragon's shape twisted and furled like a flag in the wind, its weight seeming to evaporate and vanish as it curled in upon itself. The phosphorescent eyes boiled as they advanced, leaving trails of lollipop vapor behind. Jonas dodged right, and the older knight heaved himself into the darkness to the left as the creature whipped past like an angry, hissing piece of the night sky. The dragon pulled up sharp and fluttered above their heads, laughing among the faintly gleaming planet containers.

"Okay. We need a plan. Some sort of dragon-fighting strategy," Jonas panted, picking himself up off the floor. "What've you got?"

The old hunter was already on his feet, white sword ready, and his eyes following the creature's languorous descent. "The plan remains; we keep its attention focused on us and we wait."

The Messenger, if that was the creature's name, landed lightly again a dozen paces away. It spread its long, ragged wings wide and reached out to envelop both the squire and Linus. Jonas held his sword up and slashed out at the approaching purple-black. The simple steel rebounded, nearly nicking his cheek—but the dragon howled in sudden anguish. He looked at his plain sword in amazement and then up toward the beast's lantern eyes, and his mouth dropped open.

"We wait for that." Linus nodded.

Sideways was swinging from one of the Messenger's long, crenulated horns with one hand, the other plunged his gray blade all the way to the hilt into the dragon's flesh. It screamed again, vomiting energy of a half-dozen hues as it tried to dislodge the devilkin. Sideways methodically hooked his arm around the horn and wrapped his legs around the dragon's neck—then began to plunge Chet again and again into the open wound. White blood that sizzled and smoked pulsed forward, giving off its own sick pearl light.

The Messenger began to flap its ravel-wings in desperation, and then Linus moved, as if he had waited for a signal. With surgical cuts, he sliced through the dragon's wings until they tore and peeled apart. Jonas took a step forward, then realized he had absolutely no idea what he could do to help. He looked back over his shoulder and saw Xenon standing in the distant path light, her eyes wide and her journal and quill dancing.

In maddened frenzy, the dragon reached up—Jonas at last saw the almost fragile claws at the end of its wing tips—and plucked the devilkin off its neck and hurled him away into the darkness. Sideways rolled his body in some manner of gargoyle-grace and landed lightly on his hands and feet, Chet held between his teeth. He threw Jonas a wink and trotted back toward the dying beast. Linus lunged and drove the point of the white sword deep into the Messenger's torso. Bleeding and burning and its wings unthreaded, the strange dark thing curled forward, its jaws still puking prismatic death. The squire dashed to Linus's side and bodily hauled the old man and his weapon free; they had become caught in the tangle of flesh and twisting muscle. The two humans made it out of the way just shy of the dragon's crashing head.

The Messenger wheezed and bled and light dripped out of its jaws. It was dying but not yet dead. Sideways sauntered up, Chester held loosely in one hand, its blade leaned against his shoulder. "Aww, and you had all those hundreds of years to prepare the big scary speech."

"Sideways," Linus said with quiet reproach.

The devilkin held a theatrical hand up to his ear and leaned over the wheezing dragon. "What was that, Cosmos Dragon? Blah, blah, I had time to workshop my backstory in between eons of masturbation and eating roaches?"

"I hate when he does this." Linus carefully checked the white sword for any remnants of the dragon's ichor before sheathing it again at his side. "It's tawdry."

Jonas sheathed his own sword, not knowing quite how to respond to the devilkin's elation. The squire tapped the silver hilt of Hecate; it was cold to the touch.

Sideways chuckled. "You want the honors, young sir? Not many can claim the title of dragonslayer in this day and age."

"No, that's okay," the squire said, waving to Xenon as she approached breathless.

"Whatever." Sideways shrugged and stabbed his gray blade adroitly between the Messenger's fading eyes.

The goblin leaned in close over the devilkin's shoulder, filling a full page with her sketch of the dragon's head. "Never seen anything like this in the fossil record; there's no record of such a creature. Do you suppose they were all taken by the Lost on Shame, or perhaps did this specimen mutate over the centuries as it fed off the other dragons?"

"Something to ponder later," Linus instructed and pointed toward the illuminated dome ahead. "If there is one."

The four explorers left their questions and the dead dragon behind. "How much time do we have?" Jonas looked up over the brass dome. It echoed the overall structure of the entire aster-oid, a perfect circle. But set in one side was a triangular doorway where the illuminated pathway terminated.

"Uh—maybe thirty minutes before the mile limit?" Xenon said. "Kind of lost track a bit back there!"

"Marks on the dome, claw marks." Sideways pointed.

The devilkin was right; more of the Messenger's claw marks could be seen around the triangular door, like a drunkard's key scratching at a lock. As they approached, they could now see above the curve of the dome signs of bubbled and melted metal, burn marks from where the dragon's breath had finally eaten its way inside.

"Why did it want in?" Jonas asked nervously, but the other three were already running forward into the dome. He followed, his heart thick.

The doorway led to a small room that was unsurprisingly cir-cular. Jonas joined his companions where they stood speechless, looking around the room.

The walls were covered with Precursor sigils, etched into the metal. In the center of the room was a low console, about hip height on the squire. The console's material was clean white, and its face was covered with row after row of square buttons. On each button was a different sigil, and they glowed in more colors than even the Messenger's fire. *A table of jewels, just as the king said!*

All of this was a lot for Jonas to absorb, but the most strik-ing feature of all was the vicious black punctures in the trim perfection of the Arkanic console. Some of the buttons were cracked and scattered, or hanging by the most slender of glass cylinders that apparently suspended all of them.

"It reached in here and changed the course," the goblin said. "I'm making a leap, I know—but we don't have time to ponder. Zero sent the Node here, it woke up the dragon, and then it clawed its way in here until it could reach the console. Somehow it turned the asteroid around."

Linus nodded, his eyes still making a careful inventory of the room.

The devilkin sheathed his sword. He patted the goblin on the shoulder and moved to the side of the console and settled himself comfortably on the edge.

"Well," he said, not unkindly to Xenon, "*we* got the dragon. You're up."

CHAPTER TWENTY-TWO

RIME

Rime sat on the deck of the airship and stared at the chess piece in her hands. She liked that it was a proper knight, not just the abstracted horsehead that some sets used. The white knight sat on the back of his own horse, and she could even make out fine details like the pennant curving around his lance and the feathers of his plume. The grain of the wood made her think that it was ash that had been bleached to make it the proper ivory color for the game.

Bleached. She curled a lock of bone-white hair around a finger and squinted at it. *I need a haircut.* Something to even out the lengths, at least—the white half seemed to grow slower than her regular brown. *I'll get Jonas to chop it off when he gets back.*

She had been sitting in the same spot since the others had left. The *Raven* had taken up a simple anchor-point within a half mile of Shame's impact point and waited. Rime had stared at the asteroid for the first hour, carefully drawing a schematic of light and order across the sky, numbers and arcs and lines intersecting as she then revised and rerevised her plan. After that it wasn't

242   G. DEREK ADAMS

useful to continue to stare and made her eyes start to dry out, so she stopped. The red-white orb continued its roaring progression, an impossible bulk of matter in the sky, filling more and more of it with its presence, with its moment, with its demand for attention. The mage yawned.

Why am I not getting impatient? Normally I would be losing my mind by now. She spun the chess piece slowly between her fingers, then grinned. *I want this.*

The goblin archaeologist's younger sister wandered back over. The sour-faced creature had tromped by every few minutes during the long wait, usually saying nothing, a few times growling out some vague sentence of claptrap to the empty air. Rime had not bothered to respond.

"Ruth Garamonde has cheese in her travel clutch," Mercury announced.

The mage groaned, clenching the white knight in her fist and pressing it and sharp knuckles into her forehead. The knights on board must have finally surrendered to the goblin's queries as a distraction from the approaching asteroid. "What kind of cheese?" Rime heard herself ask.

"Oblique Squamish cheddar from Valeria," the small goblin reported. "Sharp with a hint of dill."

"That sounds pretty good."

"It is." Mercury nodded, shifting slightly. "Did you know that Captain Chalk's first name is Paaen?"

"I didn't."

"Do you think my sister is dead?"

Rime stood up. *My hair is half white. In that vision or what-ever I saw in the throne room, it was all white. And I was at least ten years older. That means I don't die today, right?* "I have no idea. Probably not."

Mercury nodded again, barely acknowledging that the mage had spoken. Rime tucked the white knight piece back in the pocket of her coat and stretched. She looked out across the open air, at the space vanishing beneath the asteroid, and decided it was time. "It's close enough. Captain Chalk!" she called and waited for his responding wave from the bridge. "Keep the *Raven* at least two miles away from me. I can't be worrying about you while I do this."

"Aye," the scarred knight agreed and turned the ship's black wheel.

Rime looked down at the goblin. *Should I say something more?* She opted for a genial shrug; her mind was already racing, occupied with the four-mile-wide globe of eldritch flame and unknown construction that waited for her. Her fingers sank into the Magic Wild, a caramel burn of acid on her skin. *At last.* Her normal practice when flying was to surround herself in crackling energy and hurl herself forward like a missile—this time she would need to be more surgical, husband every ounce of her strength. Rime formed bands of silver light around her wrists and ankles and pulled herself skyward like a marionette.

Mercury watched her go but made no parting gesture.

The wind whipped past, cold and bitter, but it felt like a gospel to her. The flaming circle of Shame came down out of the heavens to meet her, and Rime realized she was laughing. She spread her arms wide and soared on, arcing upward, looking for the perfect apex, the point where two lines would meet. Curves and calculations filled her vision, the precise spot where she would stand drawn as a white circle, the formulae and numerical notation irising away from it like the tail of a peacock. Her mind was a fish in the sea of mathematics; all she had to do was take her place.

Then a scribble appeared on her mind's schematics that overlaid the sky and the asteroid. A brown scribble that quickly took the form of a stick figure holding a sword with a crude cloak drawn as a rhombus. The scribble-Jonas reached into its cloak and pulled out words.

too
much
magic
please
stop
!

The exclamation point he fashioned out of his scribble-sword and waved at her imploringly.

Rime lifted a hand and pushed the scribble away, leaving only the clean order of her design. She flew into the circle and put her feet down on nothing. The mage used the remaining seconds to straighten her coat and brush the wind-swept hair out of her eyes. To the few that watched, she was a tiny red dot standing in the naked air, surrounded and engulfed by the flame and bulk of the approaching asteroid.

Shame came closer, closer—then at once Rime lifted her hands like a symphony's conductor. For the first time ever she allowed her guard to relax, to let herself hear every cry from the beasts screaming in her head, to not just skim the surface, not just dip her hand—but let herself sink into the endless water of the Magic Wild.

Jonas had warned her, but she didn't care. To do this thing, to stop the asteroid, she had to let go. It wasn't truly the magic that tired her out, that made her fall unconscious—it was her trying to control it, to keep some part of herself safe from it. She had learned to swim, but now she would need to learn to drown.

Her eyes opened, but they were already open. Her blood turned to molten gold and then obsidian bees and then lightning and terror and the waves crashing on the bones of the earth and it was good, so good, and she could feel her heart becoming glass and a mirror and a doorway that opened on a castle of boundless star-death and comet-candy, and it was good, it was good, and maggots and oil dripped down her throat, and her jaw ripped apart as her new face burst free, and it was good, and she was a primrose-phantom screaming between beams of light and twisting in the wind of some idle atom's whim, and she was rock and copper-penny blood and lips and hands on her body and pleasure and wet, and it was good, it was good, it was good, and her knuckle bones were cities, and her teeth were nothing, nothing, nothing, and she was screaming and screaming, and still there was more and more and more and endless more and light and color and wind and fire and ice and screaming and screaming and—

Get. Yes. No. Hold. Stay. Me. Me. I am ME. I am 9. I am the square root of 7. I am my feet on the stairs and the pain on my back. I am my mother's eyes. I am . . . I am . . .

"*I . . . am a storm,*" Rime forced the words out. "*And my heart is a thunderbolt!*"

She beat back the Magic with every ounce of will she had; she wrapped herself in numbers and equations and the armor of logic. She couldn't recall where the words had come from, but they felt right. She was more than the Magic, she was distinct, she was she. *I am Rime Korvanus . . . and you . . . serve . . . ME.*

Light the color of winter frost erupted from her eyes and hands, impossible beams of force rising to meet the falling asteroid. The burning orb hit the gouts of light, and a tremendous groan filled the air as the forward momentum of Shame was halted by her magic. The vast asteroid shuddered and shook, a boulder prevented by an ant.

Fucker's heavy. Rime grunted and poured more energy down the beams but immediately began the next phase of her plan. She kept the main force going but then fashioned siphons of light that pulled energy from the asteroid itself and vented it out into the air and ocean beneath her. It created a strange energy wheel of bled force and blunted momentum. The mage kept pouring energy into the two main columns holding the asteroid back, but she could feel the drain on her own reserves begin to lessen. *It's still an imperfect system; I'm putting in more energy than I'm pulling off the flame-ball, but it will mean I can hold it longer.* The math of *how* long was stark and unpleasant, and Rime had scrupulously ignored it during her planning. She would hold as long as it took. The mage breathed out and was surprised to see the vapor immediately condense and freeze before her eyes. She risked a quick glance below—the ocean beneath her was freezing over, an ice sheet forming and spreading with her and her magic brace as the center. *Hmm—that's unexpected.*

She was glad that her red coat was thick.

The minutes ground on, and the asteroid came to a halt. Rime let the magic flow and licked away the red blood that trickled from her nose and across her lips. Strange lattices of ice were forming in the air around her, but she kept her attention fixed on the burning globe above her. Her teeth ground together, and the mage stood in the invisible circle, her feet on the skin of the air, and held. And held. And held.

CHAPTER TWENTY-THREE

XENON

Xenon stepped toward the ruined console and spread her journal open, simple leather binding and yellow paper against the immaculate not-stone and the light of the buttons. The others watched her: Sideways calm, Linus appraising, Jonas hopeful. *This is . . . the most absurd final exam ever concocted.* She spread her green fingers across the buttons, feeling their weight, tracing familiar ideograms, tugging carefully at the shattered glass pillars where the dark dragon's claws had punctured the console. *I would want to spend decades in this room, a month on every button, a lifetime of work here—happy, useful, important work about the Lost. And I have less than twenty minutes to recall every sigil, every scrap of lore—and somehow get Shame to turn itself around.*

"Please speak, Scholar Xenon," the old hunter counseled. "It will keep your thoughts focused, and if nothing else we can be an attentive audience."

Mother would love this one. Maybe they should date. The cherry bomb thought sailed across her brain. Xenon breathed out, then began. "Okay. Okay. No way to tell the amount of damage that the Messenger caused, so no point in focusing on that. Also, no way to repair that damage in the time we have, so that's out too. This console is the only thing in the room, so it's the only thing we have to contend with. It's the obvious input point. I recognize many of these sigils, but the significance of the colors escapes me. All Arkanic writing we've studied has been monochromatic, etched into stone or recovered relics."

The goblin pulled her trusty quill from behind her ear, flipped to the back page of her journal, and sketched out a hasty grid. *Ten rows, ten columns. One hundred buttons—minus the ones the dragon destroyed.* "Some of the sigils repeat! That's the symbol for 'Fire,' and it's here, here, here—three different places! Cyan 'Fire,' Red 'Fire,' Green 'Fire.'" She noted their placement on her grid, hand flying.

"What happens if we push a button?" Sideways eyed a few near his perch, then reached an orange hand out.

Xenon grabbed his hand and bared her teeth. "DO NOT DO THAT. We don't have time for random; we need every bit of information we can get. I was just about to push a button as an experiment; keep your stupid carrot hands to yourself."

The devilkin held both hands up in defeat and slid off the console to get out of her way. She scanned the rows of functioning buttons again, and her eyes lit upon a familiar symbol, an equilateral triangle with a dot in the center. "'Knowledge.' Okay, I'll press this one as a test. Everyone brace yourselves just the same."

She leaned away from the console, placed two fingers on the button, and then gave it a firm press.

The entire console shimmered, all buttons glowing white at once—sparks rumbling from the broken ones. A shape took form, hovering over the console, another orb, this one made of green light. It flashed a single symbol, then pulsed with expectation.

"What—" Linus began.

"Shh," Xenon commanded, one hand toward the knight. *I know that sigil. It means "Key."* An idea formed in her head, and she leaned in close to the green ball of light and sang a nonsense scatter of notes. "La la la la!"

The green ball flashed, reacting to the tones, then went all white. It flashed the "Key" sigil again and continued to wait. Xenon looked down at the console; all of the buttons were still glowing white.

She turned to her companions. "It's locked. I'm guessing when the Messenger broke the console to bring Shame home, it triggered some sort of protective enchantment. It's like the door we came through; we need the right key to unlock the console."

"You mean we have to sing a song to make it work?" Sideways demanded.

"What song?" Jonas mopped sweat from his face.

Xenon breathed out, feeling anxiety coiling around her limbs and heart faster and faster like black wires. "That's just it. It's an Arkanic lock, which means it's an Arkanic song. The Songs of the Lost are . . . well, lost. Even if I somehow had a recording of every song they ever had, it would be anyone's guess as to which is the correct one. And in the time we have—"

"The sword. Like the door." The squire pointed to Linus with desperation.

The goblin shook her head, but the old knight answered for her. "That was a moment of crude force—my blade could unmake this enchantment, but it would also break the console itself. We need it to be operable so we can succeed at our task."

Xenon covered her eyes with the palm of her hand and made herself focus on just breathing. The other three were silent as well, as Time skipped by them laughing. She forced herself to lower her hand and speak. "We can't give up. There must be a way. At the very least, we can sing any songs we know, on the off chance that—" Xenon snapped her fingers. "The king! She said that Time is memory and a bunch of other stuff about circles."

"Prophecy is an uncertain guide," Linus cautioned.

"Prophecy is the graffiti of history, the damp sandwich in the bottom of the scholar's picnic basket, the annoying footnote without attribution, loyalty, or regret." Xenon slammed her fist into her palm. "Archaeologists rank prophecy below sexually explicit limericks and bodily functions as proper dinner conversation. I hate them. But it's all that we got. Now think! Any songs about circles? Or Time? Or memory?"

All four bowed their heads in thought. Sideways scratched his chin. "I mean, there is that kid's song about the puppy circle? Snouts to the left, snouts to the right! If you pet our bums, then we'll get in a fight! Tails to the left, tails to the right! If you pet our heads, then we'll give you a bi—"

The devilkin trailed off into silence. Jonas coughed. Xenon turned to glance at the green ball of light; it showed no recognition. "Okay—'Puppy Circle' is out. I'll write that in my journal later. Anyone else?" Xenon spread her hands in desperation.

The squire cocked his head, then looked up at the others. "Hmm, it's not a song about circles, but it is a song that's come up a bit lately. I told Rime about it, then I heard it in . . . umm . . . prison."

"What song?" the goblin took a step toward Jonas.

"Oh, it's an old hymn from home. Kids in Gilead learn it in school; I don't have a voice for singing, though. It's the one that goes, 'Last light of the sun against gravestone sky—'"

"'Dream of the shadows all come to die.'" They all turned in surprise at the clean tenor voice of Linus. His eyes were closed and he sang as if he were alone and unafraid on a much younger battlefield.

"White sand, gray stone, green field bear the scar,
of heroes' blood and silver star.
They walk in steel, they die in stone,
Children of Gilead sing alone."

The old knight repeated, "'Children of Gilead sing alone,'" and opened his eyes as the green orb of light flashed, then disappeared with an echo of the last note.

Xenon turned to the console in shock. The buttons turned from the blank white to their customary colors; she leaned on the edge—a fortunate thing as more projections of light spun up from the console's center. They took the form of green square slates that orbited the room in a stately rhythm. As she watched in wonder, images began to appear in the windows of light. An elderly gnome served scones to a group of excited young gnomes with a ping-pong paddle. Two men wearing garish costumes chased a third who wore a red cloak and a demon's horns. King Tamar sat alone on her throne. A silver-coated werewolf held out a flower to his lover, a skinny man with red hair and a guitar. A slender sea-elf stole pearls from her mother's bower and held them to her neck in admiration. A brutish man wearing the skin of a bear punched a small blond boy to the ground. Two dwarves wearing robes sat at the feet of a much older dwarf as they watched a pebble slowly roll from his palm. Mercury stood on the deck of the *Raven*, eyes lidded, small hand in the larger hand of the scarred Captain Chalk. A silver-haired gnome coughed into a handkerchief, then hid it when her family ran into the room. A dark-eyed boy lay on the top of a wagon, a wooden sword in his hands. A thick young goblin pulled a fish from a stream with his bare hands, then laughed in delight as he turned to an older man with a long gray mustache. *What is all this?*

"How could that have worked?" Xenon sputtered, overwhelmed. "How could a children's song from Gilead open an Arkanic lock from thousands of years ago?"

The archaeologist didn't have time to dwell as one green window grew large and prominent and showed a marvelous sight. It was the exterior of the asteroid, burning flame and momentum—but halted by a gigantic lattice of ice and energy. And in the center of it, red long-coat flapping in the wind, was the wild mage.

"Rime!" Jonas exclaimed and trotted across the small room so he could get a better look. He pulled something from his pouch and held it tightly in his hands as he watched, concern leaking from his face.

"*Doma* Korvanus is buying us time. We must act now, Scholar Xenon!" Linus said.

But what? But how? No time, no time, no time. Xenon reached up, grabbed an earlobe, and pulled down hard until the pain centered her. She pulled her journal over and started filling in the grid with familiar symbols and blacking out the ones destroyed by the dragon. *That creature was able to use this console with its giant claw, so it can't be that complicated. Maybe it's as simple as telling it what you want? You select the sigils for the command, then the ship will respond?* The frantic acid in her stomach sloshed, but she seized on the idea, as flimsy a glimmer as it was. *What did the dragon ask? Something really, really simple—something that a giant claw could punch out in the dark.*

She grabbed all the broken buttons she could easily find and laid them out on the edge of the console. "Okay—there seem to be several here that reference 'Motion' in one way or the other, and the other sigil that seems to be the most common is 'Thief'? So he told the ship to 'Go to Thief'?"

"What is 'Thief'?" Sideways's voice was sharp.

"I don't know what it means; I don't know if any of this is right." The goblin folded her fingers together, joints creaking with nervous energy. "We're out on the guess of an estimation of a hunch of a wobbly premise from a leap of faith."

"We have to do something, Xenon!" Jonas begged. "Rime can't hold this thing forever."

As if in agreement, the entire room shuddered violently. On the window they could see the beams of ice surge in size and brightness as the mage struggled to keep the asteroid back. Xenon ran her eyes across the console again and finally threw up her hands. "Okay, fine! We know that the dragon said 'Go to Thief' and that brought Shame back, let's tell it to 'Go AWAY from Thief.'"

She found the right sigils for "Motion" and a bright-yellow sigil for "Away," but all of the buttons marked with the "Thief" symbol had been broken off by the dragon's claw. Each button was designed to sit on a slender cylinder of glass; she tried replacing a few buttons, but they just caused the cylinders to fracture further. *It's a fine instrument. I need something to work as a replacement button, something flat and solid. On top of that I'm not even really sure where the original "Thief" button was—I guess I should just push a bunch and hope for the best?*

"Xenon!" the squire yelled in panic. "I think she's losing her grip!"

Xenon slapped her hands together, knowing her eyes had to be bright periwinkle by now. *You're here now. Not acting is worse than guessing and being wrong.* In quick succession she pressed the buttons for "Move," "Away," "Hope," "Knowledge"—and in a burst of inspiration grabbed her journal and laid it down on the largest swath of empty cylinders and broken buttons, the ones she prayed had once been the buttons for "Thief." She placed her hand on the battered leather and pressed down firmly, activating a dozen buttons all at once. "Please work. Please work. Please work!"

A series of chimes went off and the console rippled with light. The sigils on the wall that had been blank and quiet began to glow and spin—a cascade of energy and sparks flew up from the console, erupting from every shattered glass cylinder. Xenon whirled around the room, hoping for any sign of what she had done.

One by one the green windows of light changed. Where before they flickered, showing the odd scenes of life on the planet below—now they showed only stars. And one by one they closed. The console hummed, reminding her of *Tobio,* but not a single pitch: a chord, a choir, a chorale. At last only the largest screen remained, showing the wild mage and her tower of ice and the ocean surface below.

"Did that—"

"Shh." Xenon held up a finger and then stepped closer to the large window. A score of heartbeats clipped by in silence and then all four of the explorers saw it at once. The red dot that was Rime, was getting farther away. The goblin allowed herself to breathe. "I think . . . that we did it?"

"You did it!" Jonas crowed and swept her up in a fierce bear hug, spinning her around. Xenon laughed and then shrieked when she saw that her journal was burning from where it was wedged down in the broken console.

"No!" she wailed and pulled herself free of the squire to dash over to the burning book. Sideways leapt in before her and retrieved the journal, swatting out the flames against his chest. He handed it to her sheepishly, and she felt the tears roll down her face and daggers of pain lodge in her chest as she saw the pages falling into ash.

"Sorry, Xenon, uh, sorry," the devilkin offered, clearly unsure of how to share sympathy about an inanimate object.

The goblin cradled her ravaged journal to her breast like a dying bird and could not reply.

"Come, let us return to your vehicle and depart. We have no way of knowing how quickly the asteroid will accelerate with your improvised instructions." Linus held out his arm in a courtly fashion, and Xenon leaned on it with gratitude. They started to leave with the devilkin bringing up the rear, when the squire's panicked voice pulled them up sharp.

"Something's wrong." Jonas pointed. "Rime's ice-magic tower thing. The asteroid is getting farther and farther away, but *it's still growing*. I . . . I . . . I don't think she can stop!"

CHAPTER TWENTY-FOUR

JONAS & RIME

And she held. And she held. And she held.

The flame pushed and she made more ice. The asteroid and gravity demanded and she refused. A country of cold formed beneath her on the waves and she could not feel her skin or her eyes or even her breath. She was a conduit and the Magic Wild flowed through her and bowed to her will.

Except, Rime realized, it did not truly bow. *It feels so good, with a thought I can create and bend and shape and mar. But the Magic is slipping from my hold.* But the asteroid still came and so she held.

The lattice of ice had become a tower, vast beams and girders crossing and wound and winding upward to refute the Precusors' orb. The longer she built it, the more it demanded and the more she wanted to give and the more magic she found to employ. *That's the trap. The trap that is closing. I need to back up, retreat take a breath, something.* A fresh surge of power rippled up her spine and she realized that she was contemplating just picking the asteroid up like a pebble and tossing it back out into space herself.

The thought became thicker, took form, became an itch, a hunger, a need—*so much, too much, power to be used, why not, why not, why not, WHY NOT.*

Rime gasped. And she was somewhere else. Somewhere dark. She could see out her eyes still, like vast bay windows, but she could also turn and see the rest of this place: the library of her mind. *I'm back. It's been . . . days since I came in here?* Before it had been well-lit, tidy white shelves with row after row of brightly colored books, a stool for her to sit on when she came here to get away from the outside world, a stand that held a hand-bound book of her dreams, her singular hope to escape the fate of all other wild mages. Now that stand was knocked on its side, the Book of Hope splayed, pages torn and scattered across the floor. The shelves of knowledge—everything she had ever learned, read, been taught—all covered over with a thick bramble of cruel thorns. What little light remained came from the numbers. Gentle, green, glowing sixes and sevens and nines and twos, spiraling around the center of what had once been her refuge. Rime stepped into the light to admire what her numbers guarded. A simple sword with a wooden handle, stabbed into the floor like a monument—while all around it grew the green flesh and red flowers of a geranium.

She put two fingers on the cool metal of the sword's pommel. She looked outside her windows to the magic tower of ice that she was building. She looked inside, into the darkness where the creatures of madness had howled for as long as she could remember.

Except now they were not howling. They stood, shoulder to shoulder, quiet and sure. They pressed close against the light and stared back at her.

Rime looked down at herself, at her hands, and saw that they were dissolving. A clear voice began to sing, from somewhere in the darkness of her own head. The tune was familiar, but she could not catch the words. *Oh. This is my Answer. This is the time that I break,* she thought and let her fingertips drop from the memorial. She stepped forward into the company of the waiting monsters, while she still had feet to do so. She closed her eyes.

RIME'S DREAM #5

She sat at a table in a room with three corners. In one corner Fire smiled at her. In another corner was a box lashed tight with ivy and thorn. In the last was a woman with white hair, tossing back the last drops in her glass—square cubes of ice clinked and rolled. There were no doors.

Across the table was her. But not her now, her Before. Shorter, thinner, eyes larger, whip marks still wet on her back. Her Before the Magic—before she could command it, before she could burn with it. A little girl with long brown hair, her tiny fists clenched and her jaw set.

"No one can save us," Rime Before said. "No one but you. Not then, not when, not now, not ever. No one but you. Jonas helps. And Time helps. And books help. And Music would help if you let it. But no one but you can take the hand that's offered. No one but you can turn the stone. No one but you can stand in the center and hold."

Easy for you to say.

"It is," the little girl said.

You haven't carried it yet. You haven't felt the weight.

"Not when you were I. But now I am you. You have slipped away. Surrendered. I am the final drop of you." Rime Before took her hand, her large eyes bright.

It's not just the shadows, the monsters in my head—it's the light too, the Magic—it's too much for me.

"I know."

I can't hold on forever.

"No." Rime Before smiled. "You can't."

She smiled back at the little girl and stood up from the table.

It took less than an hour to jog back to the entrance, and it was with great shuddering relief that Jonas saw that the sky-cycle remained on the small landing waiting for them. He looked down below and could see that the asteroid was picking up speed, but beyond, Rime's magic continued to work, building a tower of ice and light that surged and wound upon itself in pursuit of the fleeing globe. The squire squinted, but he could not see the smallest bit of red from her coat. He turned to the others in haste and waved them forward.

"Let's get down there! We have to help her." Jonas moved to the side of *Tobio* and was quickly joined by Xenon, who swung into the saddle and began flipping switches. The other two came more slowly—Sideways taking a measured amble to the other side of the sky-cycle, Linus walking to the edge of the landing to look out.

"No. We do not," the hunter said, his hand on the hilt of the white sword.

"What?" Jonas said, sick certainty already racing down his veins.

Linus continued, his attention still on the wild mage's tower below. "I have seen this before. She has pulled on too much of the Magic Wild and it has taken her utterly. She will pull more and more until her physical body is nothing but cinders and dust. The Hunt tries to avoid situations like this due to the collateral damage, but at least out at sea it should be minimal."

"You knew," Jonas spat, and his sword was out. "You knew this would happen. You and Sir Graham, you *planned* this."

"My boy, this was a matter for adults." Linus turned to face him, his white sword still at his side. "Can you really say the girl's life is not worth spending in exchange for that of thousands?"

"But—we don't have to spend it at all." The squire realized he was weeping angrily. "We can still save her."

"Can we discuss this, Linus?" Xenon called. "We've done an amazing thing together, seen wonders, saved the whole planet, maybe? Doesn't that count for anything?"

"The circle does not hold, boy. It breaks. How many ways do you need to hear it? Your friend is dead, your duty done. If not today, then tomorrow, or a hundred tomorrows." The white sword was out and the old knight's eyes were cold. "Kneel before the End."

Jonas felt overcome with grief and fury. There was no way he could best Sideways in a fight, but maybe with luck he could overpower Linus alone. *I can't ask Xenon to get in the middle; she just saved the whole world!* He pulled out the flat skull-face pin that Rime had thrown him and pressed his fingers tightly around its sharp edges. "It doesn't have to break today, Linus! It can hold today! It can hold even though it doesn't want to. Maybe your sword can cut our way to her, just like the asteroid. Please, please—" The squire forced his begging mouth shut.

"Save your words, boy." Linus sighed. "She cannot keep this magnitude of energy going indefinitely; soon, very soon, it will be over."

"You know, you're right." A thin voice came from over the edge of the landing. "I can't keep it up indefinitely, so I stopped."

It started small.

She opened her eyes and took a step. Then another step.

The briar and thorn tightened around her library shelves, then it relaxed and fell away as she continued to walk. Her numbers ignited phosphorescent green and whirled around her. They danced through her mind and righted the broken stool and tumbled lectern. Lights flickered on, and the darkness drew back. The eyes of her madness still watched, but they drew back as she advanced. She could begin to hear the murmur and howl as the madness was pushed back. *Good. Scream all you want.*

Rime laid a fond hand on the sword hilt in the center of the room, spared an annoyed glance at the red flowers, then leaped back through her eyes into the world outside her head.

Ice and power and song and glory and the wind at her beck and call. She was almost evaporated again by the flood of power, but she held. She had held the asteroid; she could hold herself too. Rime bit her lip and let the magic go. The beams of light, the girders and towers of frozen water erupting up into the sky slacked, then fell still. She took a breath and was empty and alone and just herself, still standing in the invisible circle of her schematic.

Rime squinted up through the lattice of ice and saw Shame retreating. She flew up, realizing why things looked so odd. Her left eye was covered with ice. The mage peeled it off, ignoring the pain. *This time I'll save the boy.*

○

Jonas's jaw worked and he pointed at the source of the voice, but no words came out.

Floating in the air, thin bracelets of light around her wrists and ankles, was Rime. Her face was haggard, eyes sunken, signs of frostbite spreading across her face like purple moss.

"Rime!" Jonas shouted dumbfounded, then again: "Rime!"

"Yes, it's me." She pointed down below. "My ice thing is breaking."

The squire noticed the telltale wobble as she looked down. *She's about to pass out!* Beyond the sounds of Shame's roaring flames could be heard the crack of ice splintering and crashing down.

"Now, you, old man." Rime turned her attention back to the hunter. "You can make your play right now and try to take me out and I'm blowing up your little sky bike first thing. *Thing first.* Then even if you kill me, you're stranded on this rock."

"You'd be leaving your friend and the Scholar Xenon stranded as well." Linus kept his sword and tone even.

"I can turn into a bat," Sideways offered helpfully, amusement clear in his voice.

"I know their lives mean nothing to you. And yeah, I killed you one time before, so maybe you have a way to come back from the grave. But I don't think you have a way to come back from fucking outer space." The wild mage bobbled again, then the light flared as she concentrated.

Linus lowered his sword slightly. "I could jump."

Rime crossed her arms. "There's hundreds of feet of water below and we're miles from land. I don't think you float very well."

The hunter sheathed his sword. "Then today we play to a draw. We have broken bread this day, a small magic, a small covenant. Today it will be enough."

"Good, great, awesome, whatever." Rime snapped her fingers and the entire landing and part of the asteroid's metal skin ripped free as if by an invisible force. "Hold on."

She flew down and the landing followed, buffeted by wind as Rime dragged them across the sky. Jonas held on tight to the edge of the landing and tried not to scream as they dodged the still tumbling spires of ice. Rime was taking the most direct route, batting gigantic columns of ice out of her way in her haste—it left little concern for the comfort or smoothness of the ride for the passengers. The squire caught sight of a vast island of ice, covered with melting wreckage in the water below. The *Raven* appeared at last, black and fierce in the sky ahead. The mage deposited the landing rudely on the deck. Mercury, the captain, and the crew were already running over, shouting words of acclaim. Jonas raised a faltering hand to greet them. He enjoyed flying, but that last trip had been a bit too severe and pragmatic for his tastes.

"None of that," Rime said. "No medals today."

She pointed and Mercury sailed through the air to land in her sister's lap on the sky-cycle's back with a squawk. A finger leveled at Jonas deposited him similarly, and then the mage herself zoomed over to wedge herself in between the goblin and the squire.

"Full throttle, please." Rime coughed, the light around her beginning to fade. Xenon and Mercury shrugged at each other, laughing, then the older goblin kicked *Tobio* into movement and they leapt from the black deck and back into the sky.

Linus and Sideways watched them go, the former holding up a hand in salute, the latter simply crossing his arms.

Jonas looked down at Rime and felt her sag against him. "That . . . that was amazing, Rime. Where are we going?"

"Just . . . fly. Not to Gilead." The mage's eyes fluttered as she clung to consciousness. "You know how when I use a lot of magic, I'm out for a long time?"

"Yeah?"

"I think I'm going to be out for a *very* long time. I'm—I'm scared I'm not going to wake up this time." Her eyes were hard and empty of tears.

"You—you will. I'm sure of it," Jonas stuttered.

"You have no idea," Rime rolled her eyes, exhaustion creeping over her.

Jonas took her hand, pressing her skull pin against her palm. "I do. I do have an idea. Today's a good day; today we win. You are a Hero True, Rime Korvanus, and they don't die in their sleep."

"You . . . are a moron." The mage snorted and then fell back quiet and unconscious against Jonas's shoulder. His eyes widened, seeing that all of her hair had turned white as snow. *Oh! Almost— one tiny bit of brown still there at the back.* He held the sprig of brown hair between his fingers in wonder. Jonas had no way of even fathoming the amount of power she had used holding up the asteroid. She had been out for hours before and days, even. *Will she be out for a week? More? How am I going to feed her?*

Mercury's head popped up over her sister's shoulder. "She seemed pretty glass-sure we'd just take her wherever. Rude-hat."

"You can drop us off somewhere if you need," Jonas apologized.

"Eh," Xenon said cheerily. "I need to get a new journal and record all my observations while they're fresh, but other than that we don't have anywhere pressing to be." The goblin laughed suddenly, long and bright. "I was just thinking that we're out of money. How stupid is that, when not an hour ago we sent an asteroid back into the heavens."

"Oh—well, we've got money," Jonas said, remembering the pouch of gold coins pushed way down in his satchel. "It's technically Rime's, but I think she's going to be out for quite a while, so I guess I'm in charge of the money."

Mercury cackled. "Perfect, then, you're the bankman."

"Uhh . . ." Jonas felt a vague sense of unease as the small goblin's smile widened with naked avarice. Then he remembered the new cauldron he had abandoned with the horses on the outskirts of Corinth, and how nice it had been to buy fresh ingredients and prepare them around the fire. *Got to cook for four now. Rime won't mind . . . right?*

The sky-cycle *Tobio* hummed across the sky, leaving a line of magenta energy in its wake. It was still bare hours before sunrise, and as the asteroid retreated, the dim of honest night returned. The four travelers headed west for the moment with the sun soon to be close on their trail. The two sisters laughed again and put on more speed. Jonas kept a close grip on Rime, his hand in hers, long after the sun found them.

CHAPTER TWENTY-FIVE

AFTERMATH

Linus the Blue stood on the deck of the *Raven*, watching his prey escape.

"Hardly proper," Sideways complained.

"You were supposed to kill that goblin the instant she fulfilled her purpose, assassin," the knight said, not breaking his eyes from the vanishing sky-cycle. "And the boy."

"Yeah, well—" The devilkin looked down at his feet uncomfortably. "Saving the planet threw me off my game. And I have a very specific asterisk in my contract: 'no killing goblin girls with cute ears.'"

Linus sighed and walked away toward the bridge of the ship. *An extraordinary moment, to be sure, in the center of the* asteroid. "Very well. That clause I will respect. It would have made no difference to the outcome today, regardless."

Sideways nodded and remained in place with his arms crossed, watching the last magenta trail of the sky-cycle evaporate.

Sir Graham came to meet him, bowing with empty courtesy. "A great deed, Linus. The king will reward you greatly for your aid in this matter."

"She already knows what I want, and I claim it now," the knight called out to the captain and the two remaining knights. "The *Raven* is hereby conscripted by the Hunt. Your king has agreed to this boon; you serve at my command. Is this understood?"

The thin knight and the one with the squashed nose looked to Captain Chalk, who squared his jaw in distaste but finally replied. "By my king's command we serve. What are our orders, sir?"

Discipline is more valuable than loyalty. "Bring the parcel from belowdecks to my quarters. Have a care; it is made of glass. Set a westerly course to pursue the sky-cycle, but make port at the first village we encounter. We will need to take on some supplementary crew, supplies, and firewood."

"Aye." Chalk spun the ship's wheel and spat out a reprimand to the two knights that weren't moving quickly enough to obey.

"You intend to pursue Lady Korvanus immediately, then?" Sir Graham inquired, coming to stand next to Linus.

"That is my purpose. She managed to regain control of the Magic Wild today—that's not something that has ever occurred in the history of the Hunt. When the abominations release something that potent, it always consumes them. That she was able to come back"—the old knight's grip tightened around the hilt of the white sword—"it does not bode well. She is *exceptional.*"

Even Linus could hear the appreciation in his voice, so he took the gnome's leer without rancor.

"Well, the *Raven* is a fast ship, and you know the way they bear. I suppose you shall have no trouble catching them swiftly." Sir Graham reached into his pocket and pulled out an amberglass figurine shaped like a whale.

"What is that, Liar?" Linus demanded, backing away and drawing his sword.

"I owe our Heroes something, No Heart." The gnome laughed and threw the whale figurine down hard on the deck, where it shattered. "A head start at the very, very least."

Linus stood on the deck of the *Raven* and looked up at the noon sun. The glass had shattered and the sun had leaped forward, or at least that was how it had appeared to him. The gnome had stolen time and stolen away. All around the deck lay the sleeping forms of Sideways, Captain Chalk, and the other two knights. The old man sighed and pinched his nose with two fingers.

He walked to the edge of his ship's rail and smiled. A few hours would not make a difference. And the Liar was right; it was only sporting. The greatest Hunt should follow all the forms with proper care.

"See you soon, Snowlock," Linus promised his prey and turned to wake his crew, his assassin, and his hound.

Enton Blake stood next to his employer and looked down into the jaws of the steel city that howled through the waves as if it would eat the sky.

"The lock-wards are in place?" Mr. Moore inquired.

"Yes. The city started to sink again when the asteroid—retreated. We have blocked the main supports with repulsor buoys; the city of Zero will stay above the water until we are done with it," Enton replied.

"Good." The president of Seafoam Trading Company did not smile but moved toward the small boat that waited. "They stole their technology from the Precursors, just as we have—but they rose to far greater heights than we have yet dared. 'Nothing more real than the chains you forge'—the watchwords of Zero. Nothing more immutable than the limits you place upon yourself. In this city lived men who sold their thought and blood for power and glory. A dangerous transaction."

Enton nodded. "Yes, Mr. President."

"I feel like I'm coming home." Mr. Moore left, but his cold remained long after.

The asteroid left the planet quietly, slipping off into the empty between worlds like a boat on a star-filled lake.

Within, the dragons slept, as they had for a vast towering wall of years. The dragons slept, but they also Dreamed.

They Dreamed and they Spoke in each other's minds. Time is a wondrous cradle and Necessity a cruel but productive caretaker.

The dragons Spoke of the Shadow that had lived among them, feeding and consuming their light, their minds. They Spoke of the tiny blips of heart and flesh that had appeared in their Dream, and how they had killed the Shadow. Then the blips had fled, as quickly as they had come, after singing a strange Song, one the Dream had not heard since they were Caged.

They had grown beyond their Names, but they still felt joy at the Shadow's death. The Dream reached out to the blips of heart and flesh, hoping to share their thanks—but the Dream could not reach them.

The Dream could feel, out beyond the metal skin of the Cage that they had been returning home in, to the City, to where the Sun Children had banished them. And now they were moving away. The Dream considered. And then they were glad they were not returning home, because in their long slumber they had also known a Nightmare.

A Nightmare reaching for the City, a machine, a colossus, a thing of light and will that brought with it only Darkness.

The Dream looked out, far down into the empty quiet they traveled, and thought.

Where are we going?

And the Dream was content. Content to be and wonder and not know the Answer.

The asteroid and its prisoners' Dream flew on, across the vast empty that some call Night.

EPILOGUE

Sand tossed his beard and robe in the back of the caravan without bothering to fold them. The rain was starting, and they needed to get the gear out of the open. Vincent as well was trotting along, his wooden sword stuffed under his cloak to protect it from the first drops. Only Toby dragged his feet, as usual, standing a few feet away from the caravan, still thumbing through the last few pages of the play script.

"Come on, Toby!" Vincent called. "We'll finish it after the rain stops. Or tomorrow if it gets late!"

The rain-spattered Demon looked up, a mule-emperor expression on his face. "I thought you said we all died!"

Sand raised his hands in exasperation and crossed through the increasing rain to grab Toby by the elbow and drag him toward the caravan. He didn't particularly care about the actor getting wet, but the script and the costume cost money. "I lied to you, Toby. You would think you would stop being surprised by that peculiar habit of mine."

"You said the Demon and the Paladin died! And the Sage too!" the blond actor yowled in existential outrage.

"That's not the kind of play this is. Death is simple and common. They each lose something, you see? The Sage loses his memory, the Demon learns that the Fountain of Purity is dry, and the Paladin—"

"How can it be a tragedy if nobody dies?" Toby threw the script down on the rain-wet ground. "It's not funny enough to be a farce, and nobody gets married, so it's not a comedy. What kind of stupid play is this?"

"I liked it," Vincent offered from under the caravan's awning.

"Tragedy isn't about death," Sand said, rain filling the square. "It's about loss. The irreplaceable, the essential, the most dear. Death is an exit, an actor changing clothes. Common, regular, expected. But when the character loses something and then must go on regardless . . . ah, then we see the shape of the knife. The Demon will never know release from his torment, but he must go on regardless. The Paladin sold his heart in return for the sword of demon's bane, but he must go on regardless. Going on is the tragedy—going on and remembering. Remembering yourself before, before you were broken."

"But they aren't really broken in this play," Toby argued, the anger in his face gone. "There's adventure and laughter and they are still together at the end. Even though they lost someone—some*thing*, irreplaceable."

"They're still in the game," Vincent added, crossing through the rain to join his fellow actors. "*We* are still in the game."

Sand bowed his head and allowed himself the actor's shame. Real tears.

"I miss her," he said.

Toby was first to embrace the bald man, and Vincent's gangly arms were not a second behind.

The three actors stood in the rain together.

Sand looked up into the face of his troupe and let the rain hide his professional lapse. "Well, let's go on, then."

And they did.

Xenon brought *Tobio* down to cruise a few meters above the surface of the waves. Mercury was curled up in her lap, snoring wildly. She kept a protective hand on her sister's stomach, feeling it go up and down with each leonine snore.

An idea struck her, and she craned her neck slightly to speak to Jonas, who was tending to his own sleeping charge.

"Hey, Jonas," Xenon said.

"Yeah?"

"You know—I just realized that you never *actually* used that silver sword that we pulled out of the well."

"Huh," the squire grunted. "I guess—I didn't?"

"So, it was completely pointless?"

"I guess so." The squire shrugged. "Sorry about that."

"Prophecies," the archaeologist snorted. "To be expected, I suppose. No offense to your king, but anyone who says they can predict the future is a fool."

THE END

FOR NOW

JONAS AND RIME WILL RETURN

AS WILL MERCURY AND XENON (APPARENTLY)

IN

A PAPER-THIN HARRY POTTER PARODY:

RIME KORVANUS AND THE COUNCIL OF NINE

OR

DON'T TELL MY CRUSH I'M A WILD MAGE!

AUTHOR'S PLEA

Gentle and Attractive Reader—please take a moment and leave a review for the book. An honest review—good or bad!—is what keeps a book alive out there in the wild. Your opinion can save this book from the dust bin of history and me from the grips of blank anxiety. Thank you for reading! And your hair looks nice today.

— Derek

ACKNOWLEDGMENTS

A t the end of this book there is a giant list of names—all of the backers of the preorder campaign. I thank them first, with a solemn nod and no jokes for once. Beyond that I thank the list invisible of everyone who has supported my writing this far in any way, big or small. Without you all, this book would not be here. It would be somewhere else, stapled together and written in crayon. Thank you for helping me dream of stranger skies and tell you stories about rocket-powered gryphons.

Unending gratitude to my editors from Girl Friday Productions: Lindsay Robinson for her blistering developmental edit, Michelle Hope Anderson for her deft and nuanced copy edit, Meghan Harvey and Bethany Davis for masterminding it all and keeping me on track with charm and aplomb. From Inkshares I would like to send tasteful heart emoji to my Publishing/ Marketing Manager Avalon Radys, Matt Kaye, and Jeremy Thomas.

Thank you, Veronica Belmont and Tom Merritt, for this bizarre turn of fate and opportunity, your support, and your undying devotion and ceaseless allegiance to my petty whims, which I am just now informing you that this Acknowledgment acts as a binding contract thereto.

And at the last, a salute to my Beloved. Carina McGeehin lets me live at her house and nobly tolerates all the stray-dog oddities that come with the way my brain operates. Without her, I'm back to knocking over trash cans in alleys and howling philosophy on street corners. Thank you for being my home.

ABOUT THE AUTHOR

In his formative college years at University of Georgia, G. Derek Adams spent his time cultivating a love of words, theater, and Dungeons & Dragons. Adams has written two previous novels and is threatening to write more. He has an abiding love for the fantasy universe and an unabashed desire to play within it. Adams lives in Athens, Georgia, with his Beloved, a dog, two cats, and a rescue warg.

LIST OF PATRONS

This book was made possible in part by the following grand patrons who preordered the book on Inkshares.com. Thank you.

Adam Shirley
Ako Cromwell
Amanda L. Dean
Amy L. Dowdy
Amy L. Miller
Andrew J. Stephens
Andrew S. Wheeler
Cameron Logan
Charles Methvin
Chrismon Hinsch
Christopher S. Childs
David C. Sibilsky
Erick Jaudon
Eric Wagoner
E. R. Moore

Fran Teague
Genevieve Marie Esquivie
George Marston
James D. Mitchell
James J. Franklyn
Jayne Lockhart
Joanna B. Eldredge
John M. Calhoun
John Waldrip
Joseph Terzieva
Joshua L. Darnell
Julie G. Daniel
Justin Sanders
Katherine Garcia
Katie Nystrom

Kat Marie Mitchell

Kristina Tanner

Lauren E. Wilson

Lauren McGeehin

Leigh Vandiver

Michaelian Ennis

Michael McGeehin

Michael Niedzwiecki-Castile

Mike Smith

Paul C. Garrett

Rebekah Lee

R. E. Long

Sayge Medlin

Sean C. Polite

Steve Wildey

Thomas Torrent

Timothy McLeod, Jr.

Tracy Carroll

William Cline

William S. Carroll

INKSHARES

Inkshares is a crowdfunded book publisher. We democratize publishing by having readers select the books we publish—we edit, design, print, distribute, and market any book that meets a preorder threshold.

Interested in making a book idea come to life? Visit inkshares.com to find new book projects or to start your own.

SWORD & LASER

Sword & Laser is a science fiction and fantasy-themed book club, video show, and podcast that gathers together a strong online community of passionate readers to discuss and enjoy books of both genres.

Listen in or join the conversation at swordandlaser.com.